Chester Himes was born in Missouri in 1909. After the war, he left the States to live in Europe. He died in Spain in 1984. He wrote several acclaimed Harlem thrillers, *The Crazy Kill, The Real Cool Killers* and *Cotton Comes to Harlem*. He also wrote an autobiography, *The Quality of Hurt*, and novels which include *Lovely Crusade* and *If He Hollers, Let Him Go*, his first book, published in 1945.

D0871028

Chester Himes

If He Hollers Let Him Go

Library of Congress Catalog Card Number: 98-86458

A catalogue record for this book is available from
the British Library on request

The right of Chester Himes to be identified as
the author of this work has been asserted
in accordance with the Copyright, Designs and
Patents Act 1988

Copyright © 1945 Chester B. Himes

First published in 1999 by Serpent's Tail,
4 Blackstock Mews, London N4

Website: www.serpentstail.com

Printed in Great Britain by Mackays of Chatham plc

10 9 8 7 6 5 4 3 2 1

CHAPTER
1

I dreamed a fellow asked me if I wanted a dog and I said yeah, I'd like to have a dog and he went off and came back with a little black dog with stiff black gold-tipped hair and sad eyes that looked something like a wire-haired terrier. I was standing in front of a streetcar that was just about to start and the fellow led the dog by a piece of heavy stiff wire twisted about its neck and handed me the end of the wire and asked me if I liked the dog. I took the wire and said sure I liked the dog. Then the dog broke loose and ran over to the side of the street trailing the wire behind him and the fellow ran and caught it and brought it back and gave it to me again.

'About the—' I began. I wanted to ask him how much it cost because I didn't have any money.

But he cut me off. 'Now about the pay. It'll cost you a dollar and thirty-five cents.'

I said, 'I haven't got any money now but I'll give it to you on Monday.'

'Sure, that's all right,' he said.

I took the dog and got on the streetcar. I liked the little dog; but when I got home nobody else seemed to like it.

Then I turned over and dreamed on the other side.

I was working in a war plant where a white fellow named Frankie Childs had been killed and the police were there trying to find out who did it.

1

The police lieutenant said, 'We got to find a big tall man with strong arms, big hands, and a crippled leg.'

So they started calling in the coloured fellows. The first one to be called was a medium-sized, well-built, fast-walking, dark brown man of about thirty-five. He was dressed in a faded blue work shirt and blue denim overall pants tied about the waist with a cord. He came up from the basement and walked straight to the lieutenant and looked him in the eye, standing erect and unflinching.

The lieutenant asked, 'Can you stand the test?'

'What test?' the coloured fellow wanted to know.

'Can you go up to the third floor and look the dead body of Frankie Childs in the face?'

The coloured fellow said, 'Frankie Childs! Sure, I can go up and look at that bastard dead or alive.' He had a fine, scholarly voice, carrying but unmusical. He turned and started up the stairs three at a time. Suddenly I began to laugh.

'Oh!' I said to the lieutenant. 'You gonna keep 'em running upstairs until you find out what one's crippled.' I fell out and rolled all over the floor laughing.

Then I turned over and dreamed on my back.

I was asking two white men for a job. They looked as if they didn't want to give me the job but didn't want to say so outright. Instead they asked me if I had my tools. I said I didn't have any tools but I could do the job. They began laughing at me, scornfully and derisively. One said, 'He ain't got no tools,' and they laughed like hell.

I didn't mind their not giving me the job, but their laughing at me hurt. I felt small and humiliated and desperate, looking at the two big white men laughing at me.

Suddenly I came awake. For a time I laid there without thought, suspended in a vacancy. There was no meaning to anything; I didn't even remember having dreamed.

The alarm went off again; I knew then that it had been the alarm that had awakened me. I groped for it blindly, shut it off; I kept my eyes shut tight. But I began feeling scared in spite of hiding from the day. It came along with consciousness. It came into my head first, somewhere back of my closed eyes, moved slowly underneath my skull to the base of my brain, cold and hollow. It seeped down my spine, into my arms, spread through my groin with an almost sexual torture, settled in my stomach like butterfly wings. For a moment I felt torn all loose inside, shrivelled, paralysed, as if after a while I'd have to get up and die.

Every day now I'd been waking up that way, ever since the war began. And since I'd been made a leaderman out at the Atlas Shipyard it was really getting me. Maybe I'd been scared all my life, but I didn't know about it until after Pearl Harbour. When I came out to Los Angeles in the fall of '41, I felt fine about everything. Taller than the average man, six feet two, broad-shouldered, and conceited, I hadn't a worry. I knew I'd get along. If it had come down to a point where I had to hit a paddy I'd have hit him without any thought. I'd have busted him wide open because he was a paddy and needed busting.

Race was a handicap, sure, I'd reasoned. But hell, I didn't have to marry it. I went where I wanted and felt good about it. I'd gotten refused back in Cleveland, Ohio, plenty of times. Cleveland wasn't the land of the free or the home of the brave either. That was one reason why I left there to come to Los Angeles; I knew if I kept on getting refused while white boys were hired from the line behind me I'd hang somebody as sure as hell. But it'd never really gotten me down. Once I threatened to sue a restaurant and got a hundred dollars. I'd even thought about making a business of it. Most times when I got refused I just went somewhere else, put it out of my mind, forgot about it.

They shook that in Los Angeles. It wasn't being refused employment in the plants so much. When I got here practically the only job a Negro could get was service in the white folks' kitchens. But it wasn't that so much. It was the look on the people's faces when you asked them about a job. Most of 'em didn't say right out they wouldn't hire me. They just looked so goddamned startled that I'd even asked. As if some friendly dog had come in through the door and said, 'I can talk.' It shook me.

Maybe it had started then, I'm not sure, or maybe it wasn't until I'd seen them send the Japanese away that I'd noticed it. Little Riki Oyana singing 'God Bless America' and going to Santa Anita with his parents next day. It was taking a man up by the roots and locking him up without a chance. Without a trial. Without a charge. Without even giving him a chance to say one word. It was thinking about if they ever did that to me, Robert Jones, Mrs Jones's dark son, that started me to getting scared.

After that it was everything. It was the look in the white people's faces when I walked down the streets. It was that crazy, wild-eyed, unleashed hatred that the first Jap bomb on Pearl Harbour let loose in a flood. All that tight, crazy feeling of race as thick in the street as gas fumes. Every time I stepped outside I saw a challenge I had to accept or ignore. Every day I had to make one decision a thousand times: *Is it now? Is now the time?*

I was the same colour as the Japanese and I couldn't tell the difference. 'A yeller-bellied Jap' coulda meant me too. I could always feel race trouble, serious trouble, never more than two feet off. Nobody bothered me. Nobody said a word. But I was tensed every moment to spring.

I carried it as long as I could. I carried my muscle as high as my ears. But I couldn't keep on carrying it. I lost twenty pounds in two weeks and my hands got to trembling. I was working at the yard then as a mechanic and every time my white leaderman started over toward me I drew up tight inside. I got so the only place I felt safe was in bed asleep.

I was even scared to tell anybody. If I'd gone to a psychiatrist he'd have had me put away. Living every day scared, walled in, locked up. I didn't feel like fighting any more; I'd take a second thought before I hit a paddy now. I was tired of keeping ready to die every minute; it was too much strain. I had to fight hard enough each day just to keep on living. All I wanted was for the white folks to let me alone; not say anything to me; not even look at me. They could take the goddamned world and go to hell with it.

Suddenly the baby started bawling in the next room and I heard the bed squeak as Ella Mae got up to feed him. I wondered if they knew how well I could hear them through the thin partition. If they did they didn't let it bother them. I heard Henry mutter sleepily, 'Goddamnit! Goddamnit!' Then all I could hear was the sound of the baby sucking greedily, and I thought if they really wanted to give him a break they'd cut his throat and bury him in the back yard before he got old enough to know he was a nigger. Then I was ashamed. Ella Mae loved that baby. If anything happened to him she'd die.

Parts of my dream started coming back and I remembered vaguely about a little black dog with gold-tipped hair, and the police lieutenant looking for a big crippled man who must be coloured. I remembered saying in my dream, 'Oh, you gonna keep 'em running upstairs until you find out what one's crippled.' Suddenly it struck me as funny, and I began laughing. But right in the middle of the laugh I felt a crazy impulse to cry. I wanted to just lie there and cry.

Hell, I oughta stay home today, I thought. I oughta go over and see Susie and take a quart of rum. She was fine if you were drunk enough. Once she told me, 'I'm not pretty but I'm wonderful.' I could picture her ducky black body with the tiny waist and round, bucket-shaped hips. I knew if I kept thinking about her I'd get up and go over and play it out and to hell with my job.

I tried to force my mind to a blank. I had to get myself together; I had to get up.

I could hear the baby still sucking. Lucky little rascal, I thought, didn't know how lucky he was. I wished I had Ella Mae in bed with me; I could lose myself with her too. I remembered how she used to let me in the evenings when Henry was at work. That was during the time I was having so much trouble trying to get my journeyman's rating at the yard and used to come home so burnt up all the time. When I found out she'd done it just because she felt sorry for me I quit speaking to her for a week. But she hadn't let it bother her one way or the other.

I'd gone to the Lincoln Theatre last night and I began thinking of how the audience had applauded so loudly for the two white acrobats. The other acts had been all-coloured – singing and dancing and black-face comedy. I thought at the time how the white folks were still showing everybody how strong they were and how we spooks were still trying to prove how happy we were. But what got me was the way the coloured audience clapped their hands off for the white acrobats – not so much just because they were white, although that was reason enough in itself, I thought – but because one of the boys was blind.

'He's blind,' I heard some woman in back of me whisper. 'He is? Which one?'

'The little one.'

'Is dat so? Well, ain't he spry?'

It went all through the audience: The little one's blind.

We're a wonderful, goddamned race, I thought. Simple-minded, generous, sympathetic sons of bitches. We're sorry for everybody but ourselves; the worse the white folks treat us the more we love 'em. Ella Mae laying me because I wasn't married and she figured she had enough for me and Henry too; and a black audience clapping its hands off for a blind white acrobat.

I thought of Ben telling Conway out at the yard, 'I was just asking the man a question, fellow, I ain't going to steal your white man. I know that's the one thing a Negro won't forgive you for – that's stealing his prize white man.'

What I was trying to do now was to keep from thinking about Alice, just to drift on my thoughts as long as they didn't touch her. I was scared if I thought about her now I'd begin to wonder, maybe to doubt her. She'd broken a date with me last night; that's why I'd gone to the Lincoln.

The next thing I knew I had opened my eyes and was looking at her picture on my dressing table. It was as if I was trying to catch some telltale expression in her eyes. But it wasn't there; she had the same warm, intelligent, confident look. I just looked at her and didn't think about her at all – I just laid there and enjoyed looking at a really fine chick. She had one of those heart-shaped faces with a cupid's-bow mouth, and coal-black hair parted in the middle and pulled tight down over her ears.

Now I didn't mind thinking about her – who she was; her position as supervisor of case work in the city welfare department. Her father was a doctor – Dr Wellington L.-P. Harrison. He was the kind of pompous little guy you'd expect to have a hyphenated name, one of the richest Negroes in the city if not on the whole West Coast.

I jumped out of bed and went over and picked up the picture. It set me up to have a chick like her. It gave me a personal pride to have her for my girl. And then I was proud of her too. Proud of the way she looked, the appearance she made among white people; proud of what she demanded from white people, and the credit they gave her; and her position and prestige among her own people. I could knock myself out just walking along the street with her; and whenever we ran into any of the white shipyard workers downtown somewhere I really felt like something.

I didn't want to think about her breaking our date. She'd called and said she ought to attend a sorority meeting she'd forgotten all about – she was president of the local chapter. And would I really mind? Of course I couldn't mind; that was where the social conventions had me. If she'd been Susie I could have said, 'Hell yes, I mind,' but I had to be a gentleman with Alice. And I really wanted to be. Only thinking about it now gave me a tight, jealous feeling. Started me to wondering why she'd want to marry a guy like me – two years of college and a shipyard job – when she could pick any number of studs with both money and position. But she was trying so hard to make me study nights so I could go back to college after the war and study law, she had to be serious, I reassured myself.

Before I lost it again I put the picture down on the dresser and went into the kitchen to make some coffee. I didn't know Ella Mae was there; I was barefooted and my pyjamas were open. She was standing before the small gas range and when I came in she turned to face me. Her robe was hanging open but at sight of me she pulled it together and fastened it, not hurried, but with finality.

'I was just getting ready to wake you,' she said.

She was a full-bodied, slow-motioned home girl with

a big broad flat face, flat-nosed and thick-lipped; yellow but not bright. She had the big, brown, glassy eyes that went along with the rest of her; and her hair was short and straightened and she had it in curlers.

'Good morning, *Mrs* Brown,' I said facetiously, then, lowering my voice, I added, 'I was just thinking about you, baby.'

She smiled self-consciously, but her look made me button my pyjamas. 'Your clock woke the baby up,' she said.

'He's cute,' I said. 'I heard him.'

She turned back to the stove so I couldn't see her face. 'She's a *she*,' she corrected.

'I forgot.' I ran my finger down her spine.

She pulled away and began making coffee in her silex. 'Go on and get dressed,' she said. 'You'll be late again.' When I didn't move she added, 'I'm making your coffee. You want anything else?'

'Yeah,' I said. She didn't answer. 'I'd get married if I could find somebody like you,' I went on. 'Then I wouldn't mind waking up in the mornings.'

'Go on and get dressed,' she said again. I made another pass at her and she said, 'Oh, go on, Bob! You'll be over it in a minute. Everybody wakes up like that.'

'So!' I said, putting my arm about her waist and trying to pull her to me. 'You oughtn' to told me that, baby.' I put my right hand on her shoulder and tried to face her to me. 'Come on, baby, be sweet.'

She gave me a hard push, sent me off balance. 'Go on now! Don't be so crazy. Hurry up or you'll be late.'

I stood back and looked at her with a sudden hard soberness. 'Do you ever wake up scared?' I asked.

She turned and looked at me then. There was a queer expression on her flat yellow face. She stepped over to me, reached up, and put her hands about my head, drew me down to kiss her. Then she pushed me away again, saying, 'Now hurry up, you'll make all your riders late too.'

'Okay, little sister,' I said. 'When Henry's gone to the Army and you get all hot and bothered and come running to me, just remember.'

She gave a slow laugh and stuck out her tongue. I felt differently now. All the tightness and scare, even the lingering traces of jealousy, had gone out of me. I just felt pressed for time.

I hurried back to my room and put on my shirt and shorts, crossed the kitchen to the bathroom, still barefooted. It was a small, four-room cottage sitting back in a court off of Wall Street in the middle fifties, and the rooms opened into one another so there wasn't any way of getting out of a certain casual intimacy, even if I'd never had Ella Mae. My room was in the back, off from the kitchen, and the bathroom was on the other side. Their bedroom was on one side of the front, and the parlour on the other.

When I'd finished brushing my teeth and washing up I started back through the kitchen in my underwear and almost bumped into Ella Mae as she was returning to bed. I patted her on the hips and said, 'Stingy.' She switched on through the parlour into her bedroom.

I got a clean pair of coveralls out of the dresser drawer, slipped them on over my underwear, pulled on my high-heeled, iron-toed boots, slanted my 'tin' hat on the back of my head, and slipped into my leather jacket. Something about my working clothes made me feel rugged, bigger than the average citizen, stronger than a white-collar worker – stronger even than an executive. Important too. It put me on my muscle. I felt a swagger in my stance when I stepped over to the dresser to get my keys and wallet, identifications, badge, handkerchief, cigarettes. I looked to see if I had enough money, saw a ten and some ones. Then I went into the kitchen and drank two cups of black coffee. All of a sudden I began rushing to get to work on time.

CHAPTER
2

I went out to the garage, threw up the door, backed halfway out to the street on the starter, telling myself at the time I oughtn' to do it. I had a '42 Buick Roadmaster I'd bought four months ago, right after I'd gotten to be a leaderman, and every time I got behind the wheel and looked down over the broad, flat, mile-long hood I thought about how the rich white folks out in Beverly couldn't even buy a new car now and got a certain satisfaction. I straightened out and dug off with a jerk, turned the corner at forty, pushed it on up in the stretch on Fifty-fourth between San Pedro and Avalon, with my nerves tightening, telling me to take it slow before I got into a battle royal with some cracker motor-cycle cop, and my mind telling me to hell with them, I was a key man in a shipyard, as important as anybody now.

Homer and Conway were waiting in front of the drugstore at the corner of Fifty-fourth and Central.

'You're kinda tardy, playboy,' Homer said, climbing in beside Conway.

I turned the corner into Central and started digging. 'She wouldn't let me go,' I said.

'You mean you had that last dollar left,' Conway said.

I squeezed between a truck and an oncoming streetcar, almost brushing, and Homer said, 'See that. Now he's tryna kill us. He don't mind dying hisself, but why he got to kill you and me too?'

'Just like that safety man said, gambling thirty seconds against thirty years,' Conway said.

I pulled up in front of the hotel at Fifty-seventh and my other three riders, Smitty, Johnson and Pigmeat climbed in the back.

Before I started I turned to Pigmeat and said, 'I own some parts of you, don't I, buddy?'

'Get over, goddamnit!' Johnson snarled at Smitty in the back seat and pushed him. 'You want all the seat?'

'Don't call me no "buddy," man,' Pigmeat said to me. 'When I escaped from Mississippi I swore I'd lynch the first sonabitch that called me a "buddy".'

'There these niggers is fighting already,' Homer said, shaking his head. 'Whenever niggers gets together that's the first thing they gonna do.'

Smitty squirmed over to give Johnson more room. 'By God, here's a man wakes up evil every morning. Ain't just *some* mornings; this man wakes up evil *every* morning.' He looked around at Johnson. 'What's the matter with you, man, do your old lady beat you?'

Homer thought they were going to fight. He decided to be peacemaker. 'Now you know how Johnson is,' he said to Smitty. 'That's just his way. You know he don't mean no harm.'

As soon as Smitty found out somebody was ready to argue he began getting bad sure enough. 'How do I know how he is?' he shouted. 'Does he know how I is? Hell, everybody evil on Monday morning. I'm evil too. He ain't no eviler'n me.'

'Shut up!' Conway yelled. 'Bob's tryna say something.' Then he turned to me. 'Don't you know what a "buddy" is, Bob? A "buddy" drinks bilge water, eats crap, and runs rabbits. That's what a peckerwood means when he calls you "buddy".'

'I ain't kidding, fellow,' I told Pigmeat.

He started scratching for his wallet. 'Now that's a Senegalese for you,' he complained. 'Gonna put me out his car 'bout three lousy bucks. Whatcha gonna do with a fellow like that?' He passed me three ones.

'This is for last week,' I said, taking them. 'What about this week?'

'Aw, man, I'll give it to you Friday,' he grumbled. 'You raise more hell 'bout three lousy bucks—'

I mashed the starter and dug off without hearing the rest of it. Johnson had started beefing about the job, and now they all had it.

'How come it is we always got to get the hardest jobs?' Smitty asked. 'If somebody'd take a crap on deck Kelly'd come and get our gang to clean it up.'

'I been working in this yard two years – Bob'll tell you – and all I done yet is the jobs don't nobody else wanta do,' Conway said. 'I'm gonna quit this yard just as sure as I live and nothing don't happen and get me a job at Cal Ship.'

'They don't want you over there neither,' Pigmeat said.

'They don't even want a coloured man to go to the school here any more,' Homer put in. 'Bessie ask Kelly the other day 'bout going to school – she been here three months now – and he told her they still filled up. And a peck come right after – I was standing right there – and he signed him up right away.'

'You know they don't want no more nig – no more of us getting no mechanic's pay,' Pigmeat said. 'You know that in front. What she gotta do is keep on after him.'

'If I ever make up my mind to quit,' Johnson said, 'he the first sonabitch I'm gonna whup. I'm gonna whup his ass till it ropes like okra.'

Conway said, 'I ain't gonna let you. He mine. I been saving that red-faced peckerwood too long to give 'im up now. I'm gonna whip 'im till he puke; then I'm gonna let 'im get through puking; then I'm gonna light in on him and whip 'im till he poot. . . .' He kept on as if it was getting good to him. 'Then I'm gonna let 'im get through pooting; then I'm gonna light in on 'im and whip 'im till he—' They were all laughing now.

'You can't whip him until you get him,' I called over my shoulder.

'You tell 'em, Bob,' Smitty said. 'We gonna see Kelly in a half-hour, then we gonna see what Conway do.'

'I ain't said I was gonna whip the man this morning,' Conway backtracked. 'I said when I *quit* – that's what I said.'

The red light caught me at Manchester; and that made me warm. It never failed; every time I got in a hurry I got caught by every light. I pulled up in the outside lane, abreast a V-8 and an Olds, shifted back to first, and got set to take the lead. When the light turned green it caught a white couple in the middle of the street. The V-8 full of white guys dug off and they started to run for it; and the two white guys in the Olds blasted at them with the horn, making them jump like grasshoppers. But when they looked up and saw we were coloured they just took their time, giving us a look of cold hatred.

I let out the clutch and stepped on the gas. Goddamn 'em, I'll grind 'em into the street, I thought. But just before I hit them something held me. I tamped the brake.

'What the hell!' Johnson snarled, picking himself up off the floor.

I sat there looking at the white couple until they had crossed the sidewalk, giving them stare for stare, hate for hate. Horns blasted me from behind, guys in the middle lanes looked at me as they passed; but all I could see was two pecks who didn't hate me no more than I hated them. Finally I went ahead, just missed sideswiping a new Packard Clipper. My arms were rubbery and my fingers numb; I was weak as if I'd been heaving sacks of cement all day in the sun.

After that everything got under my skin. I was coming up fast in the middle lane and some white guy in a Nash coupé cut out in front of me without signalling. I had to burn rubber to keep from taking off his fender; and the car behind me tapped my bumper. I didn't know whether he had looked in the rearview mirror before he pulled out or not, but I knew if he had, he could have seen we were a carful of coloured – and that's the way I took it. I kept on his tail until I could pull up beside him, then I leaned out the window and shouted, 'This ain't Alabama, you peckerwood son of a bitch. When you want to pull out of line, stick out your hand.'

He gave me a quick glance, then looked straight ahead. After that he ignored me. That made me madder than if he'd talked back. I stuck with him clear out to Compton. A dozen times I had a chance to bump him into an oncoming truck. Then I began feeling virtuous and let him go.

But at the entrance to the Shell Refinery the white cop directing traffic caught sight of us and stopped me on a dime. The white workers crossing the street looked at the big new car full of black faces and gave off cold hostility. I gave them look for look.

'What's the matter with these pecks this morning?' Homer said. 'Is everybody evil?'

By now it was a quarter of eight. It was twelve miles to the yard. I gritted my teeth and started digging again; I swore the next person who tried to stop me I'd run him down. But traffic on all harbour roads was heavy the whole day through, and during the change of shifts at the numerous refineries and shipyards it was mad, fast, and furious.

It was a bright June morning. The sun was already high. If I'd been a white boy I might have enjoyed the scramble in the early morning sun, the tight competition for a twenty-foot lead on a thirty-mile highway. But to me it was racial. The huge industrial plants flanking the ribbon of road – shipyards, refineries, oil wells, steel mills, construction companies – the thousands of rushing workers, the low-hanging barrage balloons, the close hard roar of Diesel trucks and the distant drone of patrolling planes, the sharp, pungent smell of exhaust that used to send me driving clear across Ohio on a sunny summer morning, and the snow-capped mountains in the background, like picture post-cards, didn't mean a thing to me. I didn't even see them; all I wanted in the world was to push my Buick Roadmaster over some peckerwood's face.

Time and again I cut in front of some fast-moving car, making rubber burn and brakes scream and drivers curse, hoping a paddy would bump my fender so I'd have an excuse to get out and clip him with my tyre iron. My eyes felt red and sticky and my mouth tasted brown. I turned into the tightly patrolled harbour road, doing a defiant fifty.

Conway said at large, 'Oh, Bob's got plenny money, got just too much money. He don't mind paying a fine.'

Nobody answered him. By now we were all too evil to do much talking. We came into the stretch of shipyards – Consolidated, Bethlehem, Western Pipe and Steel – caught an open mile, and I went up to sixty. White guys looked at us queerly as we went by. We didn't get stopped but we didn't make it. It was five after eight when we pulled into the parking lot at Atlas Ship. I found a spot and parked and we scrambled out, nervous because we were late, and belligerent because we didn't want anybody to say anything about it.

The parking-lot attendant waited until I had finished locking the car, then came over and told me I had to move, I'd parked in the place reserved for company officials. I looked at him with a cold, dead fury, too spent even to hit him. I let my breath out slowly, got back into the car, and moved it. The other fellows had gone into the yard. I had to stop at Gate No. 2 to get a late card.

The gatekeeper said, 'Jesus Christ, all you coloured boys are late this morning.'

A guard standing near by leered at me. 'What'd y'all do las' night, boy? I bet y'all had a ball down on Central Avenue.'

I started to tell him I was up all night with his mother, but I didn't feel up to the trouble. I punched my card without giving a sign that I had heard. Then I cut across the yard to the out-fitting dock. We were working on a repair ship – it was called a floating dry dock – for the Navy. My gang was installing the ventilation in the shower compartment and the heads, as the toilets were called.

At the entrance to the dock the guard said, 'Put out that cigarette, boy. What's the matter you coloured boys can't never obey no rules?'

I tossed it over on the wooden craneway, still burning. He muttered something as he went over to step on it.

The white folks had sure brought their white to work with them that morning.

CHAPTER
3

I climbed the outside wooden gangway from the dock and went aboard through the gangway port, an accommodation opening in the shell that put me on the third of the five decks. The compartment I entered was the machine shop; forward was the carpenter shop; aft were the various lockers, toolrooms, storerooms, and such, and finally the third-deck showers and latrine – all a part of the ship itself – where my gang was working.

The decks were low, and with the tools and equipment of the workers, the thousand and one lines of the welders, the chippers, the blowers, the burners, the light lines, the wooden staging, combined with the equipment of the ship, the shapes and plates, the ventilation trunks and ducts, reducers, dividers, transformers, the machines, lathes, mills, and such, half yet to be installed, the place looked like a littered madhouse. I had to pick every step to find a foot-size clearance of deck space, and at the same time to keep looking up so I wouldn't tear off an ear or knock out an eye against some overhanging shape. Every two or three steps I'd bump into another worker. The only time anybody ever apologized was when they knocked you down.

Bessie, one of the helpers in my gang, met me at the midship bulkhead with the time cards.

'Are you evil too?' she greeted.

'Not at you, beautiful,' I grimaced.

All I knew about her was that she was brown-skinned, straightened-haired, and medium-sized; she wore a hard hat, clean cotton waists, blue denim slacks, and a brown sweater. I'd never looked at her any closer.

'You folks got me almost scared to come to work,' she was saying.

I ducked through the access opening without answering, came to a manhole, went down a jack ladder to the second deck, threaded through a maze of shapes to the sheet-metal toolroom. The Kelly that Conway had been whipping in the car was our supervisor. He was a thin, wiry, nervous Irishman with a blood-red, beaked face and close-set bright blue eyes. He had fought like hell to keep me from being made a leaderman, and we never had too much to say to each other.

I tossed the cards on the desk before the clerk with the late cards on top. She picked them up without saying anything. Kelly looked up from a blueprint he was studying with Chuck, a white leaderman, and his face got redder. He turned back to the print without saying anything, and I turned to go out. He had given me enough jobs to last my gang another week and I didn't see any need to say anything to him either. But before I got out he stopped me.

'How's that coloured gang of yours coming along, Bob?'

It was a moment before I turned around. I had to decide first whether to tell him to go to hell or not. Finally I said, 'Fine, Kelly, fine! My coloured gang is coming along fine.' I started to ask him how were the white gangs coming along, but I caught myself in time.

'You coloured boys make good workers when you learn how,' he said. 'I ain't got no fault to find with you at all.'

Chuck gave me a sympathetic grin.

'Now that's fine,' I said. I opened my mouth to say, 'What do you think about the way we're blasting at Ireland?' but I didn't say it.

I turned to the crib girl and said, 'Let me have S-14.'

She was a fat, ducky, blue-eyed farm girl with round red cheeks and brownish hair. She widened her eyes with an inquiring look. 'What's that?'

'A print.'

'What's a print?' she asked.

She hadn't been on the job very long so I said patiently, 'A print is a blueprint. They're in that cabinet there. You have the key. Will you unlock the cabinet and give me the print – the blueprint – marked S-14?'

She unlocked the cabinet reluctantly, giving quick side glances at Kelly to see if he'd say anything, and when she saw that S-14 was marked 'Not to be taken from office,' she turned to Kelly and asked, 'Can he see this?'

My head began heating up again. Kelly looked up and nodded. She took down the print and handed it to me. 'You'll have to look at it here,' she said.

All the leadermen took out prints. I wanted to explain it to her, knowing that she was new on the job. But she had tried my patience, so I said, 'Listen, little girl, don't annoy me this morning.'

She looked inquiringly at Kelly again, but he didn't look up. I walked out with the print. She called, 'Hey!' indecisively, but I didn't look around.

A white helper was soldering a seam in a trunk while a white mechanic looked on. The mechanic and I had been in the department together for the past two years, but we had never spoken. He looked at me as I passed, I looked at him; we kept the record straight. I went up the jack ladder and came out on the third deck again.

There were a lot of women workers on board, mostly

white. Whenever I passed the white women looked at me, some curiously, some coyly, some with open hostility. Some just stared with blank hard eyes. Few ever moved aside to let me pass; I just walked around them. On the whole the older women were friendlier than the younger. Now and then some of the young white women gave me an opening to make a pass, but I'd never made one: at first because the coloured workers seemed as intent on protecting the white women from the coloured men as the white men were, probably because they wanted to prove to the white folks they could work with white women without trying to make them; and then, after I'd become a leaderman, because I, like a damn fool, felt a certain responsibility about setting an example. Now I had Alice and the white chicks didn't interest me; I thought Alice was better than any white woman who ever lived.

When I ducked to pass through the access opening in the transverse bulkhead I noticed some words scrawled above and straightened up to read them: 'Don't duck, Okie, you're tough.' I was grinning when I ducked through the hole and straightened up, face to face with a tall white girl in a leather welder's suit.

She was a peroxide blonde with a large-featured, overly made-up face, and she had a large, bright-painted, fleshy mouth, kidney-shaped, thinner in the middle than at the ends. Her big blue babyish eyes were mascaraed like a burlesque queen's and there were tiny wrinkles in their corners and about the flare of her nostrils, calipering down about the edges of her mouth. She looked thirty and well sexed, rife but not quite rotten. She looked as if she might have worked half those years in a cat house, and if she hadn't she must have given a lot of it away.

We stood there for an instant, our eyes locked, before either of us moved; then she deliberately put on a frightened, wide-eyed look and backed away from me as if she was scared stiff, as if she was a naked virgin and I was King Kong. It wasn't the first time she had done that. I'd run into her on board a half-dozen times during the past couple of weeks and each time she'd put on that scared-to-death act. I was used to white women doing all sorts of things to tease or annoy the coloured men so I hadn't given it a second thought before.

But now it sent a blinding fury through my brain. Blood rushed to my head like gales of rain and I felt my face burn white-hot. It came up in my eyes and burned at her; she caught it and kept staring at me with that wide-eyed phoney look. Something about her mouth touched it off, a quirk made the curves change as if she got a sexual thrill, and her mascaraed eyelashes fluttered.

Lust shook me like an electric shock; it came up in my mouth, filling it with tongue, and drained my whole stomach down into my groin. And it poured out of my eyes in a sticky rush and spurted over her from head to foot.

The frightened look went out of her eyes and she blushed right down her face and out of sight beneath the collar of her leather jacket, and I could imagine it going down over her over-ripe breasts and spreading out over her milk-white stomach. When she turned out of my stare I went sick to the stomach and felt like vomiting. I had started toward the ladder going to the upper deck, but instead I turned past her, slowing down and brushing her. She didn't move. I kept on going, circling.

Someone said, 'Hiya, Bob,' but I didn't hear him until after I'd half climbed, half crawled a third of the way up the jack ladder. Then I said, 'Yeah.' I came out on the fourth deck, passed two white women who looked away disdainfully, climbed to the weather deck. A little fat brown-skinned girl with hips that shook like jelly leaned against the bulwark in the sun. 'Hello,' she cooed, dishing up everything she had to offer in that first look.

'Hello, baby,' I said. The sickness went. I leaned close to her and whispered, 'Still keeping it for me?'

She giggled and said half seriously, 'You don't want none.'

I'd already broken two dates with her and I didn't want to make another one. 'I'll see you at lunch,' I said, moving quickly off.

I found a clean spot in the sun and spread out the print. I wanted an over-all picture of the whole ventilation system; I was tired of having my gant kicked down in first one stinking hole and then another. But before I'd gotten a chance to look George came up and said Johnson and Conway were about to get into a fight.

'Hell, let 'em fight,' I growled. 'What the hell do I care, I ain't their papa.'

But I got up and went down to the third deck again to see what it was all about. It was cramped quarters aft, a labyrinth of narrow, hard-angled companionways, jammed with staging, lines, shapes, and workers who had to be contortionists first of all. I ducked through the access opening, squeezed by the electricians' staging, pushed a helper out of my way, and started through the opening into the shower room. Just as I stuck my head inside a pipe fitter's tacker struck an arc and I jerked out of the flash. Behind me someone moved the nozzle of the blower that was used to ventilate the hole, and the hard stream of air punched my hard hat off like a fist. In grabbing for it I bumped my head against the angle of the bulkhead. My hat sailed into the middle of the shower room where my gang was working, and I began cursing in a steady streak.

Bessie gave me a dirty look, and Pigmeat said, 'We got Bob throwing his hat in before him. We're some tough cats.'

The air was so thick with welding fumes, acid smell, body odour, and cigarette smoke; even the stream from the blower couldn't get it out. I had fifteen in my gang, twelve men and three women, and they were all working in the tiny, cramped quarters. Two fire pots were going, heating soldering irons. Somebody was drilling. Two or three guys were hand-riveting. A chipper was working on the deck above. It was stifling hot, and the din was terrific.

I picked up my hat and stuck it back on my head. Peaches was sitting on the staging at the far end, legs dangling, eating an apple and at peace with the world. She was a short-haired, dark brown, thick-lipped girl with a placid air – that's as much as I'd seen.

'Where's Smitty?' I asked her. She was his helper.

'I don't know,' she said without moving.

Willie said, 'While you're here, Bob, you can show me where to hang these stays and save me having to go get the print.' He was crouched on the staging beneath the upper deck, trying to hang his duct.

I knew he couldn't read blueprints, but he was drawing a mechanic's pay. I flashed my light on the job and said, 'Hang the first two by the split and the other two just back of the joint. What's your X?'

'That's what I don't know,' he said. 'I ain't seen the print yet.'

'It's three-nine off the bulkhead,' I said.

Behind me Arkansas said, 'Conway, you're an evil man. You don't get along with nobody. How you get along with him, Zula Mae?'

'He's all right,' she said. She was Conway's helper. 'You just got to understand him.'

'See,' Conway said. 'She's my baby.'

Arkansas gave her a disdainful look. 'That's 'cause she still think you her boss. Don't you let this guy go boss you 'round, you hear.'

25

'He don't boss me 'round,' she defended.

'You just tryna make trouble between me and my helper,' Conway said. 'I'm the easiest man here to get along with. Everybody gets along with me.'

'You from Arkansas?' Arkansas asked.

'How you know I ain't from California?' Conway said.

'Ain't nobody in here from California,' Arkansas said. 'What city in Arkansas you from?'

'He's from Pine Bluff,' Johnson said. 'Can't you tell a Pine Bluff nig – Pine Bluffian when you see him?'

'Hear the Moroccan,' Conway sneered. 'Johnson a Moroccan, he ain't no coloured man.'

'You got any folks in Fort Worth, Conway?' Arkansas asked.

'I ain't got many folks,' Conway said. 'We a small family.'

'You got a grandpa, ain't you?' Arkansas persisted.

'Had one,' Conway said.

'Then how you know?' Arkansas pointed out.

Peaches was grinning.

'You going back?' Homer asked.

Arkansas looked at him. 'Who you talking to? Me?'

'You'll do. You going back?'

'Back where?'

'Back to Arkansas?'

'Yeah, I'm going back – when the horses, they pick the cotton, and the mules, they cut the corn; when the white chickens lay black eggs and the white folks is Jim Crowed while the black folks is—'

He broke off as Smitty came in with a white leaderman named Donald. They didn't see me. He showed Donald where he had cut an opening in his duct for an intake vent, and Donald said he'd cut four inches off the X.

'That's where Bob told me to cut,' he said.

Donald shook his head noncommittally; he was a

nice guy and he didn't want to say I was wrong. I'd often wondered if he was a Communist. He had a round moonface, pleasant but unsmiling, and that sharp speculative look behind rimless spectacles that some Communists have.

I stepped into the picture then. 'When did I tell you to cut out there?' I asked Smitty.

Donald turned red. 'Hello, Bob,' he said. 'Smitty said you was off today.'

'Jesus Christ, can't you coloured boys do anything right?' Kelly said from behind me. He had slipped in unnoticed.

Air began lumping in my chest and my eyes started burning. I looked at Kelly. I ought to bust him right on the side of his scrawny red neck, I thought. I'd kill him as sure as hell. Instead I ground out, 'Any mechanic might have made the same mistake. Any mechanic but a white mechanic,' I added.

He didn't get it. 'Yeah, but you boys make too many mistakes. You got to cut it out.'

Donald started moving off. 'I ain't made a single mistake this month, Mr Kelly.' Conway grinned up at him from where he knelt on the floor, soldering a seam.

Pigmeat nudged me. 'See what I mean? Got 'em skunt back to his ears. He thinks the man a dentist.'

Kelly heard him but acted as if he didn't. He said to Conway, 'I wasn't talking about you. You're a good boy, a good worker. I was talking 'bout some of these other boys.'

In the silence that followed Peaches said, 'Oh, Conway gonna get a raise,' before she could catch herself, having thought we'd keep on talking and she wouldn't be heard. Somebody laughed.

I kept looking at Kelly without saying anything. He turned suddenly and started out. When he had gone

Smitty said, 'How come he always got to pick on you? He don't never jump on none of these white leadermen. You know as much as they do.'

I unfolded my rule and tapped the duct he was working on. 'Cut your bottom line ten inches from the butt joint,' I directed, trying to keep my voice steady. He was just a simple-minded, Uncle Tom-ish nigger, I told myself; he couldn't help it. 'You'll have a four-inch gap. Take this duct over to the shop and get a production welder to weld in an insert plate and grind the burrs down as smooth as possible.' I turned and started out, then stopped. 'And remember I'm your leaderman,' I added.

Ben was standing in the opening, grinning at me. He was a light-brown-skinned guy in his early thirties, good-looking with slightly Caucasian features and straight brown hair. He was a graduate of U.C.L.A. and didn't take anything from the white folks and didn't give them anything. If he had been on the job for more than nine months he'd probably have been the leaderman instead of me; he probably knew more than I did, anyway.

I grinned back at him.

He said, 'Tough, Bob, but you got to take it.'

CHAPTER
4

I bumped into Red Williams in the companionway and he said he'd been looking all over for me.

'Will you get me a tacker, Bob?' he said. 'I'm tired of fooling with these people. I've had enough.'

He was a tall, rawboned, merriney-looking Negro with kinky reddish hair and brown freckles.

Me too, I wanted to tell him, but the fellows in my gang looked up to me; whenever they had trouble with the white workers they looked to me to straighten it out. So all I said was I'd see Hank.

Hank was the tacker leaderman, a heavy-set, blond Georgia boy about my age and a graduate of Georgia Tech. White mechanics could go to him and get any tacker they wanted, but he made the coloured mechanics wait until he could find a coloured tacker that was free. Most of the white tackers didn't like to work for coloured mechanics, and Hank wouldn't assign them to. He wasn't offensive about it, he'd just make the coloured mechanics wait, and if they got mad about it he gave them a line of his soft Southern jive. I found him on the quarter-deck talking to a couple of white women tackers in their welders' suits.

'How 'bout a tacker for a half hour or so?' I said.

He hadn't seen me coming toward him and when I spoke he jumped. Then he put on his special smile for coloured. 'Why, if it isn't the shot,' he said. 'Whataya say, big shot, long time no see. What's cooking?'

'All I want's a tacker,' I said. I knew it wasn't the way to go about it but I wasn't in the mood for jive.

'Say, fellow, you're getting fat – a regular capitalist.' He kept on as if he thought he was going to thaw me out. Then he turned to the two women. 'Here's a boy who's come out to California and made good in a big way; he's a leaderman in the sheet-metal department – one of Kelly's boys.'

I saw I couldn't rush him so I decided to dish out some too. 'You're doing fine yourself,' I said. 'The folks back in Georgia wouldn't know you.'

He kept his smile, but he began getting dirty. 'You said it, bo.' Then to the women, 'This boy's really a killer, got all the little brown gals in a dither about him.' To me again, 'How *does* you do it, bo?'

I got all set to curse him out; then right in the middle of it I realized that I was jumping the gun; he hadn't really said enough to start a rumpus about. I had to laugh. The three of them started to laugh with me. I said, 'Don't sell me *too* hard, buddy, you just might find a buyer.'

Hank caught it first; the creases stayed in his face but his smile went. The two women dug it from the change in his expression; neither blushed; they just got that sudden brutal look.

'You don't want a tacker, sho 'nuff?' Hank said, trying to get back his advantage.

But he had lost it. 'Sho 'nuff,' I drawled. 'An' ri' now.'

We looked at each other, measuring. His eyes were hard blue, hostile but not quite angry. I don't know how mine looked but I tried to make them as hard as his.

He decided to play it straight, where he always had the advantage. 'To tell you the truth, Bob, all of my tackers are busy, will be busy all day.'

I tried to get it back again. 'How about one of these ladies?' I'd started to say 'Southern' ladies, but decided not to press him that far.

'They're busy too,' he said. Now he got some of his smile back.

I started to turn away, saw a couple of tackers lounging over at the port rail by the generators, gabbing; turned back. 'How about one of them?' I nodded in their direction.

He glanced over at them, looked back at me. Now he had all of his smile back. 'They're busy too,' he said. 'You're just out of luck, Bob. Why don't you try Tommy?' Tommy was another cracker bastard.

I couldn't call him a liar; that's where he had me. I couldn't go down to Kelly and say, 'Hank said he ain't got any tackers' – even if I would have, which I wouldn't. He'd look at me as if I was nuts and say, 'Why, goddamn, why tell me?' I turned away, thinking. The white folks win again, trying to laugh it off. But it stuck in my craw. If I couldn't get the work done I'd have to take Kelly's riding; and in order to get it done I had to eat everybody else's. I had my usual once-a-day urge to tell them to take their leaderman job and shove it.

But half-way down the ladder I thought, what the hell, and turned around and went back to the tackers who were gabbing by the rail. I saw they were Southerners, but I asked anyway.

'Look, can I get one of you fellows to tack a couple of stays for me?'

They looked at each other. For a moment I thought neither one was going to answer, then one said, 'We's waitin' fuh Hank.'

'You're not working on a job, though, are you?'

'No, we's jes waitin'.'

31

I couldn't tell whether they were making fun of me or just talked like that. I decided to try again. 'If Hank says it's all right, can I get one of you then?'

They looked at each other again. The other one spoke this time. He said, 'Sho.'

All of a sudden I had to laugh. They knew that Hank wasn't going to assign them to me. 'Okay, boys,' I said. 'Get your rest.'

I walked off but I didn't know where I was going. I couldn't go down and tell Red that Hank wouldn't give me a tacker, either; they'd get down on me too. Then I thought of Don. I found him at the forward end supervising the installation of a cowl vent.

'Wanna do me a favour?' I said.

He turned that bright speculative stare on me. 'Shoot Kelly?' He didn't crack a smile, but I laughed once anyway to show him it was funny.

Then I said, 'Let me borrow one of your tackers for about a half-hour.'

He thought for a moment. 'There's a girl down aft – Madge. They're doing these things.' He kicked at the cowl. 'You can have her till dinner-time, anyway.'

'Fine,' I said, hurrying off. I noticed the white mechanics give him a dirty look, but I didn't think anything about it at the time.

She had her back to me and her hood up so it covered her hair, so I didn't recognize her right off. I was about twenty feet away, hurrying toward her, when one of the white mechanics looked up, and that caused her to turn. I saw that she was the big, peroxide blonde I'd run into on the third deck earlier; and I knew the instant I recognized her that she was going to perform then – we both would perform.

As soon as she saw me she went into her frightened act and began shrinking away. I started off giving her a sneer so she'd know I knew it was phoney. She knew it anyway; but she kept putting it on me. I didn't know how far she'd go and I got apprehensive. Before I got too close to her I began talking to her, like you do to a vicious dog to gentle it.

'Look, Madge, Don said you could work with me for a while.'

A wild excited look came into her eyes and her mouth went tight-lipped and brutal; she looked as if she was priming herself to scream. This bitch is crazy, I thought, but I walked on up to her and picked up her line as if nothing was happening. 'It's just a short job,' I said. 'I'll carry your line for you.'

She came out of her phoney act and jerked her line out of my hand, 'I ain't gonna work with no nigger!' she said in a harsh, flat voice.

I didn't even think about it. I just said it right out of my stomach. 'Screw you then, you cracker bitch!'

I stood there for a moment swapping looks with her. She didn't even bat her eyes; she just gave me a long hard brazen look and turned to the two mechanics squatting open-mouthed and said, 'You gonna let a nigger talk tuh me like that?'

One started up tentatively, a bar in his hand. 'Well now, by God—'

I gave them a glance. They were both elderly men, small, scrawny, nothing to worry about. I turned and walked away, went down to the head and told Red that I couldn't find him a tacker, he'd have to take the job over to the sheet-metal shop and get it welded.

'These white folks just refuse to work with us niggers this morning,' I laughed. I felt better now I'd cursed somebody out.

At eleven-thirty MacDougal, the department super-intendent, sent for me. I walked across the yard to the sheet-metal shop where he had his office.

'Hello, Bob, the boss'll see you in a minute,' Marguerite said, looking up from her desk by the door. She was a small, compact, black-haired woman with sharp brown eyes and skin that was constantly greasy. She wasn't pretty but she wore expensive clothes. She looked thirty and she was hard as nails.

'How's it going, Marguerite?' I said, but she had turned away to answer the phone and didn't hear me.

I stood there for a time then Marguerite noticed me again and said, 'Sit down, Bob. Mr MacDougal's busy now, he'll see you in a minute.'

I went over and sat in one of the chairs along the wall and looked at Mac. His desk was out from the wall across the room. He was talking to one of the white shop leadermen and didn't look at me. The shop super and two other shop leadermen came in and he talked to them in turn. Then he made a phone call. Another fellow came in and took the chair at the end of the desk with his back to me and Mac talked to him for a time; then he looked up at me and beckoned.

I went over to his desk. 'Hello, Mac,' I said.

He didn't like for the coloured fellows to call him Mac, but he wouldn't tell them outright; he'd tell Marguerite to tell them to address him as Mr MacDougal. She had told me twice; she didn't tell me any more.

He was a fat man in shirt sleeves, weighing three hundred or more. He had a jolly red face and twinkling eyes and when he laughed he shook all over. Now he sat there overflowing in his huge desk chair, beaming at me.

'Hello, Bob, I'm glad you dropped in,' he said.

'You sent for me,' I said.

He quit beaming and his face got vicious. 'You cursed a woman worker this morning,' he charged.

I was suddenly conscious that everyone in the office

had stopped to listen. 'She called me a nigger,' I said.

He carefully crossed his hands over his fat belly and leaned back in his chair. Then he began beaming again. 'You expect all kind of things when you work with people,' he began in a careful voice. 'But one of the first things people in authority gotta learn is they can't lose their temper. I can't lose my temper. My superior can't lose his temper. You didn't have no right to lose your temper about it either. Things happen every day that make me mad enough to curse somebody – but I don't do it. I couldn't keep the respect of my workers. Some of them would get mad and curse me back. I'd lose my discipline over them, I'd lose their respect, I wouldn't be able to keep my job. You can understand that, Bob, you're an intelligent boy.'

I didn't say anything.

'You know as well as I do that part of your job was to help me keep down trouble between the white and coloured workers,' he went on. 'That was one of the reasons I put you on that job. I figured you'd have sense enough to get along with the people you had to work with instead of running around with a chip on your shoulder like most coloured boys.'

I let him talk.

'You know I put you on that job against Mr Kelly's wishes. Kelly – Mr Kelly said I wasn't doing nothing but borrowing trouble but I told him you were the most intelligent coloured boy I knew and you'd be able to help us.' He took an aggrieved attitude. 'I'm surprised at you, Bob. I figured you were too intelligent to lose your head about something like that. I figured you had better manners, more respect for women than that. You know how Southern people talk, how they feel about working with you coloured boys. They have to get used to it, you gotta give them time. What makes me so mad with you is, goddamnit, you know this. I don't have to tell you what could have happened by your cursing a white woman, you know as well as I do.' He paused and jerked his head back. 'Don't you?' He pressed.

'Sure, I know,' I said.

His face got a swollen look and his eyes filled up. 'I'm not going to have you or any other coloured boy in this department who can't maintain a courteous and respectful manner toward the white men and women you have to work with,' he said. His voice shook with anger. He unhooked his hands and shook his fist at me. 'I'm not going to have it, goddamnit, that's all!'

'I'm not going to have nobody call me a nigger either,' I said. I wasn't angry; I was just telling him.

He was through with it. 'You stay on through Saturday. Monday you start in as a mechanic.' He jerked his head toward the fellow sitting at the end of the desk. 'This is Dan Tebbel. Danny's going to work with you this week and beginning Monday he takes your place.'

I'd known Mac was going to give me hell; but I didn't think he'd downgrade me and put a white boy in my place. I thought he'd be afraid of the coloured workers making trouble. It shocked me to find out he didn't give a goddamn about the coloured workers, one way or the other. I looked at Tebbel sort of vacantly. He was a thin, undernourished man with a beaked nose, pale blue eyes, and reddish hair.

But I didn't really begin to feel it until Mac said, 'You'll lose your job deferment too. You're a single boy and they'll put you in IA.'

All of a sudden I got that crazy, scared feeling I'd waked up with that morning. It had happened in a second; my job was gone and I was facing the draft; like the Japanese getting pulled up by the roots. But I couldn't find a thing to say in my defence. I had to say something, so I said, 'What's Tebbel going to do? My gang's a Jim Crow gang. Maybe they won't work for Tebbel.'

Mac reddened. 'That's all, Bob,' he said, dismissing me.

'What about Ben for my job?' I kept on; I couldn't let it go like that. 'He's a college graduate – U.C.L.A. Just as smart as—'

The phone rang. Mac picked it up. He wasn't listening to me. I stood there for a moment, listening to him talk over the phone, not knowing what to do. When I should have challenged him was when he said, 'Monday you start in as a mechanic.' But I had let it pass. Now with the bastard not even listening it was too late to quit. I turned and walked off.

Outside, I stood for a time, feeling cheated, trapped. I couldn't decide whether I'd been a coward or a fool. I debated whether to go back and split him. I'd get a fine and some days, perhaps. Probably a sapping at police headquarters. I'd lose my car. I think that was what made me decide that my pride wasn't worth it. My car was proof of something to me, a symbol. But at the time I didn't analyse the feeling; I just knew I couldn't lose my car even if I lost my job.

The whistle blew for lunch but I couldn't eat. The taste of bile was in my mouth, tart, brackish, bitter as gall. I wanted something to do with my hands, action. I began looking for a crap game. Finally I found one over between the plate racks. A dozen or so white fellows and two coloured were ringed on the concrete. There was money in the centre and two big green white-eyed dice were rolling.

I took out six ones and a ten and two of the white fellows made room for me. A big, seamed-faced, bald-headed welder with gnarled hands was shooting eight bucks. I tossed in a ten to fade him and a thin, sallow-faced man gave me a cursing look.

'He done hit me twice,' he snarled in an Okie voice. 'Think I'm gonna let you have him now?'

I took down my ten. He took his time, counted out eight ones, tossed them in the pot. He kept grumbling under his breath. 'Comin' in here tryna bull de game.' He gave me another hard, hostile look. 'One of these slick guys, think you gonna grab the gravy. Goddamn smart—' He was working himself up to call me a nigger and I figured I'd better stop him.

'If you say another word I'll knock your eyes out,' I grated in a low voice.

He popped to his feet like a jumping jack, a stooped, under-nourished, middle-aged man with the damnedest expression of baffled indignation on his face. I didn't even look up at him. He puffed and he blew. The shooter had come out on a five and he kept working at it until he made it – four, one.

'Shoot it all,' the welder said.

I looked up at my Okie friend. He had turned beet-red. 'He's all yours,' I said.

He muttered some words in his mouth, dribbling saliva. I began feeling better.

'Take down some,' somebody said to the shooter. 'You're holding up the game.'

'I got it,' I said, and tossed my sixteen bucks in the centre.

The shooter nursed the dice, blew on them, said, 'Now do your stuff, babies. Come out on seven.' He cocked his arm, turned them loose. They stopped trey, one.

'Liddle Joe from Kokomo,' one of the coloured fellows murmured, looking at me.

The big bald-headed welder picked them up and rubbed them on his leather pants leg. I looked at him.

'Come on,' a Texas drawl said impatiently. 'You're holding up the game.'

The shooter was getting ready to unlock 'em but now he rubbed them up some more. He gave the speaker a defiant look. Then he threw a beautiful seven.

'A lick too late,' I crowed. I picked up my thirty-two bucks, feeling good for the first time that day.

Then a little waspish, rat-mouthed cracker snatched the dice and tossed six bits in the centre. 'I shoot a nigger lick,' he said.

I didn't move. I squatted there with my eyes on the ground and couldn't look up. When I looked up it was toward one of the coloured fellows. He was looking down too, unmoving; and when he looked up it was toward me. A ripple went through the ring for just an instant; nobody moved. Then the third coloured fellow tossed six bits in the centre and the game went on. I caught several white fellows giving me furtive looks; but I kept looking at the shooter.

When the dice got to me I blew the air out of my lungs, got another lungful, and said, 'I'm gonna shoot my hand.' I tossed the bills in the centre.

'How much is it?' somebody asked.

The little rat-mouthed cracker started to count it. I leaned forward and pushed his hand away. 'It's thirty-two bucks,' I said.

He gave me a hard look and said, 'I got six bits of it.'

I squatted back and waited. I knew they wanted to tell me to take some down and let the game go on. If I'd been white they'd have cursed me. But because I was coloured they didn't say anything; they kept it bottled up and began getting mean.

Finally one of the coloured fellows said, 'Let's gang him.'

Every player in the game took a piece, each pulling his

bet in front of him. I picked up the dice with my right hand, passed them to my left, rolled them softly on the concrete. One came to a stop six up; the other dropped in a deep crevice and cocked with the five facing me, the six facing away.

'Throw in, good losers,' I said. 'I ain't going no farther.'

'Throw in what for?' the rat-mouthed fellow challenged.

'Cocked dice,' somebody said.

I began to choking up. 'Listen, I ain't giving away a goddamned thing. I made my goddamned eleven and now I'm gonna take my goddamned money.'

'You'll take hell, you nigger bastard,' the rat-mouthed guy said, feeling covered by the other twelve white guys.

Blood rushed to my head, stung me blind. I jack-knifed up and kicked at him with one motion. He rolled to one side and my boot heel went over his shoulder, throwing me off balance. I wheeled to my left, falling half forward, my right arm stuck out to catch my fall and my right foot flattened in a pigeon-toed stance.

'I'll cool the nigger!' I heard a voice grate, and I raised my chin, looking for the guy.

I just had time to see him: a tall young blond guy about my age and size. His mouth was twisted down in one corner so that the tips of his dogteeth showed like a gopher's mouth and his blue eyes were blistered with hate. I'll never forget that bastard's eyes. Then that sick, gone feeling came in the pit of my stomach – just a flash. And a blinding explosion went off just back of my eyes as if the nerve centres had been dynamited. I had the crazy sensation of my eyes popping out of my head and catching a telescopic photo of ringed figures, some half up, others squatting in a circle. Then I didn't know a thing.

When I came to the whistle was blowing. I lay flat on

my back in the shade of a rack of plates. Two white fellows and a coloured fellow were bent over me, waiting for me to come to. When I opened my eyes they helped me to get to my feet.

One of the white fellows gave me a sympathetic grin. 'You stuck your chin right straight into his fist.'

The other one said, 'I got some of your money for you – twenty-five dollars and some change.' He stuck it in my hand.

The coloured fellow's eyes were muddy, opaque. His flat brown face was unsmiling. He didn't say anything.

I was still dazed. I braced myself against the plates, shook my head to clear it.

One of the white fellows said, 'Take it easy, son.' They both waited a moment longer and when I didn't say anything they moved off together, grinning. They were elderly, kindly men. I wasn't angry at them; I just hadn't given them a thought. I leaned there for a while, half in the noonday sun, feeling a little faint. I put my hand up tentatively and stroked my chin. When I looked up I saw a couple of other white fellows who had been in the game standing at a distance, watching me.

Then I remembered the blond boy's eyes. I recalled his words, 'I'll cool the nigger!' I felt that sick, gone feeling again. I began trembling; I felt weak, scared. I knew I couldn't take it; but I was scared of what I might do. Scared of what might happen to me afterward. If I could just stop thinking; every time I thought of trouble I thought of death. Then I looked at the coloured fellow again. His face was impassive.

'You see which way he went?' I asked.

He studied me for a moment. 'Ah know whar he work,' he said. His expression didn't change.

I licked my lips, tried to keep the sick, scared feeling out of my eyes. 'Where?' I asked.

He stood there looking at me as if time meant nothing. A curious animal change came over his face. I noticed him take his hand out of his pocket. It struck me funny. But now we seemed closer, as if we'd struck an understanding or come to an agreement about something.

'He in de copper shop,' he said. 'He work on a 'chine down in de back end. You doan need tuh go through de shop, you ken cum in de back do'.'

I started off. My first step was wobbly, more from the sick, gone feeling in my stomach then from any effects of the blow. The coloured fellow stepped in beside me; his eyes slid from side to side.

'You got a chiv?' he asked.

I knew I didn't have one but I fanned myself. 'Musta left it in my box,' I said.

He looked around again, then slipped me his. I didn't look at it, but by its feel it must have been eight inches long. I slipped it in my pocket.

'Ah'da cut de bastard's throat mahself,' he said. 'But Ah thought you'd wanna do it yuhself.'

He split off and I kept on toward the copper shop. My hand rested on the knife in my pocket. I began thinking of how I ought to cut him. Whether I ought to slip up and begin stabbing him in the back, trying to get his heart; or wheel him about to face me and begin slashing him across the face, cutting out his eyes and slashing up his mouth. Maybe he'd be on the lookout for me, I thought, and would have a knife himself. Then we'd dodge about and keep cutting at each other until one dropped.

Bile rolled up in my stomach and spread out in my mouth. I started retching and caught myself. The sun beat down on my bared head like showers of rain. My skin was tight and burning hot, but it wouldn't sweat. Only in the palm of my hand holding the knife did I sweat. I had lost my hat; I didn't know where.

I could see the blond boy's bloody body lying half across his machine, blood all over the floor, all over the shapes; blood on my hands; his face all cut to pieces, one eye hanging out and wrinkled like an empty grape skin. I came to the copper shop, kept on around to the back. For a moment at the back door I stopped and steadied myself. I took the knife out and opened it and got it in a stabbing grip. Then I saw a piece of wood on the ground. I picked it up and held it in my left hand, the knife in my right.

I stepped through the door and stopped. The blond boy looked up at that instant and our gazes locked. He stuck his right hand out slowly and gripped a ball-peen hammer on his work-bench.

It was then I decided to murder him cold-bloodedly, without giving him a chance. What the hell was the matter with me, running in there to fight him? I thought. What the hell did I want to fight him for? I wanted to kill the son of a bitch and keep on living myself. I wanted to kill him so he'd know I was killing him and in such a way that he'd know he didn't have a chance. I wanted him to feel as scared and powerless and unprotected as I felt every goddamned morning I woke up. I wanted him to know how it felt to die without a chance; how it felt to look death in the face and know it was coming and know there wasn't anything he could do but sit there and take it like I had to take it from Kelly and Hank and Mac and the cracker bitch because nobody was going to help him or stop it or do anything about it at all.

The sick, scared, gone feeling left my stomach. I kept looking at him, thinking. There's one goddamned thing, you can't take your colour with you, until I felt only a cold disdain. I turned around and went out.

CHAPTER
5

I went to Mac's office and asked Marguerite for a sick pass to go home. She gave it to me in her cold business manner without saying a word. But I felt she was all right, she was a fine person, she didn't have anything against me. I smiled at her and said, 'Thank you,' and went out.

That was what it did for me. 'Unchain 'em in the big corral,' the boys used to say in Hot Stuff's crap game back in Cleveland. That was what it did for me; it unchained me, made me free. I felt like running and jumping, shouting and laughing; I felt something I'd felt the time Joe Louis knocked out Max Schmeling – only better.

When I checked out Gate No. 2 the gatekeeper looked at me and said, 'What, you going home already? You just got here a few minutes ago.'

I wagged a finger at him. 'You don't know how tempus fugits.'

He didn't like that. 'You coloured boys better lay off that gin,' he said, winking at the guard.

I laughed. 'The only way you can make me mad now,' I told him, 'is to get a mouthful of horse manure and blow it through your teeth at me.'

He turned red and started to say something else, but I didn't stop. I backed out my car, circled in the parking lot, crossed the Pacific Electric tracks, and turned into the harbour road, just idling along. I didn't feel like speeding. The car drove easy all of a sudden, I thought. Not a jerk in it, not a squeak; it took the bumps like a box-spring mattress. It was a pleasure just sitting there, my fingers resting lightly on the steering wheel, just idling along.

I was going to kill him if they hung me for it, I thought pleasantly. A white man, a supreme being. Just the thought of it did something for me; just contemplating it. All the tightness that had been in my body, making my motions jerky, keeping my muscles taut, left me and I felt relaxed, confident, strong. I felt just like I thought a white boy oughta feel; I had never felt so strong in all my life.

A warm glow went all over me as if I had just stepped out of a Turkish bath and had had a good massage. My mind was light, relieved, without a care in the world. As I idled along past the long line of industries I felt a sudden compelling friendliness toward the white people I passed. I felt like waving to them and saying, 'It's all right now. It's fine, solid, it's a great deal.'

A well-dressed, slenderly built middle-aged white woman stepped from the curb in the path of my car. I eased to a stop and waited for her to pass. She looked up; surprise was first in her eyes, then she gave a tentative, half-decided smile. I smiled in return, warm and friendly. It made all the difference in the world; the weights had gone out of my head.

Now I felt the heat of the day, saw the hard, bright California sunshine. It lay in the road like a white, frozen brilliance, hot but unshimmering, cutting the vision of my eyes into unwavering curves and stark unbroken angles. The shipyards had an impressive look, three-dimensional but infinite. Colours seemed brighter. Cranes were silhouetted against the grey-blue distance of sky.

I felt the size of it, the immensity of the production. I felt the importance of it, the importance of the whole war. I'd never given a damn one way or the other about the war excepting wanting to keep out of it; and at first when I wanted the Japanese to win. And now I did; I was stirred as I had been when I was a little boy watching a parade, seeing the flag go by. That filled-up feeling of my country. I felt included in it all; I had never felt included before. It was a wonderful feeling.

Glancing up, I saw a dine-dance café across from the Consolidated. I pulled into the parking lot and coasted to a stop, got out, and went inside. It was cool inside and so dark I had to pause just inside the doorway for my sight to pick out objects. The bar was flat across one side, and the dining-room circled out in front of it.

There were a number of men at the bar, a few women. A group of loud-voiced shipyard workers sat at a table playing Indian dice. They were all white. I found a seat at the bar between a woman and a man and made myself comfortable. The fear of being refused service might have come into my mind, but I didn't notice it. After a while the bar-tender stopped in front of me. He was a thin, indifferent-faced man with thinning black hair and a winged moustache. I ordered a double scotch and he grinned. The white woman next to me stopped talking and looked around. I could feel her gaze on me.

'You would take gin though, wouldn't you?' the bar-tender said.

I let my eyes rove over the stock. All I saw was gin, rum, tequila, vodka, and wine. I grinned back at the bar-tender. 'Gin's fine,' I said. 'I was nursed on gin.'

He picked up the bottle, poised it. 'Double?'

'That's right,' I said. I turned to look at the white woman at my side. Our eyes met. She had brown eyes, frankly curious; and blond hair, dark at the roots, piled on top of her head. In the dim orange light her lipstick didn't show and her mouth looked too thin for the size of her other features. She had taken off her brassière on account of the heat and the outline of her breasts showed distinctly through her white rayon blouse.

She looked away after a moment and when I looked into the mirror I met the eyes of the man on the other side of her. I smiled slightly, looked away before seeing whether he returned it or not.

The bar-tender replaced the gin bottle. 'Chaser?'

'Water,' I said.

He set up the water. 'We don't have no more whisky, only once or twice a week,' he said. 'I ain't seen no Scotch since I don't know when.'

'Scotch? What's that?' the blond girl said. She had a man's heavy voice.

'Speaking of Scotch reminds me of a joke,' the man on the other side of her began. 'Two Scotchmen went to a Jew store to buy a suit of clothes . . .'

I got interested in watching a guy down the bar balance a half-filled glass on its edge and didn't listen. When I finished my gin I went over and sat down at a table. A young dark-haired girl in a blue, white-trimmed uniform came over to take my order. She had two imitation daisies pinned on each side of her hair. Her face was impersonal.

I ordered the biggest steak they had, then a double martini as an afterthought. A big rawboned old-timer came in and looked about for a place to sit. Finally he sat at the table with me. I thought to myself, I must be turning white really and truly, and grinned at him.

'If it's one thing I don't like, it's sitting at a goddamned empty table,' he greeted.

'It is kinda bad,' I said.

'You married?' he asked.

I shook my head. 'Still in the field.'

'I been married thirty-two goddamned years,' he said. 'Got the best goddamned finest woman in the world. Got three boys in the Marines. And goddamnit, every time I come into this goddamned joint I don't find nothing but empty tables.' I thought for a moment he was going to bang on the table and complain to the management.

'You work at Consolidated?' he asked suddenly.

I shook my head. 'I work at Atlas.'

'That goddamned stinking joint!' he said. 'The Navy had to take over that goddamned yard before they could get any work done. That is the goddamnest, laziest, prissiest, undermanned, prejudiced shipyard—' He cursed out Atlas until my steak came, then he looked at it and said, 'That looks pretty good. They must be getting some better beef out this way now.' Until his steak came he cursed out the West Coast beef.

We ate silently. I'd never eaten steak that tasted so good. When I'd finished I got up, paid my bill, said, 'See you,' and left. He didn't say anything; but I felt all right about it.

I decided to go back by Figueroa, and when I turned into it a couple of white sailors thumbed me and I stopped to give them a lift. They were very young boys, still in their teens, scrubbed-faced and slightly tanned. The three of us sat in the front seat; the one in the middle put his arm behind me to make room. For a time we went along without talking, then I asked, 'What's you guy's names?'

'Lester,' the one in the middle said, and the other one said, 'Carl.'

'What's yours?' Lester asked, and I told him, 'Bob.'

'You work in a shipyard?' Carl asked.

'Atlas,' I told him. 'I'm a sheet-metal worker.'

'I worked a while up at Richmond – Richmond No. 1,

Kaiser's yard,' he said. 'I'm from San Francisco.'

'I was up there once,' I said. 'I like Frisco, it's a good city.'

The boy in the middle hadn't said anything, so I asked him, 'Where you from, Lester?'

'Memphis,' he said. 'You ever been there?'

I gave him a quick side glance; then I chuckled. 'No, I never been to Memphis,' I said. 'I'm from Ohio – Cleveland.'

'I bet you'd like Memphis,' he said as if he really believed it.

'Maybe,' I said. 'But I'll never know.'

He grinned. 'You like Los Angeles, eh?'

'Just between you and me,' I said, 'Los Angeles is the most over-rated, lousiest, countriest, phoniest city I've ever been in.'

That was one thing we all agreed on. They liked my car and we talked about cars for a time as we skimmed along the wide straight roadway. The boy from Frisco said, 'Of course if I had my way I'd take a Kitty.'

I said, 'Who wouldn't?'

We passed a couple of girls jiggling along in thin summer dresses and the boy from Memphis whistled.

I said, 'I bet you wouldn't take it if she gave it to you.'

'What you bet?' he said, and they both blushed slightly.

I got a funny thought then; I began wondering when white people started getting white – or rather, when they started losing it. And how it was you could take two white guys from the same place – one would carry his whiteness like a loaded stick, ready to bop everybody else in the head with it; and the other would just simply be white as if he didn't have anything to do with it and let it go at that. I liked those two white kids; they were white, but as my aunt Fanny used to say they couldn't help that.

When we got closer to town and saw more women on the street we started a guessing game about every one we passed, whether they were married or single, how many kids they had, whether their husbands were in the Army, if they played around at all. All the elderly women they called 'Mom.' We had a lot of fun until we came to a dark brown woman in a dark red dress and a light green hat carrying a shoebox tied with a string, falling along in that knee-buckling, leaning-forward, housemaid's lope, and frowning so hard her face was all knotted up. They didn't say anything at all. I wanted to say something to keep it going, but all I could have said about her was that she was an ugly, evil-looking old lady. If we had all been coloured we'd have laughed like hell because she was really a comical sister. But with the white boys present, I couldn't say anything. I looked straight ahead and we all became embarrassed and remained silent for a time. When we began talking again we were all a little cautious. We didn't talk about women any more.

When we neared Vernon Avenue I asked them where they were going and they said down to Warner's at Seventh and Hill. I took them down and dropped them in front of the box office. They thanked me and went off. I kept over to San Pedro and turned south. It was two-thirty when I got home. Henry had already left for work and Ella Mae had taken the baby out for a sunning.

I took a shower, shaved, put on slacks, sport shirt, and sandals; got my .38 Special out of the bottom bureau drawer, checked to see that it was loaded, went out, and got in my car and drove over to Central to get some gas. I put the gun in the glove compartment and left the car in the station for Buddy to check over while I strolled down past the Dunbar Hotel.

I felt tall, handsome, keen. I was bareheaded and my hair felt good in the sun. A little black girl in a pink draped slack suit with a thick red mouth and kinky curled hair switched by. I smelled her dime-store perfume and got a live-wire edge.

Everything was sharper. Even Central Avenue smelled better. I strolled among the loungers in front of Skippy's, leaned against the wall, and watched the babes go by. A white woman in a Ford roadster with the top down slowed for the traffic and a black boy called, 'Hello, blondy!' She didn't look around.

Tia Juana pulled up in his long green Cat and parked in a No Parking zone. He got out, a short, squat, black, harelipped Negro with a fine banana-skin chick on his arm, and went into the hotel, and some stud said, 'Light, bright, and damn near white; how does that nigger do it?'

A bunch of weed-heads were seeing how dirty they could talk; and a couple of prosperous-looking pimps were standing near by ignoring them. Some raggedy chum came from the barber shop across the street where they had a crap game in the rear and said that Seattle had won two grand. The coloured cop grabbed him for jay-walking and started writing out a ticket; and he was there trying to talk him out of it: 'You know me, man, I'm ol' Joe; everybody know ol' Joe—' Everybody but that cop, that is.

It was a slick, niggerish block – hustlers and pimps, gamblers and stooges. But it didn't ruffle me. Even the solid cats in their pancho conks didn't ruffle me. It wasn't as if I was locked up down there as I'd been just yesterday. I was free to go now; but I liked it with my folks.

A couple of my boys came up. 'You still on rubber, man?' one wanted to know.

'That's right,' I said.

'Say, run me out to Hollywood, man.' It was twelve miles to Hollywood. I laughed.

'Don't pay no 'tention to that nigger, man,' the other one said. 'That nigger's mad. Lemme take a sawbuck, man. I got a lain hooked down here and all he needs is digging.'

'That's right,' I said. 'Try a fool.'

They grinned. 'You got it, Papa.' They went off to find another one.

My people, I thought. I started to get a drink, then glanced at my watch. It was a quarter to four. I hurried over to the parking lot, got my car, circled into Central, and began digging. It was just four-thirty when I pulled up before the entrance to the parking lot at Atlas Ship.

I got out, walked over to the gate where the copper shop let out. My boy was one of the first ones through. I was thinking of him as 'my boy' now. I followed him, wondering how I could work it if he caught a P.E. train. But I got a break; he waited on one side of the street until a grey Ford sedan slowed for him and climbed in. I sprinted back across the street, got in my car, and dug off just as one of the yard cops was coming over to move me. I muscled in ahead of a woman driver three cars behind the grey Ford; kept the position until we came to Anaheim Road in Wilmington, then pulled up to one car behind and stayed there. I thought about my riders; they were burning, I knew.

The next instant I'd forgotten them. It felt good following the guy, knowing I was going to kill him. I wasn't at all nervous or apprehensive. I thought about it like you think about a date with a beautiful chick you've always wanted to make; I just had that feeling that it was going to be great.

The grey Ford had five riders besides the driver. At Alameda Street it turned north into Compton, and two of the riders in back got out, leaving my boy alone. When it stopped before a house in Huntington Park I rolled up and parked right behind it. My boy got out, said something to the fellows in the front seat, and the car moved off. He glanced idly at my car, took two steps toward the house, then wheeled about and stared into my eyes. His eyes stretched with a stark incredulity and his face went stiff white, like wrinkled paper. He stood rigid, half turned, as if frozen to the spot.

I reached into the glove compartment and got my gun, then I opened the door and got out into the street. I wasn't in any hurry. They'd probably hang me, I knew, but I'd already accepted that, already gotten past it. He turned quickly and started up the walk toward the house, walking stiff-jointed, his shoulders high and braced and his back flattened like a board. When he got to the steps a homely blond woman opened the door from the inside and two small towheaded kids squeezed past her legs and ran toward him.

He pushed the children back through the door with a rough, savage motion, then whispered something sharply to the woman. She snapped a quick frightened look toward me and her mouth opened as if to scream. She let him in and slammed shut the door and I could hear it being bolted from the inside.

I stopped. I didn't have to kill him now, I thought. I could kill him any time; I could save him up for killing like the white folks had been saving me up for all these years.

Out of the corner of my eye I saw two old ladies coming down the sidewalk with loaded shopping bags, giving me frosty looks. It didn't occur to me that my boy might stick a gun out the front window and blow off the back of my head. I felt cool, untouchable, indifferent. I thought perhaps he might be calling the police, but it didn't worry me. When the two old ladies came opposite me I gave them a wide, bright smile and said in my best manner 'It's a beautiful day, isn't it?'

I left them standing dead still on the sidewalk, twisting their scrawny necks about to stare at me with outraged indignation as I climbed into my car and dug off.

I could even go back to the shipyard and work as a mechanic, I thought. As long as I knew I was going to kill him, nothing could bother me. They could beat my head to a bloody pulp and kick my guts through my spine. But they couldn't hurt me, no matter what they did. I had a peckérwood's life in the palm of my hand and that made all the difference.

CHAPTER
6

I called the best hotel in town when I got home and made reservations for a deuce at nine o'clock. The headwaiter's voice was very courteous: 'Thank you, Mr Jones.' I grinned to myself; he'd fall out if he knew I was a Negro, I thought.

Then I called Alice. I'd decided to knock myself out and when I told her to wear evening clothes her voice became excited. 'Now I know we're going to the Last Word.' That was a new club out on Central she'd been trying to get me to take her to ever since it opened; I suppose she figured that the people in her class didn't patronize such places and the only way she'd get there was for me to take her.

'Nope,' I said. 'The Avenue's out tonight.'

'You know I want to go to the Last Word,' she said. Her low, well-modulated voice was cajoling.

'That's not the mood,' I said. 'And anyway, nobody dresses for the Last Word.'

'Where, Bob, the Seven Nymphs?' That was a Hollywood joint where Negroes went sometimes.

'Nope, bigger and better,' I said.

'Don't tease me, Bob.' A thread of annoyance had come into her voice. 'I absolutely refuse to go unless you tell me now.'

'It's a secret,' I laughed. 'I'll call for you at eight.' I

hung up before she had a chance to reply.

Ella Mae passed through the living room with the baby wrapped in a blanket. She had just finished bathing it. 'You oughta be 'shamed of yourself, teasing Alice like that,' she said.

'Don't you worry about Alice,' I told her. 'Alice can take care of herself.'

She began pinning a diaper on the baby. 'You're going to mess up yet,' she said. 'Alice don't know you like I do.'

I grinned at her. 'Nobody knows me like you do. You're my baby.' She snorted. I began peeling off my sport shirt. 'I'm just playing around with Alice until you and I figure out how to get rid of Henry,' I said. 'Then we're going to get married and I'll keep Alice as my Monday girl.'

She gave me a long peculiar look. Then suddenly she giggled. 'You'll have to raise Emerald.'

'Emerald what?' Then I laughed. 'I forgot her name was Emerald.' It always startled me. 'You sure did your baby a dirty trick,' I added.

'I think Emerald's a pretty name,' she defended. 'Prettier than Alice, anyway.'

'Emerald Brown,' I pronounced, going into my room to finish undressing. 'You must think she's gonna grow up to be one of the green people.'

She didn't reply.

'Well, it's your baby,' I said.

I took another shower and began dressing. When Ella Mae came into the kitchen to heat the baby bottle she said, 'You oughta be clean enough even for Alice now – two baths in one day.' Her voice was ridiculing.

'I'm tryna turn white,' I laughed.

'I wouldn' be s'prised none, lil as it's said,' she cracked back.

'You know how much I love the white folks,' I said; I couldn't let it go.

'You just ain't saying it, either,' she kept on. 'All that talking you do 'bout 'em all the time. I see you got the whitest coloured girl you could find.'

'Damn, you sound like a black gal,' I said, a little surprised. 'I thought you liked Alice.'

'Oh, Alice is fine,' she said. 'Rich and light and almost white. You better hang on to her.'

'Okay, baby, I quit,' I said. I wondered what was eating her.

She went into her room and closed the door. I put on dinner clothes, cloth pumps, midnight-blue trousers, white silk shirt with a soft turned-down collar, a pointed-tip dubonnet bow, and a white jacket. I'd bought the outfit a year ago, but the only chance I'd had to wear it was at the Alpha formal at the Elks Hall during the Christmas season, except when I wore it down on the Avenue late at night as if I'd just come from some affair or other. I felt sharp in it.

I stepped out into the parlour and called Ella Mae. 'Come look at your sweet man, baby.'

She looked strictly evil when she stepped into the room. She gave me one look and said, 'All I hope is you don't come home mad and try to take it out on me.' Then she softened. 'You do look fine, sure 'nough.'

I grinned. 'Well, talk to me, baby.'

She stepped forward suddenly and pulled my face down and kissed me. She made her mouth wide so that her lips encircled mine completely, wet and soft; and her tongue came out and played across my lips, forcing itself between my teeth.

I pushed her away roughly, almost knocking her down. 'Goddamnit, quit teasing me!' I snarled.

'Just like a nigger,' she said angrily, blood reddening in

her face. 'Get dressed up and can't nobody touch you. Shows you ain't used to nothing.'

'Hell, I wasn't even thinking about my clothes,' I said, stalking out.

Outside the setting sun slanted from the south with a yellowish, old-gold glow, and the air was warm and fragrant. It was the best part of the day in Los Angeles; the colours of flowers were more vivid, while the houses were less starkly white and the red-tiled roofs were weathered maroon. The irritation ironed quickly out of me and I got that bubbly, wonderful feeling again.

I glanced at my watch, saw that it was a quarter to, and hurried to the car. At Vernon I turned west to Normandie, driving straight into the sun; north on Normandie to Twenty-eighth Street, then west past Western. This was the West Side. When you asked a Negro where he lived, and he said on the West Side, that was supposed to mean he was better than the Negroes who lived on the South Side; it was like the white folks giving a Beverly Hills address.

The houses were well kept, mostly white stucco or frame, typical one-storey California bungalows, averaging from six to ten rooms; here and there was a three- or four-storey apartment building. The lawns were green and well trimmed, bordered with various local plants and flowers. It was a pleasant neighbourhood, clean, quiet, well bred.

Alice's folks lived in a modern two-storey house in the middle of the block. I parked in front, strolled across the wet sidewalk to the little stone porch, and pushed the bell. Chimes sounded inside. The air smelled of freshly cut grass and gardenias in bloom. A car passed, leaving the smell of burnt gasoline. Some children were playing in the yard a couple of houses down, and all up and down the street people were working in their yards. I felt like an intruder and it made me slightly resentful.

The door opened noiselessly, and Mrs Harrison said, 'Oh, it's you, Bob. Come right in, Alice will be ready shortly.'

I had to get my thoughts straightened out in a hurry. 'How are you today, Mrs Harrison?' I said, following her into the small square hallway. 'How is Dr Harrison?'

She was a very light-complexioned woman with sharp Caucasian features and glinting grey eyes. Her face was wrinkled with countless tiny lines and sagged about the jowls. She wore lipstick but no other make-up, and her fine grey hair was bobbed and carefully marcelled. She was aristocratic-looking enough, if that was what she wanted, but she had that look of withered soul and body that you see on the faces of many old white ladies in the South.

'Oh, the doctor is busy as usual,' she said in a cordial voice, turning left down three carpeted steps into the sunken living room. 'I've told the doctor a dozen times that he's just working himself to death, but there's nothing to do with him. He says there's a shortage of experienced physicians now and he's such a humanitarian at heart.'

I could picture the doctor, a little cheap, small-hearted, lecherous, cushy-mouthed, bald-headed, dried-up, parchment-coloured man in his late sixties, who figured he was a killer with the women. He was probably out chasing some chippy chick right then and I caught myself about to say, 'Strictly a humanitarian.'

Instead I said, 'Yes, he is,' lifting my feet high to keep from stumbling over the thick nap of the Orientals. Their house reminded me of a country club in Cleveland where I worked summers when I was in high school; you knew they had dough, you saw it, it was there, you didn't have to guess about it. 'Of course the money he's making ought to compensate in part,' I added evenly.

'Well, we could do without some of the money,' she began. 'It's so hard on all of us. You know Charles, our chauffeur, was drafted, and Norma left us to take a defence job. We only have Clara now, and she's getting so temperamental, I do declare—' She broke off, looking at me. 'Bob, you look very nice tonight. You wear evening attire very well indeed.'

'Almost as if I was a gentleman – or a waiter.' I grinned, dropping into a chair before the fireplace and fumbling for a cigarette. 'The boys out at the shipyard wouldn't know me now.'

She took a seat across from me and smiled graciously. 'I imagine some of the white young men at the shipyard in some of the more advanced departments are college-trained; but I understand our Negro workers are mostly Southern migrants.'

'Oh, there're quite a few Negro college graduates working in the various yards,' I said, and got my cigarette going.

'Oh, is that so?' She raised her eyebrows slightly. 'However, I don't imagine any of them have much occasion to wear evening attire.'

I blinked at her; I wondered why she was giving me all that. I knew her, I was one of the family, more or less. But I played along with her. 'No, I guess not. You can't be a gentleman and a worker too.'

'The doctor tells me that most working people spend their leisure time at the movies or in bars,' she went on. 'I think that's really a shame. Of course the doctor and I enjoy the legitimate theatre best, but since the war he hasn't been able to leave his practice long enough for us to visit New York City for the season. We have our season tickets to the Hollywood Bowl, of course – we're on the sponsor list, you know – but I do so wish we could go East this fall and see some of the new shows—'

I caught her digging for a breath and put in, 'Can I fix you a highball?' I knew it was crude, but if I had to listen to her I was at least going to have a drink.

'No thanks, dear,' she declined. 'The doctor has stopped me from drinking entirely. It aggravates my high blood pressure, you know. But fix one for yourself, do, if you like – and one for Alice too. She'll be down in just a moment, I'm sure.' When I stood up she added, 'You know where everything is, of course.'

'Yes, thanks,' I said. I went across the hallway into the doctor's pine-panelled study and mixed a couple of Scotch-and-sodas at his built-in bar. Then on second thought I took a couple of slugs straight to get even for the three drinks I'd bought him the last time I met him at a bar. I was grinning when I returned to the living-room.

'You look quite pleased about something today, Bob,' she observed. 'I suppose you're elated at the prospect of returning to college this fall.'

'This fall?' I looked at her.

'Alice tells me you're going to arrange your work so you can attend the university in the mornings,' she informed me.

'Oh yes, that's right.' I didn't want to tell her that was the first I'd heard about it. 'Yes, I'm going to join the ranks of the Negro professionals.'

'It gives me a feeling of personal triumph, too, to see our young men progress so,' she said. 'I like to think that the doctor and I have contributed by setting an example, by showing our young men just what they can accomplish if they try.'

That was my cue to say, 'Yes indeed.' But she looked

so goddamned smug and complacent, sitting there in her two-hundred-dollar chair, her feet planted in her three-thousand-dollar rug, waving two or three thousand dollars' worth of diamonds on her hands, bought with dough her husband had made overcharging poor hard-working coloured people for his incompetent services, that I had a crazy impulse to needle her. The Scotch had gone to work too.

So I said, 'Well now, to tell you the truth, Mrs Harrison, what I'm so pleased about today is I've just found out how I can get even with the white folks.'

She couldn't have looked any more startled and horrified if I'd slapped her. 'Bob!' she said. 'Why, I never heard of such a thing!' Her hands made a fluttery, nervous gesture. 'Why on earth should you feel you have to get even with them?' But before I could reply she went on, 'Bob, you frighten me. You'll never make a success with that attitude. You mustn't think in terms of trying to get even with them, you must accept whatever they do for you and try to prove yourself worthy to be entrusted with more.' Now she was completely agitated. 'I'm really ashamed of you, Bob. How can you expect them to do anything for you if you're going to hate them?'

'I don't expect them to do anything for me they can get out of doing anyway,' I said.

'You've been talking to those Communist union agitators out at the shipyard,' she accused. 'You mustn't let them influence you, Bob, you mustn't listen to them.' She was genuinely concerned; I felt sorry for her. 'Take the advice of an old lady, Bob. The doctor and I have many, many white friends. They come here and dine with us and we go to their homes and dine with them. We have earned their respect and admiration and they accept us as social equals. But just a few of us have escaped, just a few of us.'

I started to say, 'Maybe they think the few of you are white,' but thought better of it.

'I'm really hurt and worried about you, Bob,' she went on incoherently. 'You must talk to Alice about this. White people are trying so hard to help us, we've got to earn our equality. We've got to show them that we're good enough, we've got to prove it to them. You know yourself, Bob, a lot of our people are just not worthy, they just don't deserve any more than they're getting. And they make it so hard for the rest of us. Just the other day the doctor went into a restaurant downtown where he's been eating for years and they didn't want to serve him. Southern Negroes are coming in here and making it hard for us . . .' Tears came into her eyes. 'We must pray and hope. We can't get everything we want overnight and we can't expect the white people to give us what we don't deserve. We must be patient, we must make progress . . .' She was just rattling off phrases now that didn't even make any sense to herself.

'Maybe the white folks can run faster than we can,' I muttered. 'Then what do we do?'

But she didn't even hear me. 'You must read Mrs Roosevelt's article in the *Negro Digest*,' she was saying.

The old sister was so sincere I felt ashamed; I had no idea I'd touch her that much. I got up and took her hand. 'You're right, Mrs Harrison,' I said. 'Perfectly right, you and Mrs Roosevelt both.' I had to bite my tongue to keep from saying, 'How could you and Mrs Roosevelt possibly be wrong?' Instead I said, 'I really didn't mean it the way you construed, but you're right about it.'

'Right about what?' Alice said from the foot of the spiral stairway, and fell into the living-room like Bette Davis, big-eyed and calisthenical and strictly sharp. She was togged in a flowing royal-purple chiffon evening gown with silver trimmings and a low square-cut neck that showed the tops of her creamy-white breasts with the darker disturbing seam down between; and her hair was swept up on top of her head in a turbulent billow and held by two silver combs that matched the silver trimmings of her gown – a tall willowy body falling to the floor with nothing but curves. Black elbow-length gloves showed a strip of creamy round arm. I gave her one look and caught an edge like a rash from head to foot, blinding and stinging. She was fine, fine, fine, so help me.

She must have caught it in that instant before I got it under control, for she blushed, and before she cut it off she showed me it was there. Then she smiled complacently and said, 'Thank you, darling. You look very nice yourself.' In her best social worker's voice. Everything went. It really and truly let me down.

'We're certainly going to be the people if we keep on trying,' I said. 'Either that or some reasonable facsimiles.'

Neither of them got it and I let it go. 'We were just talking about the Negro problem, and I was telling your mother she was right,' I explained as Alice came across the room and perched on the arm of my chair. 'I got a drink for you, honey,' I said, handing her the highball from the cocktail table.

Alice wasn't going to be concerned about the Negro problem. 'Mother, Loretta Fischer has bought a new mink coat,' she said as if positively shocked. 'I don't see how she does it.'

'I suppose Loretta will be the grand lady if William goes to Congress at ten thousand a year,' Mrs Harrison said; then she turned to me. 'You know, Loretta's people never had anything and her mother worked in service to give her an education. Now that William is making a little money she's spending every penny.'

'I suppose she thinks that's what it's for,' I said absently, glancing at my watch. I patted Alice on her thigh. 'We're going to have to go, baby.'

'I think our people who're making money at this time should save it,' Mrs Harrison said. 'That's all many of us are going to get out of it.'

'Some of us are going to get killed out of it,' I said.

Alice gave me a sharp look. 'You haven't been called, have you, Bob?' she asked.

'No, of course not,' I said too fast, then slowed up some. 'I don't think I'll be called.' I tapped the cocktail table. 'I'm knocking on wood anyway.'

'You won't be called,' Mrs Harrison said. 'You're what they call a key man.'

'They better not call him,' Alice said, brushing her fingers lightly down the back of my neck. 'Where are we going, darling?' she asked, standing up.

I grinned at her. 'It's still a secret.'

She made a face at me and ran upstairs after her wrap. Mrs Harrison looked curious but didn't say anything. Alice returned with a black velvet cape and I held it for her, pressing her shoulders. Mrs Harrison followed us to the door.

'You both look so nice, it's a pity you're not going to some inter-racial affair,' she said. 'I think now is the time we should make more social contacts with white people.'

'Oh, Mother, I don't want to always be running after white people whenever I go out anywhere,' Alice protested. 'I want to go slumming down on Central Avenue.'

'You sound just like the other white people,' I said to Alice.

Mrs Harrison followed us out on the porch. 'You shouldn't feel that way about it,' she said to Alice. 'You should take pains to show them that you're not seeking their company, but you should seek more social association with them, I'm sure.'

'I'd really like to see how that's done,' I mumbled under my breath. Alice pinched me.

We said good-night and climbed into the car. At Western I leaned over and said, 'Kiss me, gorgeous.'

She touched my lips lightly with hers so as not to muss her make-up.

CHAPTER
7

It was just turning dark when I pulled to the curb in front of the hotel. Alice clutched my arm and whispered, 'Oh, no, Bob, no! I don't feel like being refused. I'm not in the mood for it.'

'What the hell!' I said, startled. Some other girl, but not Alice; she was always going to some luncheon or dinner conference at the downtown hotels. Not so long before, one of the Negro weeklies had carried a picture of her knocking herself out down there with a bunch of city big shots. Then I got annoyed.

'You couldn't be getting cold feet after all the bragging you've been doing about never being refused at all the hotels you're supposed to've stayed in all over the world? What're you tryna do, make it light on me? You don't have to feel you got to look out for me. These folks don't worry me, not today.'

'It's not that,' she argued tensely. 'It's just that it's uncomfortable and it takes too much out of me.'

'I got reservations,' I said. 'You don't think I'm taking you in cold.'

'It isn't that,' she tried again. 'It just takes an effort, Bob, and I wanted to let my hair down and have some fun.'

I was getting sore. 'You seem to have enough fun with the other people you go here with. Scared because you haven't got the white folks to cover you?'

'Shhhh!' she cautioned under her breath. 'Here comes the doorman.'

'Goddamn, let him come!' I said. 'Am I supposed to shut up for the help?' I knew I was being loud-mouthed but she'd shaken my poise and I was trying to get it back.

A big, paunched man in a powder-blue uniform with enough gold braid for an admiral and a face like a red-stained rock put a white-gloved hand on the car door and pulled it open. He helped Alice to the curb, touched my elbow as I followed her.

'Tis a lovely evening,' he said in a rich Irish brogue. His small blue eyes were blank.

'Fine,' I echoed, giving Alice my arm. 'I'll pick the car up after dinner.'

He didn't bat an eye. Beckoning to his assistant, a tall, sallow-faced youth in the same kind of uniform, he said, 'Park the gentleman's car,' then walked with us to the glass door and held it open. That went off all right.

But when we mounted the red-carpeted stairs and stepped into the full view of the lobby we brought on a yellow alert. The place was filled with solid white America: rich-looking, elderly couples, probably retired; the still active executive type in their forties and fifties, faces too red and hair too thin, clad in expensive suits which didn't hide their paunches, mostly with wives who refused to give up; and the younger folks no more than half of whom were in uniform, with their brittle young women with rouge-scarred mouths and hard, hunting eyes. There was a group of elderly Army officers, a brigadier-general, two colonels, and a major; and apart from them a group of young naval officers looking very white – ensigns perhaps. I didn't see but one Jew I recognized as a Jew, and nobody of any other race at all. And I only noticed a few couples in evening dress.

It seemed that to a person everyone froze. It started at the front where we were first noticed, and ran the length and breadth of the room, including the room clerks, the porters, the bellmen, the people behind desks. Many were caught in awkward positions, some in the middle of a gesture, some with their mouths half open. Then suddenly there was a concerted effort to ignore us and only a few continued to stare.

'The great white world,' I said flippantly, leaning slightly toward Alice as we walked the gauntlet of the room. 'Strictly D-Day. Now I know how a fly feels in a glass of buttermilk.'

She moved like a sleepwalker, her nails biting into my arm as she clung to it. Her shoulders were high, square, stiff, and her face was set in rigid lines, making her seem a hard, harried thirty. She didn't speak.

'Relax, baby,' I said as we passed a group of middle-aged people. 'I'll show 'em my shipyard badge and if that don't help, all they can do is lynch us.' I didn't try to keep my voice lowered and the people must have heard; they drew away as we passed.

Alice blushed a deep dull red, but some of the stiffness left her. 'You don't have to prove it,' she said. 'They expect you to be a clown anyway.'

'Well anyway, I'm running true to form,' I said. We were both just making words.

Looking up, I caught a young captain's eye. He didn't turn away when our gazes met; he didn't change expression; he just watched us with the intent stare of the analyst.

The head waiter came quickly up the four steps from the dining-room with bleak eyes and a painted smile. He was a slight, round-faced man with a short sharp nose and thin, plastered hair. 'We are sorry, but all the tables are reserved,' he greeted us blandly in a high, careful voice.

I looked down at him with a broad smile that went all down in my throat and chest. It was all I could do to keep from putting my finger in his face. 'Don't be sorry on my account,' I said, slightly slurring the words with too much throat. 'I have one reserved. Jones – Robert Jones.'

The painted smile came off, leaving slackness in his face, and his eyes looked trapped. 'Jones, Mr Jones . . .' The 'Mr' almost strangled him, but he recovered quickly. 'Certainly, sir. I'll have to consult my lists for tonight. We have so many unexpected officers whom we must serve, you know.' This time his smile included me.

But I wouldn't accept it. Alice squeezed my arm.

He turned, left us standing on the platform at the head of the entrance stairway, walked the length of the dining-room, and disappeared through the doorway into the pantry.

'He must keep his lists in the icebox,' I said, and Alice squeezed my arm again.

I jerked a belligerent look at her, then suddenly felt good all over. She had regained her control and she looked so poised and assured and beautiful, standing there among the white folks, I filled right up to the throat. I noticed a number of the white men sliding furtive glances of admiration at her, and I thought, 'You just go right on and keep yours, brothers, and I'll keep mine – and won't miss a thing either.' Alice looked up and caught me looking at her and I winked.

'You're a cute chick,' I said. 'How 'bout a date?'

She smiled. 'It's nice to go out with you,' she whispered. 'I feel so well protected.'

I didn't get it so I just grinned. But when several other diners came up, walked past us down into the dining-room, and were seated by the captains, her smile faded. I began getting on my muscle again; I looked down over the sea of curious faces disdainfully. Breath started choking up in me and I thought, Tomorrow I'm going to kill one of you bastards, and it loosened up again. I lit a cigarette to steady my hands, thumbed the match toward the sandbox.

Finally the head waiter returned from the pantry and now he was affable. It was more insulting than hostility. He led us down to the last table by the pantry door and beckoned a crooked-faced, slightly stooped Greek waiter to take our order.

'We came here to get something to eat out of the kitchen, not to eat in it,' I said.

The head waiter lifted his brows. 'I don't understand.' He shrugged indifferently. 'This is the only table we have vacant, sir. You were fortunate, sir, to get reservations at all at such a late hour.'

'—at all, period,' I said.

Alice looked extremely embarrassed. The head waiter hovered hopefully. The Greek waiter held the chair for her and the head waiter departed. The orchestra began playing something sticky, sweet. I sat down and looked at the menu, determined to get my money's worth out of the joint. Most of the courses were listed in French and I had an impulse to sail it across the room. Then I laughed.

'Bring us a couple of martinis while I consult my dictionary,' I said to the waiter, and when he left I said to Alice, 'I'm going to have some broiled pheasant and champagne and I know the white folks are going to say, "That's the nearest that nigger can find to chicken and gin," but I don't even give a damn.'

Alice's eyes frightened me; I thought for a moment that I'd lost her. Then she said in an even voice, 'A good sauterne would be better with your pheasant,' and I breathed again.

When the waiter returned with the martinis she became

more at ease. The knowledge that she could order a meal with confidence set her up again. I started to bring her down but decided against it; she needed whatever she could get from any source, I thought.

'You order for both of us,' I said.

She and the Greek had a fine time discussing food. He was enjoying it too, it seemed, and she was getting her kicks until a woman at a nearby table giggled. Chances are the woman hadn't given her a thought; but she went into her shell again. Even the waiter noticed it. She finished ordering and the waiter left.

I looked across at the party next to us. A young ensign with chiselled features sat across from a very blond girl in a gorgeous print dress. Her hair was drawn in a bun at the nape of her neck, showing a small, shell-like ear. I let my gaze rest on her for a moment, taking in the delicate lines of her chin and throat, the sensitive lines about her mouth and the clean curved sweep of her neck. My gaze moved slightly and I looked squarely into the eyes of the ensign. There was no animosity in his gaze, only a mild surprise and a sharp interest. There were two elderly people at the table, probably the parents of one of them, and the man laughed suddenly at something that was said. After a moment he switched his gaze to Alice; it stayed on her so long the blond girl looked at her too. Her face kept the same expression. Alice didn't notice either of them; she was drinking her martini with a rigid concentration.

I had a sudden wistful desire to be the young ensign's friend. I would have liked to send him a note inviting them to join us after dinner and go to some night spot. Then I met the frosty glare of the elderly lady. I looked away.

Alice began one of her one-sided monologues, this time about literature. I knew suddenly that she was fighting; that she'd been fighting before, I let her fight.

'Don't you like to go out with me?' I asked her suddenly.

She stopped talking and gave me a long solemn look. 'I always like to go out with you, Bob,' she said. 'You make me feel like a woman. But this is the first time you've ever made me feel like an exhibit.'

'But I really thought you liked to go to places like this,' I said.

She said without thinking. 'But, Bob, with you everybody here knows just what we are.' I didn't get it at first. She hadn't meant to state it so baldly, so she began covering up. 'I'm not trying to justify it, I'm just stating how it is.'

'You mean—' I burst out laughing and people from several tables turned about to stare with disapproval. Finally I got it out: 'You mean when you go in with the white folks the people think you're white.'

There was pure murder in her eyes. 'You don't have to be uncouth.'

'On top of being black too, eh?' I added, chuckling. 'Hell, they probably think we're movie people anyway, or that you're white as it is. I'll tell them I'm an East Indian if you think that'll help. Next time I'll wear a turban.'

The nearby diners had quieted to listen. Alice got a strained smile on her face and began talking politics. But I wouldn't let her get away with it. 'What are you trying to do now, educate me?' I said.

Neither of us said another word; we were both relieved when it was over. The waiter brought me a slip of paper clipped to the bill face down on the tray. When I picked up the bill I read the two typed lines:

We served you this time but we do not want your patronage in the future.

I started to get up and make my bid, to do my number for what it was worth. But when I looked at Alice I cooled. I could take it, I was just another nigger, I was going to lynch me a white boy and nothing they could do to me would make a whole lot of difference anyway – but she had position, family, responsibility.

The bill was twenty-seven dollars and seventy-three cents. I figured they'd padded it but I didn't beef. I simply borrowed the waiter's pencil and wrote: 'At your prices I cannot afford to eat at your joint often enough for you to worry about,' and put the note, three tens, and some change on the tray.

The waiter leaned over and said, 'If it will make you feel any better I'm going to quit. And you can read what I think about it in the *People's World*.'

I looked at him a moment and said, 'If you're thinking about how I feel, when you should have quit was before you brought the note.'

When I held Alice's wrap I could feel her body trembling. A tiny vein throbbed in her temple and nerve tension picked at her face. On the way out it was an effort to walk slowly; she pulled at me as if she wanted to run. We had to wait for the car. Passing people looked at us curiously. I thought we should have waited inside, but it didn't make any difference now. When the car came Alice ran out to it and slipped beneath the wheel. I gave the doorman a five-dollar bill, his assistant a couple of ones.

The doorman fingered the five, hesitated for an instant, then said impassively, 'Thank you, sir, and good evening,' in his thick impersonal brogue. The assistant said nothing.

'You can always tell a shipyard worker by the tips he gives,' Alice sneered when I got in beside her and dug off with a jerk.

'A fool to the bitter end,' I said, slumping down in the

seat. 'I'm sorry you didn't like it.'

I didn't like Alice very much then, didn't even respect her.

'I did like it,' she snapped. 'Even with you acting boorish. The food was excellent.'

'Yes, the food was delicious,' I murmured.

She gave me a quick angry look and almost bumped into a car ahead as it stopped for the light.

'But for thirty dollars,' I added, 'I could have bought a hunting licence, gone hunting and shot a couple of pheasants, bought a quart of liquor and got drunk and gone to bed with two country whores and had enough money left over to buy gasoline home.'

She said, 'You don't have to insult me any more, Bob. I don't intend to see you after this anyway.'

I took a deep, long breath, let it out. 'It had to end sometime,' I said. 'I suppose you knew I wasn't going back to college.'

After that she didn't say anything. She kept out Hill to Washington, turned west on Washington to Western. I thought she was going home, but at Western she turned north again to Sunset, jerking the big car from each stop, riding second to forty, forty-five, fifty, before shifting into high. She pushed in the traffic, shouldered in the lines, tipped bumpers, dug up to sixty, sixty-five, seventy in the openings as if something was after her.

At Sunset she turned west, went out past the broad-casting studios, past Vine, turned left by the Garden of Allah into the winding Sunset Strip. At the bridle path she began tipping off her lid: seventy, eighty, back to seventy for a bend, up to ninety again. I thought she was trying to get up nerve to kill us both and I didn't give a damn if she did.

At Sepulveda Boulevard she turned south to Santa Monica Boulevard, then west again toward the beach. It was early, not eleven o'clock, and there was plenty of traffic on the street. But she didn't even slow.

'I like to go places in a party,' she said suddenly. 'Then to the theatre and a night club afterward.'

'With the white folks,' I remarked.

'You go to hell!' she flared, pushing back up to ninety.

CHAPTER
8

Weget the ticket just as we were coming into Santa
Monica. Two motor-cycle cops pulled up and
flagged us down. They rolled to a stop in front of us,
stormed back on foot, cursing.

'All right,' one said, pulling out his book. 'Start lying.'

Laughter came up inside of me. If they wait a couple of
days they can get me for murder, I thought. 'The lady's
going to have some babies,' I said.

The cop leaned over to see me better. 'A coon,' he said.
Then he looked at Alice again. 'Both coons.' Then on
second thought he asked her, 'Are you white?'

'She's a coon, too,' I answered for her.

'Well, we'll just run you in,' the cop said.

'That's fine,' I taunted. 'You on your puddle jumper
and me in my Buick Roadmaster.'

The cop's mouth opened and his face got blood-red.
The other cop started back toward me.

'Wait a minute,' Alice said. 'I don't like this, I don't
like any of this.' The cold hard authority in her voice
stopped the cop. 'I am a supervisor in the Los Angeles
Department of Welfare,' she went on, enunciating each
syllable with careful deliberation. 'My father's a prominent Los Angeles physician, a personal friend of the
mayor's, and one of the civic leaders of our community. I
don't like the way you have spoken to me, the words you

have employed, nor the tone of your voice. If you cannot give me the respect that is due me I'll see to it that you are both discharged from the police force.'

Both the cops looked at her as if they didn't believe they were hearing right. I had to look at her too.

Finally one of them asked her, 'Your car?'

'Mine,' I said.

He gave me a long hard look. 'I suppose your pa is a senator,' he said.

I didn't say anything. The other one said to Alice, 'Lemme see your operator's licence.'

'I left it in another bag,' she said imperiously. 'Mr Jones called to escort me to dinner and I didn't think I'd need it.'

The cop grinned evilly. 'Been to a gin party, eh?'

Alice turned a slow red. 'May I have your names and identification numbers?' she said.

The cop looked at the other cop, then said, 'Okay, fall in behind me.' As an afterthought he added, 'And move over and let Rufus drive. You got your licence, haven't you, Rufus?'

I got out and walked around the car. He blocked my path. The other cop closed in beside me. I took a breath, let it out, said: 'Rufus isn't the name on it.'

'Lemme see it,' he said.

I let him see it. He spat, moved aside, and let me get into the car. They took us to the station in Santa Monica. I put up cash bail and the desk sergeant said, 'Now get back where you belong and stay there.'

We went out and got into the car and I drove down to the beach. I parked and we sat for a time looking out over the Pacific Ocean. There were two bright red spots in Alice's cheeks and she clenched and unclenched her hands.

'You could kill 'em, couldn't you?' I said. Suddenly I

felt sorry for her. I put my arm about her shoulder and tried to pull her to me. 'Don't let it get you down, baby,' I said, trying to turn her face around to kiss her. 'You're not just finding out you're a nigger?'

She jerked away from me. 'I wish I was a man,' she said.

'If you were a man what would you do?' I asked.

Suddenly she began crying. 'I never had anybody talk to me like that,' she sobbed. 'People have always respected me. My father's known all over California.'

I reached for the key, kicked on the motor. 'Too bad they don't know me,' I said.

I turned the car and drove down to Venice, came back into Los Angeles on Venice Boulevard. By the time we reached the city Alice had stopped crying and repaired her make-up. I glanced at my watch. It was eleven-thirty.

'Shall I take you home?' I asked.

'No, let's go by some friends of mine,' she said. 'I want some excitement.' Her voice had a hard dry gaiety and her face kept breaking apart like glass.

I followed her directions, drove over to a little cottage on San Pedro, past Vernon. A short, dumpy, brown-skinned girl with slow-rolling eyes and a tiny pouting mouth let us in.

'Alice,' she greeted, then to the others in the room, 'Her Highness.'

A light-complexioned, simple-looking girl with a pretty face and dangling hair sat on the arm of an empty chair, the skirt of her loud print dress pulled high over her thighs. She looked at Alice and jerked her head disdainfully.

A slim, good-looking fellow about her colour with conked yellow hair and a hairline moustache sat on the middle of the davenport. He was dressed in tan slacks, tan and white sport shoes, and a cream-coloured rayon shirt. His face was greasy and his eyes were muddy from drinking. I followed Alice into the small, cramped room, wondering how she knew such people; they were more the kind of people I should know.

'Stella, Bob,' she said. I nodded to the dumpy girl.

Stella said, 'Bob, Chuck,' waving her finger.

The blond boy stuck up a sweaty languid hand. I dropped it as soon as possible.

'Bob, Dimples,' Stella went on.

I nodded to the long-haired girl. She didn't look at me; she was eyeing Alice with a petulant, jealous look. I flopped down on the chair beside her and looked at her smooth yellow thighs. 'Nice gams,' I commented. She stood up and let her dress fall.

A gallon bottle of wine and three dirty glasses sat among the littered ashtrays and half-emptied cigarette packages on the little cocktail table in front of the davenport. Against the back wall was a Philco combination player with records stacked on its top. Beside this was a door leading into the bedroom. Across the room was another door into the kitchen, where Alice had gone with Stella. After a moment they came back with two clean glasses and Stella filled them with the cheap warm Tokay.

'Champagne?' I murmured facetiously. Stella rolled me a look, grinned, showing a gaping hole in the middle of her upper teeth.

She moved over to the player and said, 'We were just getting ready to play some jive.' She had a husky liquor voice with queer undertones and she wasn't even half pretty. But there was an animal sensuousness in her actions and she moved with a slow slinky grace. My gaze followed her on its own.

She put on Harry James's 'Cherry,' stacked several other records on the arm drops, and did a slow-motion boogie to the hot licking lilt of James's trumpet, rolling her body from breasts to knees in undulating waves. Near the end of the piece she broke the slow, smooth motion of her boogie and put frenzied jerks in it.

'Well, knock yourself out, girl,' Dimples muttered.

'Goddamn, that knocks me out!' Stella said with feeling when the piece came to an end. Then she asked suddenly, 'Where you kids been, all sharpened up?'

Dimples said, 'Doesn't Alice look lovely?' in a saccharine voice.

'We had dinner and went for a drive,' Alice murmured affectedly.

I stuck a cigarette in my mouth and said, 'Alice had a wonderful time,' talking around it. I looked up just in time to catch her furious glance.

Stella looked curiously from one to the other of us. 'What happened?' she asked. 'Didn't they want to serve you?'

I didn't answer.

'Men are such boors,' Alice commented acidly.

Stella took her cue and dropped it. The box was playing 'All For You' by the King Cole Trio, and I closed my eyes to listen. '. . . life would be a symphony, waiting all for you . . .' It went off into an instrumental trio and I opened my eyes again. For an instant my vision was out of focus and I knew I was getting drunk. I got up to fill my glass again.

'Who wants some more wine?' I asked, then began filling everybody's glass without waiting for an answer. I quoted:

> 'A Jug of Wine . . . and Thou
> Beside me singing in the Wilderness—
> Oh, Wilderness were Paradise enow!'

Stella gave me a quick darting look and stood up. 'I've got a pint of Sunnybrook stashed if you want some,' she said, looking at Alice.

'Fine,' I said, starting to get up. She stepped past me and put her arm about Alice's waist and they went into the kitchen. I looked at Dimples and said, 'Wanna dance?' The box was blaring Erskine Hawkins' 'Don't Cry, Baby.'

'Not with you,' she said in a harsh, sullen voice, looking sidewise into the darkened kitchen.

Things began getting a little blurred. It was hot and sticky in the room and my eyes began to burn. Stella and Alice returned from the kitchen.

'It's hot in here,' Stella said. 'Why don't you take off your coat, Bob?'

I slipped out of my coat. Alice and Stella were sitting side by side on the davenport, whispering. Dimples sat on the arm of the davenport watching them, her face a mask of sullen envy.

I got slowly to my feet. The room began spinning and my stomach peeled into my mouth. I caught it a couple of times, my mouth ballooning, then Chuck jumped up and helped me into the kitchen and I let it go into the sink. I stood there and retched for what seemed like an hour.

I knew what was going on and I wasn't having any of it. I felt shocked, sickened. I went back into the room and said to Alice, 'You can't do this to me.'

She gave me a look of raw hatred. I'd slapped her before I knew it. She half fell, caught herself, and went over and lay on the davenport, burrowing her face in her hands, and began crying as if her heart would break.

My mind went into a stupor when I tried to figure out why she should be mad at me. When I came out of it I noticed that she was crying. I felt like a dog. I lurched toward the davenport and stood over her. 'I didn't mean to make you cry,' I began.

She raised her head and looked at me and all the frustration in the world was bottled up in her eyes. 'Don't think you made me cry,' she said in a cold, level voice, spacing the words apart. 'You can't make me cry. You never could make me cry. Every time I cry, I cry for many reasons.'

I stood there swaying drunkenly for a moment, trying to figure out what she meant, I gave it up.

Chuck stood up then and said, 'Take it easy, Jack.'

I looked at him a moment. I knew I had to hit something, so I drew back and hit him. He fell back against the wall, slumped to the floor.

Stella said, 'What'd you have to hit Chuck for?'

I picked up my coat, put it on without replying. I lifted my hand and waved foolishly, then I went to the door and went out and got into my car. I remember turning around; I banged the curb hard with my front tyres and cursed.

CHAPTER
9

I dreamed I was lying in the middle of Main Street downtown in front of the Federal Building and two poor peckerwoods in overalls were standing over me beating me with lengths of rubber hose. I was sore and numb from the beating and felt like vomiting; I was sick in the stomach and the taste was in my mouth. I was trying to get up on my hands and knees but they were beating me across the back of my head at the base of the skull and every now and then one would hit me across the small of my back and I could feel it in my kidneys. Every time I got one knee up and tried to get the other one up I couldn't make it and would fall down again and I knew I couldn't last much longer. But when the peckerwoods started to stop, a hard cultured voice said peremptorily, 'Continue! I will tell you when to stop.' I turned my head and looked up to see who was talking and it was the president of the shipyard corporation dressed in the uniform of an Army general and he had a cigar in one side of his mouth and his eyes were calm and undisturbed. One of the peckerwoods said: 'The nigger can't take much more.' The president of the shipyard said, 'Niggers can take it as long as you give it to them.' Somebody laughed and I looked around and saw two policemen standing by a squad car to one side nudging each other and laughing. There was no one else on the street. The other peckerwood said, 'It ain't right to beat this nigger like that. What we beating this nigger for anyway?' The cops stopped laughing and looked at him and the president of the shipyard got hard and said, 'Continue! It's an order!' So they started beating me again and I was hoping I would become unconscious but I couldn't.

Then I felt myself rolling over in bed, struggling with the covers, but I couldn't wake up, and the dream kept right on with the two peckerwoods beating me not quite to death. Then two old coloured couples in working clothes on their way to work came up and the peckerwoods stopped beating me and the cops came up and stood over me with their hands on their guns and their chins stuck out as if they were scared I might get up and hurt somebody. The coloured people looked at the peckerwoods with dull hatred and then the president of the shipyard smiled at them and said, 'There should be something done about this,' and they looked at him gratefully and said: 'Yassuh, it's a shame to go beating a man like that,' and the president of the shipyard said, 'All of us responsible white people are trying to keep these things from taking place, but you boys must help us.' I tried to tell the coloured people what he had been doing before they came but my voice wouldn't come out and they just looked at him as if he was a good kind god and said, 'Yassuh, some of these heah boys do git out of their place, but usses don't cause no trouble at all. We working in defence and we don't cause nobody no trouble.' The president of the shipyard said, 'I knew the minute I saw you that you were good coloured folks,' and they went away feeling good toward him and hating the peckerwoods. The cops picked me up and threw me into the squad car and when I asked them where they were taking me they said they were taking me to jail. When the squad car started with a jerk, I woke up.

I was lying in bed. Outside the sun was shining bright. I've overslept, I thought suddenly, and jumped out of bed. Pain shot through my head like summer lightning. My mouth was full of quinine and cottony-dry. I frowned, turning my head carefully to look into the mirror.

Then I remembered. I tried to stop it about Alice but it came back anyway. I felt an odd sort of embarrassment for her; a sort of mixture of shame and betrayal and repulsion. I hoped I wouldn't have to see her for some time; not until I could get myself prepared to think about her again.

I sat slowly down on the bed and looked about. The night kept coming back in brown, dirty memories. Parts of my dream were mingled with them. I began feeling remorseful. I despised myself. I wondered if I would ever be able to face people again. I was too ashamed to leave the room.

All of a sudden I thought about my job. I could see it coming and couldn't stop it. Danny Tebbel would be taking my place, bossing my gang around. The fellows in my gang would be sullen, resentful – ashamed too. Just ashamed of being black. They'd know what had happened to me; they'd see it in the white workers' eyes.

When I thought about Madge that cold scare settled over me and I began to tremble. Just scared to think about her, about living in the same world with her. Almost like thinking about the electric chair. I knew if I kept sitting there thinking about her I'd get up and go out to the shipyard and kill her.

But I couldn't move. I couldn't even stand up any more. I'd forgotten about the dice game and the white boy I was going to kill. It was just Madge and me in an empty world, with Alice pulling at me not quite hard enough to get me out.

I'm a goddamned coward, I told myself. I'm afraid to

die, that's my trouble. Afraid of getting hurt. Acting a fool. Being made ridiculous. Being offended, ignored, despised. Afraid to make the one final decision in my soul that would settle everything one way or another forever. I knew I was going to do it, but I was afraid to do it then.

I bowed my head in my hands and groaned. I felt like I was going to be sick a long, long time and never get well. I wrapped my robe about me and went in and took a quick shave and bath and put on some clothes.

The phone rang and I went to answer it.

'Bob?' It was Alice. Her voice was tense.

The bottom dropped out of my stomach. 'Yes, this is Bob,' I said.

'I feel like a slut,' she said.

I wanted her to stop talking about it; I wanted her to go on as if it'd never happened. 'Look, can't you forget about last night?' I said tightly. 'All it was, it just got me for a chick like you to go for a hype like that. But hell, I've forgotten about it already.'

'But I'd die if anyone knew . . .' She left it hanging.

So that's it, I thought. 'If you're worrying about me talking – don't,' I grated. 'I don't talk about anybody—'

'It's not that, Bob, darling,' she cut in quickly, but her voice sounded relieved. 'I just want to atone, darling; I just want to prove to you I'm not really that type of person.'

I kept right on as if she hadn't spoken. 'But if you're trying to buy my silence it isn't worth it. I know any number of chicks I can go to bed with, but I always thought of you—' She hung up.

I banged the receiver on the hook and turned toward the kitchen. I thought, Goddamnit, everything I do is wrong. I slipped on my jacket, got my identification and money, and went out without saying anything at all.

When I looked in the garage I didn't see my car. My stomach went hollow. Now if I'd banged it up and left it somewhere on the side of the road, that would really do it, I thought, hurrying out to the street. It was parked across the street with the front wheels cut sharply up over the curb as if I'd started to drive into the people's house and had caught myself.

The keys were still in it and the ignition was on, although the lights were off. It must have stalled when the wheels went over the curb. I walked around it, looking for dented fenders and flat tyres, but it didn't have a nick. I climbed in, mashed the starter; the motor kicked on. A better car than I was a man, I thought.

When I started north on Wall Street I had no idea where I was going. Anywhere, just to get away from the people I knew for a while. I just wanted to get away from the so-called respectable people of the world, the decent people. They were playing it too close for me, playing it harder than lightning bumps a stump, taking too many techs.

I turned over to San Pedro and headed downtown toward Little Tokyo, where the spooks and spills had come in and taken over. It was a hot, lazy day and the drain from my hangover left me lightheaded. I pulled up in front of a hotel near First and San Pedro and went into the combination bar and restaurant called the Rust Room. I climbed on a stool and ordered a double brandy straight, then looked in the mirror to see who was there.

In the mirror I saw a chick get up from a table with a couple of sailors in a booth and start over towards me. I turned to face her and began talking before she could open her mouth. 'Now don't start performing, baby, before you know what it's all about—'

'What kind of nigger are you anyway?' she broke in. 'Puleeze elucidate. Just what is your jinglet that you are now about to recite?' She was a long tall yellow chick, named Veda, who worked as a waitress on the day shift. She had a longish narrow face and a thick-lipped nice-made mouth; her thick black curly hair grew low on her forehead like a man's and her heavy black brows met over the bridge of her nose, not a pretty chick but good for a change. I'd broken a date with her a week before.

'I'm tryna tell you, honey,' I grinned. 'My car broke down and I tried to get you on the phone but couldn't anybody find you. Where were you, anyway? Having your sport I suppose.'

'Don't hand me that hockey,' she said, leaning one hand on the bar and looking at me. 'That is the saddest jive; that is pitiful, puleeze bulieve me.'

'Now look, baby, you're getting loud,' I said. 'It doesn't become you.'

'You're sad, too sad, puleeze bulieve me,' she said. 'You're just a chickenshit nigger, too sad, just too sad for words.'

'Now listen, darling, don't lose your pretty ways,' I said, trying to quiet her. 'You're too refined for all this notoriety jive.'

'You're just a sad nigger, goddamn. Why in the hell didn't you call me?'

I turned to the bartender. 'Give this chick a drink.' Then back to her. 'What you drinking, baby?' I put my arm around her and pulled her toward me. 'You're a fine-looking chick out of uniform, strictly exotic.' I was trying to stop her from talking but it didn't work.

'Exotic my fanny,' she said. 'You're just a corn-fed nigger, a mealy Moe.'

'What you drinking, girl?' the bartender asked.

'Singapore sling,' she said, then changed it: 'No, just brandy and water.' Then back to me. 'You're really too, too sad. I laid off to give you something you ain't never had before and what do you do—' She broke off. 'I'm too, too tall, really running and leaping, if I'm lying I'm dying. Puleeze bulieve me.'

'Let me get like you,' I said.

She gave me a look. 'Waste my good earth on you, a sad nigger like you, to have you duck out on me again? You must wanna die, nigger.'

'What you doing now?' I asked.

'I'm going up and go to bed, darling. What do you care?'

'Let me go up with you and put you to bed, honey,' I said. 'You just might not be able to make it.'

'I just might not at that,' she said. 'But you ain't gonna help me. You gotta have a date with me before you fall in my pad, darling. I just don't pick up anybody at the bar.' She went back to the table with the two sailors in the booth and sat down and began eating the dinner she had left.

Suddenly the brandy took hold and I began feeling melancholy. I thought of my second year at State when I subbed at end on the football team – the one game I played and the one touchdown I made and the people cheering. I had never felt so powerful, so strong, almost as if I'd become the hero I used to dream about being when I grew up. Then I thought about a motion picture called *A Guy Named Joe*; about that cat making that last bomb run, sinking a Nazi flat-top. Going out in a blaze of glory. See you, Gates. See you, Jaxon. See you, stud . . . *In the bright blue forever . . .*

Just a simple nigger bastard, that was me. Never would be a hero. Had a thousand chances every day; a thousand coming up tomorrow. If I could just hang on to one and say, 'This is it!' And go out blowing up the white folks like that cat did the Nazis.

My throat went tight, began to ache. My Adam's apple

90

swelled until it choked me and began to hurt. My face wrinkled like a piece of paper beginning to burn; and my mouth spread, lips flattening against my teeth. I began to cry. Not openly. But all down inside.

Two white soldiers and a white chick came in, looked about hesitantly, then went back and sat at a table near the juke box and ordered beer. Every eye in the room was on them.

The soldiers were ordinary boys, didn't look too bright; but the girl was strictly an Arkansas slick chick, a rife, loose, teenage fluff, with a broad face and small eyes and a hard mouth and straggly uncombed hair, dressed in a dirty white waist open at the throat and a dirty blue skirt, barelegged and muddy-shoed. She looked like she had just got off an S.P. freight – but she was white.

The waitress looked as if she didn't want to serve them but didn't know how to refuse. All the coloured women in the place sneered at the chick; one black girl at a nearby table looked at her as if she wanted to spit on her; and I heard some woman down the bar mutter.

But the men had different reactions. Some studiedly ignored her; a couple of black boys at the bar kept turning around to look at her; two Filipinos sitting directly in front of her stared at her with hot burning eyes and forgot to eat their scoff.

A couple of beers made the chick high and she got that frisky white-woman feeling of being wanted by every Negro man in the joint; she couldn't keep still. She got up to put a nickel in the juke box and stood there shaking herself. But one of the black boys at the bar wouldn't let her spend her money; he slid off his stool and went over beside her and played all the pieces she wanted to hear. Then one of the soldiers thought he ought to stand up and protect her, so she sat down.

A couple of well-dressed guys were eating dinner at a

table in the rear; they looked slick, like pimps perhaps. The chick spotted them and began flirting with the dark one. By that time the white boys were trying to get her out, but she didn't want to go. She got noisy and began singing one line over and over in her flat Southern voice – ' "I can't see for looking" ' – rolling her eyes about at the black boys in the joint. I had to laugh. She snapped a sharp disdainful look in my direction and tossed her head.

When she got up to play her nickel again both of the black boys at the bar went over and started talking to her. The soldiers stood up and tried to make her sit down. One of them took her by the arm and tried to force her into her chair but she jerked loose and said, 'Just go on out and let me alone. I can take care of myself all right.'

The two slick studs passed her on the way out and she grabbed the dark boy's arm.

He said, 'Take it easy, baby,' and brushed her off.

The soldiers got salty. They whispered something to each other, then called the waitress to pay for the beer. Another waitress went after the manager and he came from the lobby and stood by the bar. When the soldiers started to leave he headed them off.

'You can't go out and leave her here,' he said.

'She don't want to come,' one of the soldiers said.

'She came in with you, she's got to go out with you,' the manager said, taking the soldier by the arm.

They went back to the juke box and the soldier said, 'Come on, let's get out of here.'

'Listen,' the manager said to her. 'You'll have to leave with these soldiers you came in with.'

'Why?' she asked in her flat voice. 'It's a free country, ain't it?'

'Aw, come on,' the soldier said, getting red. 'Let's get

out this nigger joint.' I don't think he meant to say it, but after he'd said it he got defiant.

Where before there had just been race, now there was tension. We could call ourselves nigger all we wanted, but when the white folks did it we wanted to fight.

'Well, go on then,' she said to the soldier, then turned to the manager. 'Why I got to go out with 'em? I don't know nothing 'bout 'em. I just come in with 'em, that's all.'

All she's got to do now, I thought, is to start performing. She could get everybody in the joint into trouble, even me just sitting there buying a drink. She was probably under age anyway; and if she was she could get the hotel closed, the liquor licence revoked, probably get the manager in jail. She could take those two black chumps flirting with her outside and get them thirty years apiece in San Quentin; in Alabama she could get them hung. A little tramp – but she was white.

Then all of a sudden I thought of Madge; the two of 'em were just alike. I hadn't thought of her all that day, and now the whole bitter memory washed over me. The indignity of it, the gutting of my pride, what a nigger had to take just to keep on living in the goddamned world. I thought about killing the white boy again, but it didn't do anything at all for me now. It seemed childish, ridiculous, so completely futile; I couldn't kill all the white folks, that was a cinch. The cold scared feeling started clamping down on me; it nailed me to my seat, weak and black and powerless.

I heard the manager saying to the Arky Jill, 'You've got to go out with them.'

His voice wasn't exactly rough, but the white boy didn't like it. His defiance was riding and he turned a white look on the manager. I thought he was going to say something; and I knew if he said the wrong thing the manager would likely pop him because he was a rugged stud, formerly a Negro copper. I thought hopefully: Well, here it goes. If the boy got hurt, or if there was any kind of rumpus with the white chick in it, there wouldn't be any way at all to stop a riot – the white GIs would swarm into Little Tokyo like they did into the Mexican districts during the zoot suit riots. Only in Little Tokyo they'd have to kill and be killed, for those spooks down there were some really rugged cats; the saying was they wouldn't drink a white cow's milk. I wanted it to come and get it over with. But the white boy caught himself and didn't say anything; I felt a sense of disappointment.

'Well, all right, I'll go out with 'em,' she finally consented. 'But I'm coming back by myself.' Then she said to the soldier: 'Pay the boy and le's go.'

'I done paid him already,' the soldier said angrily, taking her by the arm and almost dragging her out.

She turned her head and grinned at the two black boys before she left. The manager walked to the door and held it open for them.

'All you got to do is go outside and get it,' the bartender said to me.

I looked at him. 'I wouldn't have her with your help,' I told him, then I asked for my bill.

He gave it to me and I paid him and started out. Veda's drink was still sitting on the bar untouched. When she saw me leaving she headed me off at the door. 'Well, how 'bout you?' she said. 'I thought you were buying me a drink.'

'It's on the bar,' I growled.

She caught me by the arm. 'Can't you wait for a minute until I get rid of my company? Just what *is* your story?'

I shook her off.

I got in my car and dug off in a hurry. I was tense, jerky, at loose ends; almost got bumped by a P.E. train turning into the station beyond Sixth. Now I didn't know where to go, what to do. All the guys I used to run around with were in the Army – Willie, Freddie, Bill, Chet. I hadn't seen any of that group of girls we used to run around with since I'd started going with Alice. Ruth was married, I'd heard; Gussie was still working in service. I saw Josie on the street-car one day and she said she was working at Lockheed. There was Vivien Williams; there used always to be something going on at her house back in the days before the Communist Party dealt the race issue out. But I decided against her. With all the pressure on me, I couldn't have listened to a Negro spouting the party line if my life had depended on it.

I was still scared to think about Alice. I wanted time to let it cool. If I thought about her now I'd hate her guts, I knew. I could understand how she'd gotten upset. After all, she wasn't used to the pressure we'd gotten last night – hard enough to beat her down. I could sympathize with her on that rap. But the breakout . . . I rubbed my hand down over my face . . . She'd known where she was going, had known what the play was from the first. I could overlook it happening once – happening accident- ally. The white folks' pressure would make a monkey eat cayenne pepper – once.

I tried to shake it from my mind, looked about me. I'd gone out past Washington. I turned around, headed back downtown, decided to go to a show, get my mind clear of everything. I parked in the lot at Sixth and Hill, stopped a moment to look at the rows of white faces on the magazine covers at the book stand, thought sardonic- ally: The white folks sure think they're beautiful, walked up to the drugstore at the corner for a pack of smokes. The little prim-mouth girl back of the counter let me stand there while she waited on all the white customers first. When she started to wait on another one who just came in I banged my hand down on the counter. 'Give me some cigarettes, goddamnit!' I said.

She jerked a look at me as if she thought I was raving crazy; everyone within earshot looked at me. I felt my face burning, my body trembling from the sudden fury.

'Never mind!' I said, wheeled outside, walked fast out Hill Street, bumping into people. There was nothing at Paramount that interested me – just a lot of white faces on the marquee billboards – nothing at Warner's. I turned down Seventh, stopped in front of Bullock's at the corner of Broadway, watched the people pass. The sidewalk was heavy with pedestrian traffic, mostly white, a sprinkling of Mexicans, here and there a coloured face. Every second man was in uniform; four out of five women were unescorted.

The servicemen were always hostile towards a Jodie, especially a black Jodie in his fine Jodie clothes. Two little Mexican slick chicks passed; I caught them looking at me and they turned up their noses and looked away disdainfully. I wasn't trying to flirt with them; I wasn't trying to flirt with anybody.

It beat me. I began to feel conspicuous, ill at ease, out of place. It was the white folks' world and they resented me just standing in it. I crossed the street and went into Loew's just to get out of sight. The seat I found was between two couples; on one side the man was next to me, on the other side the woman. The woman said something to the man with her and they got up and changed seats so the man sat next to me. It had never happened to me before. I began burning again but I tried to ignore it. I concentrated on the picture.

I never found out the name of the picture or what it was about. After about five minutes a big fat black Hollywood mammy came on the screen saying: 'Yassum' and 'Noam,' and grinning at her young white missy; and I got up and walked out.

I was down to a low ebb. I needed some help. I had to know that Negroes weren't the lowest people on the face of God's green earth. I had to talk it over with somebody, had to build myself back up. The sons of bitches were grinding me to the nub, to the white meatless bone.

I started hurrying back to the parking lot, got my car, and turned toward the West Side. In a way I still respected Alice; whatever else she might be, she'd still make the grade in the white folks' world. And I loved her too, I knew. I didn't know how I expected her to help me; what she could say or do. Maybe I wanted her to lean on me and tell me I was strong and that she belonged to me; or to hold my head against her breast and let me get it all straightened out. Or maybe I wanted to give her a chance to fall on her knees and ask for my forgiveness and tell me it was an accident and would never happen again. I didn't know.

All I knew was I needed help. Needed it the very worst way. Needed it then. Or I was gonna blow my simple top. And she was the only one I knew who could give it to me.

CHAPTER
10

D r Harrison answered my ring. He was dressed in a
brown flannel smoking jacket with a black velvet
collar. He waved a soggy cigar butt in his left hand, stuck
out his right.

'Hello, Robert, it's good to see you, boy.'

We shook hands; his felt dry, lifeless, and his mouth
looked nasty. I said, 'It's good to see you, Doctor.'

He closed the door behind me and steered me into his
study.

'You're just in time to join me in a nip.'

'Well, thanks,' I said. I always felt a sharp sense of
embarrassment around him. I didn't like him, didn't
respect him, didn't have anything to say to him, didn't
like to listen to him. But he always cornered me off for a
conversation and I didn't know how to get out of it short
of blasting him one.

He went over to his bar. 'What'll it be, Scotch?'

'Scotch is fine,' I said. 'A little water.'

'A gentleman's drink,' he said, mixing it. 'Now I prefer
rye.' Then he noticed I was standing and said: 'Sit down,
sit down. As Bertha says, "We're all coloured folks."
You know Bertha Gowing, head of the South Side Clinic?'

'No, I don't,' I said, taking the drink and sitting down.

'A fine person, charming personality, very capable,
very capable,' he said, returning to his easy chair across

from me. He waved at the Pittsburgh *Courier* on the floor. 'I was just reading about our fighter pilots in Italy; they're achieving a remarkable record.'

I said, 'That's right.'

'Makes the old man wish he was young again,' he went on.

'Think of it, the first time in the history of our nation that Negro boys have served as pilots. We can thank Roosevelt for that.'

'That's right,' I said. My mind was on Alice. I wondered how she was going to react to seeing me.

'The Nazi pilots say they'd rather engage any two white pilots than one of our Negro boys,' he said.

'Yeah, they're some tough customers,' I said.

'I was talking to Blakely the other day, and he said we should send them a cablegram saying, "The eyes of the world are on you." You know Blakely Moore, the young attorney who fought that restricted covenant case for the Du Barrys?'

'No, I don't,' I said.

'Bright young man,' he said. 'Has a wonderful future. I attended his birth.' He took a sip of rye. 'Well, how is your work progressing, Robert? I understand you have been made a supervisor.'

I stole a look at him, looked away. 'Well, not exactly a supervisor. I'm what they call a leaderman.'

'A leaderman, eh? I'm always intrigued by the titles applied to industrial workers. Now what is a leaderman?'

'I just have charge of a small crew of workers,' I said.

'But you're in authority?' he insisted.

'Well . . .' To hell with trying to explain it, I thought, and said, 'Yes.'

'That's what I like to see,' he said. 'Our Negro boys in authority. It proves that we can do it if we are given the opportunity.'

A little bit of that went a long way. 'How's everything with you, Doctor?' I asked, changing the conversation. My vocal cords were getting tight.

'I keep pretty busy,' he chuckled. 'Walter and I were just talking the other day about the tremendous change that's taken place in Los Angeles—'

'Yes, it has,' I cut in rapidly. 'The city's really growing up.' If he asked me if I knew Walter Somebody-or-other I was subject to tell him to go to hell. 'Is Alice in?' I asked before he could get it out.

'I'll see,' he said, getting up. 'You know, this house is so arranged we can go for days without running into each other.' He went into the hallway and called, 'Alice!'

After a moment she replied from upstairs, 'Yes?'

'Robert is here.'

'Oh!' A pause. Then, 'Tell him to come right up.'

He turned to me. 'You can go right up, Robert.'

'Thanks,' I said.

He stopped me to shake hands again. 'It was nice seeing you, Robert.' He always made it a point to let me know he didn't have anything against me, even if I didn't belong to his class.

'It was nice seeing you too, Doctor,' I said.

Alice was waiting for me at the head of the spiral stairway. 'How are you, dear?' she greeted. Her cool contralto voice was under wraps and her eyes were controlled. She wore a scarlet velvet housecoat and her cheeks were slightly rouged. I couldn't help but think she was a regal-looking chick.

' 'Lo, baby,' I said, kissing at her.

She dodged. 'Don't!'

'All right, if that's the way—' I broke it off, looking beyond her into the sitting room. 'Goddamn, you've got company,' I accused. I was ready to turn and go.

But she said quickly, 'Oh, you'll like them,' took me

100

by the hand and led me into her sitting-room.

It was a large pleasant room with a love seat and three armchairs done in flowered chintz. There were white scatter rugs on the polished oak floor and white organdie curtains at the double windows facing the street. Her bedroom was to the rear.

'You know Polly Johnson,' she said, and I said, 'Hello, Polly,' to a sharp-faced, bright yellow woman with a mannish haircut, dressed in a green slack suit.

'Hi, Bob, how's tricks?' she said around her cigarette.

'And Arline,' Alice went on. 'Arline Wilson.'

'Hello, Arline,' I said. She was a big sloppy dame in a wrinkled print dress with her black hair pulled tight in a knot at the back of her head, giving her a surprised, sweaty look. I imagine she thought it made her look childish. She was a schoolteacher.

'Here's that man again,' she said. I gave her a quick, startled look; she was too old for that, I thought.

'And this is Cleotine Dobbs,' Alice said of the third dame. 'Miss Dobbs, Mr Jones.'

I shook hands with her. 'How do you do, Miss Dobbs.'

She was a long, angular, dark woman dressed in an Eastern suit. She was strictly out of place in that light bright clique.

'Cleo has just come to our city to direct the Downtown Settlement House,' Alice said sweetly. 'She's a Chicago gal.'

'That's fine,' I said, figuring on how to escape. Then to Alice: 'I really can't stay. I just dropped by to say hello.'

'Oh hush, Bob, and sit down,' she said. 'You know you haven't got a thing to do.'

I gave her a lidded look. 'Don't be too sure,' I said.

She put her hands on my shoulders and pushed me down on the other half of the love seat with Cleo, the dark dame.

'That's right, girl, don't let a man get away from us,' Arline said. I sneaked another look at her.

'Maybe Bob's afraid of all us women,' Polly said. 'We must look like dames on the make.' She had a blunt, sharp-tongued manner that could soon irritate me.

'Although God knows I haven't started picking them up off the street,' Arline said, and she and Polly crossed glances.

'I'm overwhelmed,' I choked, then got my voice under better control.

'We were just discussing the problems that confront the social worker in Little Tokyo,' Cleo said, coming to my rescue, I supposed. 'I was saying that first of all there must be some organization within the community through which a programme of integration may be instituted into the broader pattern of the community. There must be adequate provisions for health care, adequate educational resources and opportunities for recreation,' she enumerated. She sounded as if she'd just gotten her Doctor's.

'What they need down there more than anything else is public housing,' Polly said bluntly. 'Have you seen some of those places that those people live in? Twelve people in a single room and not even any running water.' I remembered then that she worked with the housing authority. 'That place is a rat hole. Without adequate housing you can't even start any programme of integration.'

I sat there with my hands clasped in my lap, looking from one speaker to another with a forced interested smile, wondering what the hell had brought all of this on and getting tighter every second.

'Housing takes time,' Arline put in. She had the soft manner of the appeaser. 'And you know how they'll do even if they build a development down there; they'll allocate about one-fourth to Negroes and the rest to whites and Mexicans.'

'Mexicans are white in California,' Polly said.

'I know,' Arline said. 'That's what I mean. What they should really do is to stop all these Southern Negroes from coming into the city.'

By now I was tense, on edge; what they were saying didn't have any meaning for me – just some cut-rate jive in social workers' phraseology that proved a certain intellectualism, I supposed. But I didn't have to listen to it; I was going to get the hell out.

'But these people are already here,' Cleo pointed out. 'The ghetto's already formed. The problem now is how best to integrate the people of this ghetto into the life of the community.' She turned to me; I'd been silent long enough, 'What do you think, Mr Jones?'

'About what?' I asked.

She threw a look at me. 'I mean what is your opinion as to the problem arising from conditions in Little Tokyo?'

Well, sister, you're asking for it, I thought. Aloud I said: 'Well, now, I think we ought to kill the coloured residents and eat them. In that way we'll not only solve the race problem but alleviate the meat shortage as well.'

There was a shocked silence for an instant, then Polly broke into a raucous laugh. Alice said softly, 'Bob!'

All I wanted was for them to get the hell out of there so I could be alone with Alice, but I lightened up a little out of common courtesy. 'All kidding aside,' I said, 'If I knew any solution for the race problem I'd use it for myself first of all.'

'But this isn't just a problem of race,' Cleo insisted. 'It's a ghetto problem involving a class of people with different cultures and traditions at a different level of education.'

'Different from what?' I said.

'The mayor's organizing a committee to investigate conditions down there,' Arline said. 'Blakely Moore is on it.'

'Would you gals like a drink?' Alice asked, and at their quick nods, turned to me, 'Bob dear . . .'

I went down to the kitchen with her for the rum-and-coke setups, glad to get a breather. 'Can't you get rid of 'em?' I asked. 'I want to talk to you, baby.'

She put her arms about me and kissed me. 'Be nice, darling,' she said. 'Tom's coming by and they want to meet him.'

'Tom who?' I asked, but she just smiled.

'You'll like him,' she said. 'He's something like you.'

The drinks got them gossipy.

'Herbie Washington has married a white girl.'

'No!'

'I don't believe it!'

'Who is she?' Alice asked.

'She's white,' I muttered to myself. 'Ain't that enough?' They didn't even hear me.

'Nobody knows,' Arline said. 'Some girl he met at one of Melba's parties.'

That started Cleo off. 'I can't understand these Negro men marrying these white tramps,' she said. You wouldn't, I thought, black as you are. 'Chicago's full of it. Just as soon as some Negro man starts to getting a little success he runs and marries a white woman. No decent self-respecting Negro man would marry one of those white tramps these Negroes marry.'

'I wouldn't say that exactly,' Polly injected. 'I know of Negro men married to decent white women – as decent as you and I.' She was taking up for herself – her father was a Negro married to a white woman.

But Cleo didn't know that. 'Nothing but tramps!' she

stormed, getting excited about it. The veneer came off and she looked and talked just like any other Southern girl who'd never been farther than grammar school. 'Nobody but a white tramp would marry a nigger!' she shouted, almost hitting me in the mouth with her gesticulations. 'And nobody but a nigger tramp would have 'em. I was at a party in Chicago and saw one of our supposed-to-be leading Negro actors sitting up there making love to some white tramp's eyebrows.'

I laughed out loud. 'To her eyebrows?' I said. 'Now I'd like to see that.'

Polly and Arline were exchanging strange looks, as if to say, 'Where did this creature come from?' And Alice looked positively pricked.

But Cleo didn't pay any attention to any of us; she went on beating up her chops, looking wild and agitated. 'One of my teachers at Chicago U. was talking 'bout some girl 'bout your colour' – she indicated Alice – 'and I just up and told him that it was an insult to mention light Negroes' colour to 'em; it was 'most the same as calling 'em bastards, saying their mamas had been slipping off in the bushes with white men . . .'

Alice looked horrified; I knew she'd never be invited there again. But it tickled me. It was all I could do to keep from falling out laughing.

'Just as soon as a Negro marries one of them they start going down,' Cleo went on vehemently. 'Decent Negro people won't accept them in their homes—'

The doorbell chimed and Alice went down to answer it. Cleo was still raving when Alice ushered a tall, nice-looking, well-dressed white fellow into the room. He had sandy hair and a pleasant smile and looked like a really nice guy. But he was white, and I was antagonistic from the start.

'This is Tom Leighton, one of my co-workers,' she introduced him about.

For a moment there was an embarrassed silence; then the dames became intellectual again.

'Perhaps Mr Leighton can give us some suggestions on our Little Tokyo problem,' Polly prompted, and they had it and gone.

Leighton said something that didn't make any sense at all to me, and Cleo gushed. 'Oh, that's it! That's just the thing!' I jerked a look at her; she'd blown coy to the point of simpering. I thought, well, whataya know; this white animosity didn't go as far as the men.

Finally, when they got through kicking Little Tokyo around, Leighton turned his bright friendly smile to me. 'Did I understand Miss Harrison to say you were an attorney?'

'No, I'm a shipyard worker,' I said.

'Oh, I'm sorry,' he apologized.

I let him dangle. There was another embarrassed silence.

Then Alice said, 'Bob's going into law after the war. He's fighting on our production front now.'

Leighton gave me another of his bright friendly smiles. 'I imagine it's a very interesting occupation,' he said.

'It's a killer,' I said. He blinked a little.

'Tom has just finished reading *Strange Fruit*,' Alice said. 'He thought it was fascinating.'

Something about the way she pronounced his name made me throw a quick searching glance at her, started me to wondering what her relations were with Leighton. I began watching both of them under lowered lids, half ashamed for the crazy suspicion that had come into my mind, jealous of the guy against my will. I'd seen so many light-complexioned Negro women absolutely pure nuts about white men, it scared me to think that Alice might be like that herself. I started thinking again of some excuse to get away.

He was saying, 'I was particularly interested in the characterization of Nonnie.'

You would, I thought, since she was so goddamned crazy about a white man.

'I didn't like Nonnie at all,' Polly said. 'I can't even imagine a Negro girl who's been to college doing any of the things Nonnie was supposed to do.'

'That was it,' Alice said. 'She didn't do anything.'

Watching her furtively, I began getting so tight inside I could hardly breathe. She might be having an affair with Leighton sure enough, I thought. She wouldn't count that, just like she wouldn't count that stuff at Stella's. She'd probably be proud of it, I thought; probably feel that I shouldn't resent it even if I found out . . .

Arline was saying, 'Oh, I know a girl just like Nonnie. She's a good friend of mine – at least I went to school with her – and she's just like Nonnie.'

'Did you read the book, Mr Jones?' Leighton asked.

'Yes, I did,' I said, and dropped it.

He waited for me, and when he saw I wasn't coming he said by way of appeasement, 'Of course I think that Richard Wright makes the point better in *Native Son*.'

'Oh, but what Lillian Smith does is condemn the white Southerner,' Arline said. 'All Wright did was write a vicious crime story.'

'Personally, I think the white Southerner doesn't mind being just like Lillian Smith portrays him,' I said.

'I think Richard Wright is naïve,' Polly said.

'Aren't we all?' I said.

'*Native Son* turned my stomach,' Arline said. 'It just proved what the white Southerner has always said about us; that our men are rapists and murderers.'

'Well, I will agree that the selection of Bigger Thomas

to prove the point of Negro oppression was an unfortunate choice,' Leighton said.

'What do you think, Mr Jones?' Cleo asked.

I said, 'Well, you couldn't pick a better person than Bigger Thomas to prove the point. But after you prove it, then what? Most white people I know are quite proud of having made Negroes into Bigger Thomases.'

There was another silence and everybody looked at me. 'Take me for instance,' I went on. 'I've got a job as leaderman at a shipyard. I'm supposed to have a certain amount of authority over the ordinary workers. But I'm scared to ask a white woman to do a job. All she's got to do is say I insulted her and I'm fired.'

Leighton looked concerned. 'Is that so?' he said. 'I didn't realize relations between white and coloured were that strained in our industries.'

'Of course Bob's problem is more or less individual,' Alice apologized. 'He's really temperamentally unsuited for industrial work. As soon as he enters into a profession his own problem will be solved.'

'Yes, I can understand that,' Leighton said. 'But as far as the problem of the Negro industrial worker is concerned, I feel that it is not so much racial as it is the problem of the masses. As soon as the masses, including all of our minority groups, have achieved economic security, racial problems will reach a solution of their own accord.' He turned to me. 'Won't you agree with me to that extent, Mr Jones?'

'No,' I said. 'It's a state of mind. As long as the white folks hate me and I hate them we can earn the same amount of money, live side by side in the same kind of house, and fight every day.'

He got one of those condescending, indulgent smiles. 'Then how would you suggest effecting a solution to a minority group problem?'

'I don't know about any other minority group problem,' I said, 'but the only solution to the Negro problem
is a revolution. We've got to make white people respect
us and the only thing white people have ever respected is
force.'

'But do you think a revolution by Negro people could
be successful?' he asked in that gentle tone of voice used
on an unruly child.

But I tried to keep my head. 'Not unless there were
enough white people on our side,' I said.

'By the same token,' he argued, 'if there were enough
white people on your side there wouldn't be any need for
a revolution.'

'There's a lot of 'em who don't do anything but talk. If
we had a revolution it'd force you to act, either for us or
against us – personally, I wouldn't give a goddamn which
way.'

'Suppose your revolution failed?' he asked.

'That'd be all right, too,' I said. 'At least we'd know
where we stood.'

His smile became more indulgent, his voice more
condescending. 'I think that you will discover that the
best course for Negroes to take at this time is to partici-
pate and co-operate in the general uprising of the masses
all over the world.'

'Are you a Communist?' I asked him.

Everybody else looked shocked, but he didn't even
flinch. 'No, not that I have anything against the Communists, but I believe in the same, sensible way of doing
things. And there's just one solution for the Negro—'

All of a sudden I burnt up. I'd been trying to get away
from the white folks to begin with. And I wasn't going to
have this peckerwood coming down here among my
people, playing a great white god, sitting on his ass,
solving the Negro problem with a flow of diction and

making me look like a goddamned fool in front of my girl, when all I could do around his people was to be a flunkey and get kicked in the mouth. And what was more, his goddamned condescending smile was getting under my skin.

I cut him off with a sudden violent gesture and jumped to my feet. That broke it up.

CHAPTER
11

When the last of Alice's guests had gone she came upstairs and stood in the doorway looking at me with a wide-eyed condemning stare. I shook a cigarette loose and puffed at it and let her stand there and stare. She had a hell of a lot of gall at that, I thought. When she saw that her silent scrutiny wasn't going to beat me down she came into the room and took a seat, crossed her legs, and looked up at me with a Bette Davis pose.

'Bob, are you trying intentionally to make me dislike you?' she asked.

I dropped into a chair facing her, gave her back some of her own scrutiny, said nothing.

'Or is it that you dislike me now?' she kept on.

I wanted her to drop it. Last night had happened and was gone and if I said anything about it at all it'd just make us hate each other. I didn't want it that way. So I said, 'I'm sorry, baby, but I took as much of Leighton as I could. If I'd known you were going to have all the wizards here I'd have stayed away. I just came because I wanted to talk to you.'

'But you insulted Tom deliberately,' she charged. 'He hadn't said anything that should have offended you. He was merely trying to tell you something for your own good.'

'Well, I ain't for it,' I said.

She frowned. 'It isn't just that. That's just one incident. You always have a chip on your shoulder.'

All of a sudden I knew she was trying to put me on the defensive. 'Now what are you getting at?' I asked. 'I suppose I'm to blame for everything that happened last night?' I said it before I thought.

She got a hurt look on and said, 'So that's it? So you're trying to get even with me now?'

I started getting mad. 'Goddamnit, if I'd wanted to get even I know plenty ways of doing it besides sitting up listening to your goddamned friends,' I told her.

'I can't stop you from hating me if that's the way your mind works,' she said.

'All right, baby,' I said harshly. 'You said it, now let's skip it.' I knew if the thing started riding me we wouldn't have anything at all for each other any more.

'Is that why you told me, this afternoon when I called, about your affairs with other women?' she went on. 'Is it because you want to hurt me now?' The thing was eating into her; she couldn't let it go.

I spread my hands. 'That isn't what I said,' I denied. 'What I said was I knew plenty chicks I could go to bed with if that was all I wanted—'

'Isn't that all you want of me too?' she cut in.

'What do you want me to say, that I believe it was an accident – a drunken episode – that I still believe you're the finest, most wonderful chick on earth?' I asked her. 'Is that what you want me to say?' I blew a stream of smoke into the air. 'Okay, I say it. Now let's drop it.'

'You have an egocentricity that borders on a disease,' she informed me, getting a high and mighty air. 'You begin by attacking my character, and then when I point out some of your own weaknesses you say, "Let's drop it, I can't be criticized, I'm too—"'

'Baby, please,' I said. 'I didn't mean it that way. I'm

not trying to bring you down. I was only—'

She didn't let it touch her. 'I know you will find it hard to realize that anyone could be thinking about anything besides you,' she said. 'But believe it or not, I am thinking about myself. I am wondering why I put up with you, why I continue this farce—'

It was getting brittle now, acid, raw. 'All right, god-damnit, let's quit!' I flared. 'I'm willing to let it go, why in the goddamn hell aren't you?'

But she wasn't satisfied; she went on as if something tight inside of her was driving her. 'You're rude and uncouth and unintelligent.' She paused to light a cigarette, and I let myself go limp. I was tired of fighting with everybody; I decided to let her get it out of her system so we could have some understanding.

'There are three men who sit on my doorstep who are superior to you in every respect. They are cultured, intelligent, sensitive, prominent in the community; and any one of them could support me if I married him . . .'

I closed my eyes and tried not to listen.

'They understand the niceties a woman enjoys. They do anything in the world I ask them and it's a pleasure to be in their company . . . You're anti-social, boorish, ill at ease,' she kept hammering. 'You're not especially hand-some – you're darker than I like; you dress like a gangster, you're not acceptable socially in any respect, and yet I impose you on my parents and my friends—'

It was beginning to ride me now. I kept telling myself that she just felt beat because she'd let me see her the night before and now she was trying to get over it by digging me. But it wasn't working so well; it was all I could do to keep from blowing.

'Too true, baby,' I said, trying to keep it inside of me.

'You're insanely belligerent,' she continued. 'You think you can solve all of your problems with your brawn.

You have a really staggering inferiority complex, amounting to a fixation. You're disrespectful, quite ignorant, simply impossible.'

I had enough of it. 'You know what you can do for me,' I grated, leaning forward in my seat.

She gave me a long clinical stare of appraisal and then smiled contemptuously. 'I've been tremendously worried every minute since you left me last night that you would be so hurt and angry I would never see you again,' she began, then waited for it to sink in. 'I have even considered going to your room to plead with you.' Now she was sneering at me. 'I find that you are not worth it,' she said. 'You are not only willing to take it, believing that I am such—'

I told her right out of the hollow chagrin in my guts: 'That's because you're a nigger. If you were a white woman—'

She was out of her chair and across the room and had slapped me before I could finish. It was a solid pop with fury in it and stung like hell. I came up blind mad, grabbed her by her shoulders, and shook her until her teeth rattled.

'Goddamnit, I'll kill you,' I mouthed. 'I'll – I'll – who in the goddamned hell do you think you are, you – you –' I couldn't think of anything bad enough to call her.

When I stopped shaking her she looked up at me with a funny docile expression and said in a low controlled voice: 'You are a filthy Negro,' and I said: 'What about you? You're no goddamned angel.'

She sighed and said: 'But for some strange reason I love you,' and went candy. Her eyes got limpid and her mouth got suddenly wet and her body just folded into mine.

Whatever she had, it was really and truly for me. I couldn't help it. I went soft as drugstore cotton and fell

114

into her arms as if I was going home. I kissed her eyes, her nose, her throat; I pulled her housecoat away from her neck and kissed the curve of her shoulder. I could hear her soft throaty gasping as she pressed her body hard against mine.

Right in the middle of it the thing got me again. I couldn't help it. I asked her, 'Did you ever really do that?'

She went instantly cold, put her hands against my chest, and pushed me away from her so quickly I almost fell.

'Do you just have to do it?' she asked, her eyes condemning me. 'Do you just have to keep bringing it up?' She went over and sat down and put her face in her hands. 'You destroy every emotion I have for you.'

I stood there, clenching my fists, sucking for breath. I got a crazy feeling of being penned in by my own emotions; of getting out of my own grasp; of not being able to control my actions any longer. I didn't know whether to be mad, indifferent, or sympathetic; whether to turn and walk out, or sit down beside her and try to work it out. Finally I dropped back into my chair.

'Baby, I wish you'd try to understand,' I said. 'I don't want to think about it either. Goddamn, it hurts me too. Probably more than you. Can't you understand that? I feel like a damn simple fool.' I took a breath, let it out, felt my legs tightening so they lifted my feet off the floor. 'Every time I kiss you now I'm scared you might be laughing.'

She opened her eyes and looked at me for a long time. It was as if she was searching for something. Then suddenly her whole face took on a soft tender look and way back in her eyes there was something like a shadow of hurt. She got up and came over and sat on the arm of my chair. 'You're just a baby,' she murmured. 'Just a big little baby.' And lifted my face and kissed me like she never had before.

I put my arm about her waist and pulled her down into my lap and rubbed my face in her soft silky hair, smelling its faint perfume and feeling its soft caress. I felt all alive inside for the first time in days, on the brink of something wonderful. I felt as if all of a sudden everything was going to be all right; as if I was going to know all the answers and never have anything to worry about again as long as I lived.

She drew back her head and shoulders to look at me. Her gaze was level, pure, but not tender any more. 'Bob darling, won't you believe me when I tell you that I am not a Lesbian?' she said.

I could feel the frown pop between my eyes. 'But you'd been there before,' I said.

She broke away and jumped to her feet, wheeled to look down at me. 'So that's it,' she said. 'So that's why you came here tonight – to cross-examine me.'

I put my hands on the arms of the chair, stood up. I felt resigned, tired, let down, as if I was locked up and would never get out. 'You wanna know why I came here tonight?' I asked her. It didn't make any difference one way or another now. I could tell her. I didn't even give a damn what she might think about me. 'Not because I wanted to, I'll tell you that. I didn't want to see you again until I could get you straightened out in my mind. I sure as hell didn't come here to argue with you about all that mess that happened last night. I didn't come here to argue at all.' I took a breath. 'I came here because I had to. Because I thought you were my girl and I didn't have no other goddamned place to go. Maybe that don't sound so bright, but it's the truth. I had to get somewhere to cool off, to get myself straightened out. I had to get off the goddamned streets out of the goddamned peckerwoods' eyes before I killed some son of a bitch and went to the chair.' I let my breath out, sighed, started turning away. 'Now I'm gonna quit bothering you with it and go home,' I said.

She stepped around in front of me, clutched me by the arms, held me, made me look down into her eyes. 'What is it, darling?' she asked. 'Tell me, please.'

'I don't know,' I muttered. I wanted to tell her; I wanted to get it out of me. 'Every goddamn thing. My nerves are on edge. I keep expecting trouble every minute. Everything's going wrong all at once – it's pressing me too hard. Goddamnit! You! And the job! And just living in the world—'

'Has anything happened on the job?' she asked quickly.

I looked away from her. 'No, just the same old grind,' I lied. 'The white folks trying to see how much we'll take.' I paused, then said, 'But it don't never lighten up. I tell you, I can't take much more of it.'

She let go my arms and turned away from me. 'Bob, if you continue brooding about white people you are going insane,' she said.

'You're not just saying it.'

She sat down again. 'How do you expect me to help you, Bob?' she asked. 'I've talked to you time and time again about your attitude toward white people. I've exhausted every argument, and still you don't listen—'

'I'll listen to anything you've got to say tonight,' I told her.

'No, you won't.' She sighed. 'All you've done tonight is fight against me. You've tried to hurt me in every way you know. You won't even give me a chance to help you, darling. You keep throwing what happened last night back into my face. Nothing I say about it seems to make any difference to you.'

117

I dug out another cigarette and lit it, drank the melted ice in my highball glass, sank down on the love seat. 'Do you really want to know, Alice?' I asked her.

'How to help you?' She was looking at me steadily. 'Yes, I really do.'

'Well, I'll tell you,' I said, puffing at my cigarette. 'There are three ways—' I spread my hands. 'Maybe you couldn't do any of them anyway, but I'll tell you.' I took another puff. 'You can sit up and drink with me until I go blotto,' I said. 'That'll keep me put as long as I stay blotto. Or you can let me go to bed with you. If I go to sleep afterward that'll hold me until tomorrow morning – I don't know for how long after that.' I got up and found an ash tray, mashed out my cigarette, walked over to the window, and looked down into the soft warm night. A man and a woman were getting out of a car across the street; she looked like a girl I knew slightly named Monica; I watched them go into the house. 'Or you can talk to me, let me talk to you,' I said without looking around. 'You can tell me why you went to Stella's; how it happened you went there the first time.' I paused and when she didn't say anything I went on, 'I'll tell you everything I know about myself, about my waking up scared every morning, about the way I feel toward white people, why I resent them so goddamned much – resent the things they can do when all they got is colour – tell you all about what happens inside of me every time I go out in the street.' I waited for her a moment, then went on. 'Maybe we can find out what's wrong with both of us, even find out how we really feel toward each other. Maybe you can convince me I'm wrong about a lot of things – I've got an open mind tonight, honestly, baby.' I breathed again. 'Or if you can't convince me maybe you can make it worth while for me to try to be different. If I was really sure about

118

you—' I broke off without finishing, turned to look at her.

She had her head turned around toward me, but when I looked she looked away. I went across and sat down facing her again. 'Listen, baby,' I said. 'If I have to keep on like I'm going – not being sure about you – and getting kicked around by every white tramp who comes along, I'm gonna hurt somebody as sure as hell.'

She sat quite still for a long time after I'd stopped speaking, studying me. 'Bob, your greatest difficulty stems from your not knowing what you want to do in life,' she said. I don't think she put on her social worker's attitude intentionally; she just couldn't help it. 'If you concentrated your energies on a single objective and worked very hard toward that end – for instance if you applied yourself to your studies and thought more about re-entering college this fall – these minor incidents and day-to-day irritations would not affect you so greatly.' She paused to let it sink in.

I gave a long deep sigh and looked away from her, wondering if it was too much to ask of her to face it for a minute. Maybe she really couldn't, I thought – maybe none of her class could face it. Maybe that was why it was so insane when it broke out – because she had to keep it buried as much as possible, refuse to look at it, to recognize it, to discuss it; maybe that was her way of keeping on living, to keep her frustrations hidden, covered over with compromises, just like staying on my muscle and trying to fight back and getting kicked in the mouth every minute was mine. Maybe we'd never get together, I thought. But I listened.

'A certain amount of frustration is latent in most people – people of all races,' she went on. 'But in you—'

'It won't help to generalize,' I cut her off. 'I'm willing

119

to talk about myself without any prompting or analysis or—'

Now she cut me off. 'Bob, I've been thinking seriously that perhaps I'm not the type of woman for you. I'm ambitious and demanding. I want to be important in the world. I want a husband who is important and respected and wealthy enough so that I can avoid a major part of the discriminatory practices which I am sensible enough to know I cannot change. I don't want to be pulled down by a person who can't adjust himself to the limitations of his race – a person who feels he has to make a fist fight out of every issue – a person who'd jeopardize his entire future because of some slight or, say, because some ignorant white person should call him a nigger—'

'That lets me out,' I said, standing up. 'I may as well tell you, baby, a white woman called me a nigger at the yard Monday morning and I called her a cracker slut and lost my job.'

'Lost your job?' She recoiled as if I had slapped her. 'So that's what's wrong with you.' She was suddenly indignant. 'So that's why you need my help—'

'Hear my story first,' I said, and told her about my run-in with Madge and my getting downgraded.

She jumped up and took a turn about the room. 'If the white people hated you as much as you hated them—'

'They'd kill me now and have it done with,' I supplied. 'And that'd be fine with me.'

She stopped and looked at me. 'Do you want to be white, Bob?'

'All I want is to be able—' I began, but she cut me off.

'Let me put it another way. Will the fact that you are a Negro deter you from attempting to succeed as white men do?' I started to interrupt, but she stopped me. 'No, Bob, this is important. Your present attitude has no place for me in your life, it has no place for anyone except yourself. When you lost your temper with the girl you were not thinking about me.'

'I suppose I should have just said, "Yes ma'am, I'm a nigger," and let it go at that.'

She went over and sat down again. 'It's not just you any more, Bob,' she said. 'I have to think about myself. If we're going to be married you will have to begin thinking about the future – *our* future—'

She got me then. 'Look, baby, I'm going to make the grade,' I told her. 'Next fall I'm going back to college like you want, but right now—'

'But it's more than that Bob,' she cut in. 'I've been trying to tell you. I'll have to have confidence in you. I'll have to believe that you will make good, and I just can't see you doing it unless you learn how to get along with the white people with whom you have to work.'

I felt myself getting tight inside; the bands started clamping on my head again and the rocks started growing in my chest.

'Will you go to the girl tomorrow morning and apologize?' she asked. 'I think father knows the president of Atlas Corporation. Will you—'

'No,' I said.

'But it's not just you now, Bob,' she said. She was pleading now. 'It's you and I now, Bob. Don't you understand? In the things you do and the decisions you make you just can't think of yourself alone. You have to consider *our* future. Is that too much to ask?'

'But you don't understand either,' I began. 'I just can't take it and keep on living with myself. I simply can't—'

'Bob,' she said. 'I'm not going to plead with you any more. If you don't go to that girl and apologize and try in every way you know to get reinstated—'

'Look, baby—' I cut in again; I was trying to stop her; I didn't want her to say it. 'Look, Alice, will you listen to me? Will you let me tell you what'll happen to me if I do that? That's what I've wanted to talk about all night—'

'No, Bob, I won't listen,' she said. 'It's such a little thing. If you can't do that much, Bob, don't consider me as being with you any more.' She paused, then added, 'We have to walk together – don't you understand?'

'Okay,' I said, turning toward the door. I felt crushed inside, as if a car had run over me and left me lying there. I hadn't wanted her to say it before I'd had a chance to tell her that I didn't have a choice.

CHAPTER
12

I went home and went to bed and dreamed Alice and I were in a drugstore and when I got ready to leave I started toward the door with two packages in my hand and then I couldn't find Alice. I went around holding the two packages looking for Alice and finally found her in a hall off from the prescription room talking to the proprietor's wife who had her two hands on Alice's shoulder. I thought something funny was going on and got mad and said, 'I was looking for you.' She looked at me as if she was surprised and said, 'I thought we had a date with these people,' and I said, 'Naw, we ain't got no date,' and yanked her by the arm and pulled her out into the store and then I thought about the packages in my hand and looked down and saw that I had a half a dozen or so grapefruit wrapped in a grey vest and a .45-calibre short-barrelled revolver. I went back into the hall and put the grapefruit on a table and then I stood there and tried to put the gun in a holster I had strapped around my chest, but when I got the gun in the holster the butt end of the holster stuck out so it showed under my overcoat and I had to open my trousers and stick the end of the holster down in my trousers but still it showed when I buttoned my coat so I held my coat with my left elbow pressed against the holster to keep it from showing and went to look for Alice but she had gone outside again. I went outside and saw her up on the other side of the street about half a block ahead. Off to her right was a weedy park that slanted down to a river and when I crossed the street I saw Alice turn into the park and I hurried to catch up with her. But before I got in sight of her she began screaming for help and I fumbled with the holster until I got the gun out in my hand and ran down the sidewalk, looking into the park for her, but the park was hilly and rocky and covered with a dense growth of scrub and I couldn't see Alice. I ran ahead to a break in the brush and turned right up a hill and saw millions of swine with bony sharp spines and long yellow tusks running about in the brush and I shot at one right in front of me and I could see the hole pop in his side where the bullet went through. Then I heard Alice screaming again, horribly as if she was being torn apart, and I ran up the hill toward the sound of her voice as fast as I could, my overcoat holding me back, and my heart beating with fear. When I came to the top I saw a dry sandy wash and I started looking about in the wash for her. A woman leaning on a fence at the top of the wash said, 'There,' and I looked in a clump of bushes and saw what at first looked like a little rag doll, but when I turned it over I saw it was Alice. Her head and shoulders were the same but her eyes were closed and her body had shrunk until it was no more than a foot long and she was dead. I felt shocked and scared and all torn up inside and then I looked up for the woman who was leaning on the fence but instead of one woman there were millions of white women leaning there, looking at me, giving me the most sympathetic smiles I ever saw.

I woke up overcome with a feeling of absolute impotence; I laid there remembering the dream in every detail. Memory of my fight with Alice came back, and then I saw Madge's kidney-shaped mouth, brutal at the edges, spitting out the word 'nigger'; and something took a heavy hammer and nailed me to the bed.

I was scared to think about my gang; I started drawing in my emotions, tying them, whittling them off, nailing them down. I was so tight inside, I was like wood. My breath wouldn't go any deeper than my throat and I didn't know whether I could talk at all. I had to get ready to die before I could get out of the house.

When I picked up Homer and Conway they didn't say anything; they just looked at me out of the sides of their eyes. Then I stopped for Pigmeat, Smitty, and Johnson, and they had their usual morning squabble.

Finally Smitty asked, 'Where was you yesditty, Bob?'

I had to think about it before I answered. 'I was off,' I said.

Pigmeat turned to Smitty and said, 'Now that's that man's own business. S'pose he tell you he was with you mama.'

'I don't play no dozens, boy,' Smitty growled. 'You young punks don't know how far to go with a man.'

I went out Central trying my brakes, timing my stops so thin and my turns so tight that if any chump in front of me had dug to a sudden stop I'd have climbed up on him.

Conway leaned across Homer and said, 'What's the matter, chief? You look down in the mouth this morning. You old lady quit you?'

I felt fragile as overheated glass; one rough touch and I'd burst into a thousand pieces. 'Could happen,' I said in a thin shallow voice out of the top of my mouth.

'Bob's got his own troubles, nigger, why don't you worry 'bout yours?' Pigmeat said.

Conway turned around and gave him a dirty look. 'You getting too big for yo' britches,' he said.

A big air-brake Diesel gripped the ground in front and

I almost went inside of it. I braked so short I scrambled my riders.

Homer rubbed his head where he'd butted into the windshield and said, 'Bob sho ain't got his mind on driving this morning.'

'What Bob got his mind on this morning would get yo' black ass hung where you come from,' Johnson said.

'Where who come from?'

'You, nigger, I s'pose you from Alaska.'

'Now Bob ain't said a word,' Smitty said. 'If he was to cuss you somoleons out and put you out his car you'd say he was a bad fellow.'

Conway got it out in the open. 'Say, chief, what's that grey boy doing in yo' job? He say he taking your place. You ain't gonna quit us, chief?'

That silenced them; they knew the story, but they all waited to hear what I had to say.

'I had to get a cracker chick told yesterday – or rather, day before yesterday – and Mac demoted me,' I said.

'What to, a helper?' Pigmeat wanted to know.

'No, a mechanic,' I said.

'You know they can't 'mote the man to no helper,' Homer said. 'What the union gonna say?'

'What the union gonna say? What you think they gonna say? They white too, ain't they?'

'Did she go to the man herself?' Conway asked.

I found suddenly I'd been holding my breath. I let it out and said, 'I suppose so.'

'That's what I tell this lil old boy,' Conway said, talking about Pigmeat. 'Always messing with those white women. All they good for is trouble.'

'Was she that big Gawga pink work as a tacker?' Pigmeat asked. 'She in Hank's gang, ain't she?'

I didn't say anything; I didn't want to talk about it.

'She always signifying with you,' he went on. I

didn't know he had noticed; I wondered who else had noticed.

I'd gone away from them; I was playing a game. Whenever I saw some white people crossing the street in front of me I stepped on the gas and blew. If they jumped they could make it; if they didn't I'd run 'em down. All of 'em jumped. I felt a dead absolute quiet inside; I didn't give a damn whether they jumped or not.

'That's all you niggers think of,' Smitty was saying. 'I think it's damn shame they can Bob for something like that . . .' You're probably laughing like hell, you Uncle Tom bastard, I thought to myself. 'Those grey boys cuss them white women out going and coming,' he went on.

'Bob ain't no grey boy,' Johnson said.

'What make Bob so mad is he ain't got to get none of it yet,' Pigmeat said.

'What Bob shoulda did is to gone to the man,' Smitty said sanctimoniously.

'Man, where this nigger come from?' Pigmeat said. 'Man, where is yo' grey kinks and yo' rusty frock? Uncle Tom from way back.'

'What make me so mad,' Johnson said, 'is the white folks got it on you at the start, so why do they have to give you any crap on top of it? That's what make me so mad.'

I turned on the radio. One of Erskine Hawkins' old platters, 'I'm in a Lowdown Groove,' was playing. Alice and I had discovered it together shortly after we'd met at the Memo on the Avenue. I welled up inside, turned it off. But the words kept on in my mind. I got a hard, grinding nonchalance. To hell with everybody, I thought. To hell with the world; if there were any more little worlds, to hell with them too.

Conway was saying, 'We oughta get together and go to the man,' when I wheeled into the parking lot at Atlas.

'Reason niggers ain't got nothing now, they don't stick together.'

I found Tebbel already down in the stuffy compartment when I got there. He was Johnny on the spot, but when he started collecting the time cards I said, 'I'll take 'em.'

He jumped. 'Oh, I didn't see you,' he said. 'How you making out?'

'Fine,' I said without looking at him.

He stood there for a moment. Then he said, 'What're the boys doing today?'

I turned and looked at him then. He had a nice friendly smile on his face and was trying to co-operate. But I wasn't for it. 'They're doing what I tell 'em to as long as I'm in charge,' I said in a hard level voice, looking through him.

He reddened slightly but didn't retreat. 'Kelly said he wanted them to—'

'Damn that!'

The other workers took their cue from me. 'Come on, let's get together and back Bob up,' Red said. 'Let's go down and see the man and tell him what's what.'

'Look, fellows, let me handle it,' I said, but they weren't listening to me now.

They were going to have their say about it so they gathered around Red. All of them joined but Ben; he went about his work and had nothing to do with them.

Each one had a different idea. Red said they all ought to quit. Smitty was for talking to Mac. Pigmeat said they ought to mess up the work so it'd have to be done over. Conway thought they ought to form a committee to go see some of the big shots in the front office. George said they ought to organize all the coloured workers in the yard and strike.

Tebbel stood at a distance, red and undecided. I knew he wanted to tell them to go to work; I wondered if he would try it. I didn't say anything to them; I let 'em beef.

I didn't care whether they worked or not; I didn't look for 'em to climb any limbs for me; but it made me feel good that they thought about it.

Two white pipe fitters came into the compartment, but they went about their work without asking any questions. They had a tall, angular, coal-black fellow as their helper. He leaned over Homer's shoulder and asked him what it was all about. Homer told him. He came closer, was included.

All of a sudden Pigmeat snatched up a hammer and smashed a cast-iron fire pot. It broke into pieces, rang like a gong in my brain. Everybody jumped. Pieces flew through the air; one hit one of the white pipe fitters on the leg. Kerosene ran all over the deck.

'I wish that was a peckerwood's head,' Pigmeat said. His face was distorted, uncontrolled.

Then everybody reacted at once. The white pipe fitter glanced at Pigmeat, reached over, knocked the piece of iron out of the way, went back to work. Ben stopped work just long enough to give Pigmeat a cold, sardonic look.

Red said, 'Don't nobody light no match until these fumes blow outa here.'

Tebbel hurried out. Then suddenly Pigmeat grinned. 'I scared hell outa that sonabitch, didn't I?'

George said, 'I don't know whether you scared hell outa him. You sure scared hell outa me.'

Conway was tearing at his vest, trying to get a burning cigarette out he'd dropped from his mouth. He finally got it, stamped it out, then turned to Pigmeat and said, 'The man'll come up here and kick your ass.'

'Kick whose ass?'

'Well now, ef'n it come to that,' Arkansas said, 'I s'pect just usses in here could whip all these pecks on board this ship.'

Ben had to look up again. One of the white pipe fitters stole a glance at Arkansas.

George said, 'Man, you are a fool. These pecker-woods'll come up here and beat all the black off'n us. I bet you be the first one to holler calf rope.'

'What you bet?' Arkansas said. 'You ast anybody 'bout me. I'll fight a peck till—'

'Aw, man, hush!' George cut him off. 'The worst whipping I ever got come from me thinking I could whip every grey boy I seen. I was in Chicago, man, and I was going down to the A.C. on Thirty-fifth Street, learning how to duke. Man, I was bad, I was beating up all the little studs on State Street. Man, I dared them chumps to open their chops. Then I run into this grey boy over on Clark and we got to jawing 'bout a ruff we found on the street. He said it was hisn and I said it was mine and we went back in a vacant lot to settle it. Well, man, I got to dancing around, showing off my footwork I'd learned at the gym and hitting this grey boy anywhere I wanted. All he'd do was just duck his head and bore in. Man, I beat this chump till he was bloody as a hog, and he kept coming in. Man, I got so tired from beating this chump I couldn't get my hands up no higher'n my belt and this chump kept gritting his teeth and ducking his head and coming in. Just about time I'd decided to broom, this chump hauled off and hit me a haymaker and killed me a year. I'm telling you, man—'

'Thass you,' Arkansas said. 'That ain't me.'

They had all just about got over their defiance and were about ready to go to work when Tebbel came in with Kelly. Then they just stood there, milling around, looking sullen. Kelly walked around and looked at the work; he stopped and looked at the broken fire pot. Finally he came up to me and said, 'What's the matter these boys aren't working, Bob?'

I looked at him. 'Ask 'em,' I said. I didn't care whether he fired me or not.

He reddened and looked away. His gaze rested on Smitty. 'What's the matter you aren't working?' he said.

'I was just waiting to ask Bob 'bout this here joint,' Smitty said. 'I'm going to work right now.'

Pigmeat said loud enough for everyone to hear, 'Nigger, you got crap up your back.'

Kelly said hurriedly, 'Well, you better all get to work, I'm telling you,' and beat it.

They were all silent for a moment and then Peaches said, 'Bob done just right. There's more'n one of these dirty white tramps needs cussing out. Course it's too bad he lost his job,' she added lamely.

'What he oughta done 'stead of cussing her out is to trick her some kinda way,' Homer said. 'He shoulda slipped up to Hank and said she was lorating him, or somp'n like that, and get Hank down on her. Ain't no need of none of us running round here fighting these white folks. All you gotta do is get 'em fighting 'mongst themselves. Look what they doing in Europe right this minute, killing each other off like flies.'

'That reminds me of when I used to be a water boy for a bunch of Irish ganny dancers in Arkinsaw,' Conway said. 'They was laying track for the Yellow Dog and it was hotter'n a West Virginia coke oven. Them paddies kept holl'ing, "Come on, coon, with the water! Water Jack, you oughta been here and halfway back! Where's that black coon?" They made me mad but I knew I couldn't fit 'em all. So when I'd go atter a bucket of water I'd pee in it every time.'

'Conway!' Peaches said.

Conway gave a shamefaced grin. 'Well, that's the truth,' he said. 'Every time.'

The three girls withdrew to the end of the

131

compartment, not out of hearing distance but far enough so no one would think they were included.

I took a deep breath and thought, Well, here it goes. I hadn't expected anything anyway, so I wasn't disappointed. I'd known from the first that, whatever was done for me, I'd have to do it for myself. But I still stuck around; I didn't want the guys to think I didn't appreciate their thinking about me anyway.

Murphy took the ball and started telling dirty jokes. That morning was the first time I'd seen him; he'd been transferred into the gang yesterday when I'd been absent. He was a medium-sized, stoop-shouldered, lean-framed guy, black as the ace of spades, with a long, narrow, egg-shaped head getting bald at the extreme back tip, and eyes that slanted upward at the edges like an Oriental's.

George bobbed his head at Murphy and winked at me. 'Come in talking and ain't let down.'

Johnson said, 'We oughtn't be telling them dirty jokes. There's ladies present.'

'We ain't listening to you,' Zula Mae said. 'We's talking 'bout you.'

Two or three of them looked around to see if Tebbel was still there. He was standing off to one side, listening to everything.

Pigmeat said, 'That Willie! When he was a little baby he was so black his mama used to have to put flour on his mouth to tell where to feed him.'

'That's all right,' Willie said. 'You was so black you was four days old before anybody knew you was here.'

'Gentlemen! Gentlemen!' George said. 'I beg you desist.'

The three girls started out. It was getting too rough for them. When Peaches passed Willie she pinched him on the leg with a pair of pliers. He jumped and yelled.

'That's what you get,' Johnson said.

Then all of a sudden Arkansas asked, 'Kin you run?'

'Who you talking to?' Johnson asked.

'You,' Arkansas said.

'Sure, I can run,' Johnson said. 'Can you run?'

'Kin I run!' Arkansas echoed. 'Takes three to tell it.'

After a moment Johnson asked dutifully, 'What they say?'

'One to say, "Here he come!" The other to say, "Where he at?" The third to say, "I didn't seen him!" ' Arkansas didn't crack a smile.

'That reminds me of the coloured fellow what went down to the river—' Smitty began.

'Now how that remind you of a man going to the river?' Arkansas wanted to know.

'Anyway,' Smitty went on, 'this coloured fellow was sitting down by the bank of the river when an alligator came up out of the water. The coloured fellow watched the alligator for a while, then he started laughing. "Look at that old funny alligator," he said. The alligator rolled his eyes at the coloured fellow and ast, "What so funny 'bout me? I'se just an alligator." The coloured fellow jumped up and looked all about, looked in the bushes and up and down the bank, then he look back at the alligator. "Did you say somp'n?" he ast. "I say what's so funny 'bout me?" the alligator said. The coloured fellow's eyes popped near most out his head. "Kin you talk, or is I just hearing things?" he ast the alligator; and the alligator rolled his eyes and said, "Sure, I kin talk. All us alligators kin talk. The difference between us and you coloured folks, you coloured folks talk too much."

'Well, the coloured fellow lit out running and didn't stop till he come to the field where a white man was ploughing, and he said, "Mistah Jones, Mistah Jones, I just hear an alligator talk." Mistah Jones said, "Go on, boy, you know can't no alligator talk." The coloured fellow said, "I swear I heard him talk. Just lak a natural man. Come on down to the river, Mistah Jones, I'll show you." Mistah Jones say, "I ain't got no time for no foolishness; I got to git dis corn ploughed." But the coloured fellow said, 'I swear I heard him talk. I laughed at him and say, "Look at dat old funny alligator," and he say, "What's so funny 'bout me?" ' So Mistah Jones say, "All right, boy, I'll come 'long and see. But I swear if that alligator don't talk I'se gonna beat the stuffings outa you." The coloured fellow said, "Oh, he gonna talk."

'Well, they come down to the river bank and the old alligator was laying out in the sun; and the coloured fellow said, "Hey, alligator, show this man you kin talk." The old alligator just rolled his eyes at the coloured fellow. The white man looked at the coloured fellow and the coloured fellow said, "Now come on, Mistah Alligator, and talk. You was talking up a breeze a while ago." But the alligator don't say nothing. Ain't nothing the coloured fellow can do to make him say nothing. So the white fellow got tired of standing there and jumped on the coloured fellow like he said and beat the stuffings out of him. Well, the coloured fellow sat down beside the alligator, his head knotty as fat pine; man, his head knottier than the alligator's. "Why didn't you talk?" he ast the alligator. "I told that man you could talk and you made him beat the stuffings outa me." The alligator rolled his eyes at the coloured fellow and said, "That just what I says, you coloured folks talk too much." '

Willie and Arkansas rolled on the floor. 'Dat was some alligator,' Arkansas said.

I caught Ben's eye and grinned at him. Ben made twirling motions with his index finger at the side of his head, and I laughed.

Nobody could top that one, and they were silent for a moment. Tebbel took advantage of the pause to tell his.

'Old Aunty was out in the back yard washing.' All of us gave him a startled look. 'And she said—'

'You mean old Aunty Loo?' Pigmeat cut him off.

'It don't make any difference what her name was,' Tebbel tried again; but Pigmeat cut him off again, 'Or do you mean old Aunty Coo?'

Tebbel began getting red. 'Just old Aunty,' he snarled. 'Old Aunty was out in the back yard—'

Conway picked up a duct and banged it on the deck. 'We done told enough jokes, now let's get to work,' he said.

I had to laugh. I felt better than I'd felt all morning.

'We all know that one about old Aunty,' Johnson said.

'You know that one, don't you, Johnson?' I winked.

'Everybody knows that one, boy,' Pigmeat said to Tebbel. 'You go think up another one and then come back.'

'What I wanna know now is whether to make a butt joint here or a lap joint,' Conway said, turning over the duct.

'Tebbel will tell you all about it,' I said. 'Tebbel's gonna be your boss next week.'

Tebbel looked dubious. 'What does the print say?'

'If I had the print I wouldn't be asking you,' Conway said.

'Better get the print to be sure,' Tebbel said, and walked out.

'I done run him,' Conway grinned.

'It's a lap joint,' I said.

'I know,' he said. 'I was just trying to stop him from telling that dirty joke to keep from having to knock out his teeth.'

The three girls came in and Peaches asked, 'Are you all through telling dirty jokes?'

I laughed. 'Tebbel broke it up.'

'What did he tell?' Bessie wanted to know. 'Something dirty about some coloured people, I know.'

'They ganged up on him and wouldn't let him tell it, so he left,' I told her.

'That's good,' Peaches said. 'Don't let him get started on that stuff.'

I winked at Peaches. 'Think I'll go out and give my white woman a break,' I said.

'You ain't no trouble,' she said slyly. 'You done found that out.'

But it didn't even ruffle me. 'Wanna bet?' I teased.

'Who gonna be the judge?'

'I'll let you judge. If you holler more than once—'

'What I've got will kill a little boy like you dead,' she cut me off, and then if she had been light enough she would have turned fiery red.

'All right, let our helpers alone,' George said. 'We'll take care of everything that needs taking care of. You go on and give your white woman a break.'

Kelly had popped his head in just in time to hear the last of it. He gave a startled look and beat it without saying a word.

Pigmeat laughed. 'Did you chalk the walker?'

I glanced at my watch. It was nine-fifteen. We had clowned up more than an hour. But they had got it off their chests; almost all of them had started back to work. I felt better about it too. Now I could go up and talk to the union steward without blowing my top.

Then all of a sudden Conway snapped his fingers. 'We done plumb forgot all about Bob—' he began, but I cut him off, 'No, no, we're not gonna do that any more. You guys go on and do your work. I'll take care of everything.'

'Well, we behind you, chief,' Smitty said.

'Way behind you,' Pigmeat said.

I gave them the okay sign, hitched up my pants and

started out. Ben stopped me. 'Some folks, ain't they?' he said, shaking his head.

'Remember what the monkey said when young Mose ran over him and cut off his tail?' I asked.

'My people, my people,' we chorused, grinning at each other.

CHAPTER
13

I found the union steward, Herbie Frieberger, on the weather deck, enjoying his privileges. He was a tall, lean, stoop-shouldered guy in his early thirties, with frizzly gopher-coloured hair, a flapping loose-lipped mouth, and a big hooked nose. His face was narrow and his brownish eyes were set close together; he had a shiny tin hat tipped to the back of his head and a union button big as a saucer pinned to the front of his shirt. I didn't exactly hate the guy, but I despised him from the word 'go.' It was strictly personal.

There were five guys standing around him, four white and a coloured fellow who was something or other in the union, probably the proof that it wasn't discriminatory. Herbie was beating up his chops about Lend-Lease to Russia when I walked up.

'Comrades,' I greeted.

They all looked around. One of the white guys winked; the other three didn't speak.

'Comrade,' the coloured fellow saluted. A black Russian, I thought.

Herbie looked salty. ' 'Lo, Bob,' he growled.

'May I have a word in private with you, Commissar?' I said. Herbie didn't like that either. 'Come on, can the corny jive,' he grated. 'Next thing you'll be asking me to get you out of a jam.'

I kept my face under control. 'Okay, you know the story,' I said. 'I want to talk to you about it.'

He got important again. 'Say look, Bob, can't you see me in about a half-hour? Maybe I can do something for you, old man.'

'Whatever you can do in a half-hour, you can do right now.'

'Jesus Christ, all you guys do is gripe,' he complained. 'You don't want a union, you want a court of human relations. Write a letter to Mr Anthony.'

If he knew what I thought about both him and the union he wouldn't be so cute, I thought. I kept my voice level. 'Come on, Jew boy, don't be so loud,' I said, dragging him in front of the white boys.

He jerked a look of solid malevolence at me, then gave the others a you-see-how-it-is look, spread his hands in a despairing gesture, and walked with me to the starboard rail.

'The thing for you to do is to write out a grievance and give it to me tomorrow,' he began blabbing before I'd said a word. 'I'll present it before the executive board when we meet next week.'

'You're jumping the gun, sonny boy,' I told him flatly. 'What I want you to do is straighten out this cracker dame. I'll handle the rest of it. I want you to tell her she has to work with Negroes here or lose her job.'

I knew that'd put him on the spot; he didn't want to butt heads with those crackers any more than I did.

'Jesus Christ, Bob, you know the union can't do that,' he began tracking back. 'The union can't force anybody to quit—'

'You can if they don't pay their dues,' I said.

'But this is different,' he contended. 'This is dynamite. If we tried that, half the workers in the yard would walk out. I hate to even think what might happen.'

'Don't try,' I said. 'Think of what's already happened. If a third-grade tacker can get a leaderman bumped every cracker dame here is going to figure she can make a beef and get any Negro bumped—'

'Well, Christ, I'll talk to her,' he said. 'That's the best I can do. I've been intending to talk to her.' He wiped mock sweat from his brow. 'Damn, old man, take in some of your muscle, you'll get us all shot. Just take it easy and you'll live longer. Listen, if you take it easy for a month or two, I promise you—'

'If you can't talk to her now, and with me there to hear what you say, then to hell with you and this lousy Jim Crow union too!' I said.

'That's no way to talk about the union,' he began ducking and dodging again. 'You know we have always fought for the coloured people. Christ, learn something about your union, man. Most of the nationals have Negroes on their executive boards—'

'That don't mean anything to me,' I cut him off. 'When I came to this lousy city in '41 all I did was bump my head against Jim Crow shops that were organized by your union. They organize me *in*—that's fine – when I get *in* . . .'

'Hell, the union isn't an employment agency. If it hadn't been for the union you wouldn't be working here now—'

'That's a goddamned lie!' I said. 'The only reason this company started hiring Negroes is because they couldn't get enough white workers who wanted to work in this dirty yard. This lousy local never fought for Negroes to be hired – probably fought against it—'

'Okay, okay,' he cut in. 'This local is a stinker. Christ, don't you know I know it? But don't judge the whole movement by—'

'The whole movement ain't little Jesus Christ to me,' I

said. 'Either you're all the way for me, or you're all the way against me. I don't play the middle.'

'That's the trouble with you coloured people,' he shouted, getting agitated. 'You forget we're in a war. This isn't any time for private gripes. We're fighting fascism – we're not fighting the companies and we're not fighting each other – we're all fighting fascism together and in order to beat fascism we got to have unity. We got to have unity in the union and unity on the job—'

'That's fine, Comrade Marx, that's wonderful,' I cut him off. 'Let's you and me unite and start right here fighting fascism. Let's go down and give this cracker dame some lessons in unity and if she doesn't want to unite let's tell her about the war—'

'Aw, goddamnit, you want to agitate!' he shouted. 'I'm no Communist and you know it. Mrs Baker had an editorial in her paper about Negro people like you. She said—'

'Whatever she said, I don't want to hear it,' I said. 'Mrs Baker's not my mama.' Mrs Baker was a Negro woman who published a weekly paper in Los Angeles. 'And as for all that gibberish about unity! Get these crackers to unite with me. I'm willing. I'll work with 'em, fight with 'em, die with 'em, goddamnit. But I ain't gonna even try to do any uniting without anybody to unite with. Do you understand that?' I put my finger on his chest. 'What the hell do I care about unity, or the war either, for that matter, as long as I'm kicked around by every white person who comes along? Let the white people get some goddamned unity.'

He gave me a funny look, 'I'm white,' he said. 'I'm not kicking you around.'

That made me blind mad for him to put me on a spot like that. I blew up. 'Dammit to hell, don't look at me!' I said. 'I believe you. Tell it to some of these crackers around here who don't. They'd refuse to work with you as quick as they would me.'

Now he got a hurt enduring look. 'Jesus Christ,' he said. 'I never saw a guy so confused.'

'Okay, I'm confused,' I said. 'I knew that was coming.' I took a breath and pinned him down. 'All I want to know are you coming with me to talk to this dame?'

'Bob, you know damned well I can't do that. I'd start—'

'Well, go to hell!' I said, and walked off.

I rubbed my face with the flat of my hand, dug my finger tips into my scalp. That guy could really get on my nerves. He could give more phoney arguments in five minutes than the average chump could think up in a day. And the hell of it was he could make a weak-minded chump fall for 'em. All I'd wanted was for him to straighten out the dame, and he'd damn near shown me where she was right and I was wrong.

Now I didn't know what to do. I hadn't turned in the timecards because I didn't want any stuff out of Kelly. I stood there on the deck for a time, looking out across the harbour. A cruiser was silhouetted against the skyline. The white folks are still going strong, I thought; then I thought about the black sailors aboard waiting on the white. In the good old American tradition, I thought; the good old American way.

My face felt drawn in, thin, skin-tight on the bone. I wondered what would happen if all the Negroes in America would refuse to serve in the armed forces, refuse to work in war production until the Jim Crow pattern was abolished. The white folks would no doubt go right on fighting the war without us, I thought – and no doubt win it. They'd kill us maybe; but they couldn't kill us all. And if they did they'd have one hell of a job of burying us.

The thought pushed a laugh through my nose, loosened me slightly, then I remembered that Mac had said I'd lose my job deferment. I'd be in there soon myself, if I didn't get my job back, I thought, looking at the long lean cruiser. I gripped the rail until my knuckles showed white through the brown, clamped my teeth until my jaws ached. I wouldn't take it, I told myself; I just wouldn't take it, that was all.

Then I thought of Alice saying, 'But it's not just you now, Bob. It's you and I . . . Don't you understand?' I began hurting inside, all down in my chest and stomach. I could see the planes of her face moving, the smooth mobile motion of her lips. 'In the things you do and the decisions you make you just can't think of yourself alone. You have to consider our future . . .' The plea in her eyes . . . 'Is that too much to ask?' The finality of her voice . . . 'If you don't go to that girl and apologize and try in every way you know to get reinstated – If you can't do that much, Bob, don't consider me as being with you any more . . .'

I felt something hammering on my brain, banging away with a ten-pound sledge. I gave a violent shake of my head, trying to get it off. Me and my goddamned two-cent pride, I thought; my cut-rate muscle and my blind dukes. Who in the hell did I think I was?

I took a deep breath and pushed away from the rail. I really liked that chick, I thought – she was strictly tops.

Then I started looking for Madge. But not to apologize. I was going to rack her back, I told myself. I was going to ask her what the hell she meant by saying she wouldn't work with a nigger, where did she get that stuff calling me a nigger, anyway? And if she didn't like it I was going to kick in her teeth. And if it meant losing Alice I was going to lose her. Goddamnit, I was a man like any other man; I wasn't asking any favours, and I wasn't taking no kicks.

I found her on the deck below, working with the same two mechanics, tacking a conduit to the deck plating. She was sitting on the deck with her feet drawn underneath her, bending forward over the arc. Her skin showed in a white line where her jacket and waist hiked up, and below her hips spread tight in her leather pants like an hour-glass. Don stood to one side, shading his eyes against the flash with his outstretched hand.

'What say, Don,' I greeted, coming up. 'How's things breaking?'

He looked around, didn't exactly give a start at sight of me, but his sharp brown eyes behind their rimless lenses got spark-bright. 'Oh, hello, Bob,' he said. 'I want to see you.'

The arc died for a moment and he took a quick squint at the job, looked away before a flash could catch him, and said to her, 'That's good.'

The two mechanics took off their flash glasses, gave me nervous looks, and began piddling about. It wasn't tense, but it was itchy.

I pulled the edges of my mouth down, dropped a flat-eyed evil glance on her hooded head, then looked at Don. 'A rugged playmate,' I said. 'Must have snake in her. Will she bite you too?' I wanted her to hear me, but she didn't.

She kicked back her hood, flipped the rod butt across the floor, unhooked her stinger, and began chipping the scale off the weld burrs with her iron hand chipper. She didn't see me either.

Don put his hand to his chin, worried at his lip with his index finger, then headed me off. 'I'm sorry about it, Bob. Now don't get down on me,' he said. 'I told Mac I'd let you have her; I told him how it was. I had no idea—'

Her sudden movement stopped him and we both turned startled looks on her. She came to her feet like a jack-in-the-box and went right straight into her act. She cringed back into the bulkhead and her big blue mascaraed eyes peered out at me in sheer terror.

I wouldn't let her have it. 'Get a load of this,' I said to Don, dipping my head at her; then turned and found him studying me with that sharp speculating curiosity of white men watching Negroes' reactions to white women.

She said something under her breath and now her face took on a wild raw excitement that shook me. She looked crazy enough to call me a nigger again, and I tightened instinctively against it; this time I knew I'd smack her. But instead she pumped a mean, hard contempt into her eyes and said in her flat, unmusical, nigger-baiting drawl, 'Sometimes I sho wish I was back in Texas.'

I took a breath and held it. One of the mechanics said gruffly, 'Come on, Madge, we got a divider to put in before noon.'

Now I was ready to shoot her. I wrenched my gaze away, then felt Don's eyes on me again.

But all he said was, 'I want you to believe me, Bob, I had no idea she'd give you any trouble. If you want me to I'll go with you to Mac and—'

'Naw, I'm going to fight it through the union,' I said. 'I want some of Mac too.'

He was curious to know just what had happened, but he didn't want to ask right out, so he said, 'Did you have a fight with her before?'

'Hell naw,' I said. 'I ain't never seen her before.' Then I decided to tell him; I felt I could talk to him all right. 'When I went to get her, she started that phoney act you just saw and said she wouldn't work with a nigger, and I called her a cracker slut.'

Red came up in his face in slow waves, but he didn't

pull away from it. 'Some stinker,' he said. 'What she needs is a good going over by someone.' I knew he wanted to say by some coloured fellow but just couldn't bring himself to say it. Instead he got redder and said, 'It'd take some of the stinking prejudice out of her.'

'What she really needs is just some discipline,' I said. 'Some of these officials to tell her what's what, to lay the line down and make her walk it.'

He blinked at me and his eyes got bright again. 'I told you her name, didn't I? Madge Perkins.'

I gave a little laugh. 'I found that out. What I want to know is what's eating her. She knows goddamned well nobody wants to rape her.'

He hesitated a moment, then said, 'She hasn't got a phone,' digging out a little black address book. 'But I'll give you her address.' He grinned sheepishly. 'I knew her room-mate, but she joined the WAC's.'

I gave him a quick startled look; I didn't get it. 'What do I want with her address, man?'

Now he began getting red again, but he gave me a curious little look. 'Maybe you can cure her,' he said.

'Look, man . . .' I began, then didn't know what to say. I couldn't tell whether he figured I was making a play for the dame and was using the beef as an opening, or was trying to tell me how to get even with her, or whether he was trying to prove he didn't have any racial bias himself. It could have been he felt badly about it from a white point of view and wanted to show me that all the men in his race didn't approve of that sort of thing.

Whatever it was, he went on giving me her address with a painful insistence. 'It's the Hotel Mohave on South Figueroa . . .' He gave me a downtown street number. 'Room 202, that's the front room on the second floor.'

'Say, man, look,' I began again. I wanted to tell him I

didn't want to go to bed with her, I wanted to black her eyes; but just the idea of her being a white woman stopped me. I felt flustered, caught, guilty. I couldn't realize what was happening to me, myself. It was funny in a way. I couldn't tell him I *didn't* want her because she was a white woman and he was a white man, and something somewhere way back in my mind said that would be an insult. And I couldn't tell him that I *did* want her, because the same thing said that that would be an insult too.

I started shaking my head and laughing. He looked put out, slightly offended, and his eyes blinked like butterfly wings. But he got it all out with the white man's eternal persistence, 'There's a phone in the hotel, but I don't know the number. It's one of those joints, you know.'

I was blowing laughs through my nose; I felt light-headed and giddy. 'Now anybody in the world would think we were two fairly ordinary, reasonably sane guys,' I said.

I wondered what a white man and a Negro could talk about that wouldn't touch at some time or other on one of those taboo subjects that would embarrass one or the other, or both. Either both the Negro and the white man would have to accept the fact and even justification of white supremacy – then they could talk about what the white folks were doing and thinking and what the Negroes were taking and aping; or both would have to reject the theory of white supremacy and condemn all of its institutions, including loyalty and patriotism in time of war; or the white man could retain it and the Negro reject it, which didn't make for conversation at all.

I began shaking my head again. 'I'm telling you,' I said. 'It's a killer.'

He didn't get it. He blinked and his eyes went blank,

absolutely lost; and I didn't know where to go from there either. We'd taken it too far to back out; now we stood there at a loss for words, each wanting to escape the other but neither wanting to be the first to make the break.

'There're a lot of stinkers like her in the yard,' he was saying, and I said, 'Too many.'

It was a relief to both of us when Zula Mae came up and said, 'Red wants you, Bob, he's up a tree.'

'Again,' I said, and took her by the arm. 'See you, Don.'

'Take it easy, Bob,' he said with a peculiar baffled look in his eyes.

'Baby,' I said to her. 'You sure look good to me.'

She gave me a half-incredulous, half-hopeful look, and her red lips flowered in her dark face. 'Are you kidding?' she said in her husky plaintive voice, and I gave a long loosening sigh.

But the things had gotten me. Now I felt depressed, walled in, black again. Red noticed it right away.

'What the hell happened to you, Bob? Don't the union wanna help you?' he asked.

'I got it all fixed,' I lied, but my voice was flat, dispirited.

'He been reading in the paper where all young men gonna be called to the Army,' Peaches said. 'He got the GI blues.'

'Got something,' Conway said.

Red didn't want anything in particular; just wanted me there so Tebbel couldn't take charge. I stood around for a time.

'I don't know what the hell I'd do if they called me,' Ben said. 'Every time a coloured man gets in the Army he's fighting against himself. Of course there isn't anything else he can do. If he refuses to go they send him to

148

the pen. But if he does go and take what they put on him, and then fight so he can keep on taking it, he's a cowardly son of a bitch.'

Smitty had stopped his work to listen. 'I wouldn't say that,' he argued. 'You can't call coloured soldiers cowards, man. They can't keep the Army from being like what it is, but hell, they ain't no cowards.'

'Any man's a coward who won't die for what he believes,' Ben flared. 'If he's got principles he'll die for them. If he won't he's a cowardly son of a bitch – excuse me, ladies.'

The other fellows stopped to listen now.

'Any time a Negro says he believes in democracy but won't die to enforce it – I say he's a coward,' Ben declared. 'I don't care who he is. If Bob lets them put him in the Army he's a coward. If you let them put you in the Army you're a coward. As long as the Army is Jim Crowed a Negro who fights in it is fighting against himself.'

'If Bob gets called sure 'nough and listens to you and gets sent to the pen, he's a fool,' Zula Mae said.

Ben gave me a swift look. 'Bob's all right. If they call him he'll go on and make the best of it. Nobody expects him to be a martyr. But one thing I'll tell you, and you remember it—'

Tebbel stepped from one of the shower nooks where he'd been standing and Ben gave him a glance and kept on. 'One thing . . . You'll never get anything from these goddamn white people unless you fight them. They don't know anything else. Don't listen to anything else. If you don't believe it, take any white man you know. You can beg that son of a bitch until you're blue in the face. Argue with him until you're out of breath and no matter how eloquent your plea or righteous your cause the only way you'll ever get along with that son of a bitch is to whip his ass – excuse me, ladies.' He looked around defiantly. 'Bob'll tell you that's right. Isn't that right, Bob?'

'That's right,' I said.

'Then he gonna be your friend from then on,' Conway chuckled.

'That reminds me of a story,' Tebbel said. 'There were two coloured soldiers—'

'Was one named Moe?' Pigmeat cut in.

I chuckled and went out.

CHAPTER
14

When I went down to turn in the time cards Kelly said, 'Wait a minute, Bob, I want to talk to you.' Then he went on telling this joke to the two white guys from the shop.

'So he took this gal out in the shed out of respect for old Aunty, see, because all old Aunty had was this one-roomed shack where she and the gal lived.' He took a quick glance to see if the tool-crib girl was out of hearing and lowered his voice slightly. 'It'd been raining like hell, see, and the shed didn't have any floor and it was all sloppy and muddy where the hogs had been wallowing. But this guy was hard up, see, he'd been on the road for two weeks . . .'

I wasn't ready for that one; wasn't even looking for it. I didn't even have time to dodge it. He'd tricked me into listening by having me wait, and now without giving me time to get mad he said, 'How's Danny Tebbel getting along Bob? Do you think he's going to be able to handle your gang?'

The other two guys looked at me curiously to see how I was taking it, and the tool-crib girl came over and said, 'Those boys in your crew are breaking too many of those 9/32 bits; they'll just have to stop it or they can't have any more.'

They couldn't have done it any better if they'd

rehearsed it. I couldn't take offence because Kelly didn't tell the joke to me and he could always say if I hadn't wanted to hear it I didn't have to listen. And even if I still wanted to take offence, the girl had stepped into the picture and whatever I might say to Kelly was sure to offend her. I never wanted to get out of a place so bad in all my life; I wanted to just take my tail between my legs and slink on out. It was a gut punch and my stomach was hollow as a drum; it took all I had to keep standing up straight, to keep on looking at him.

I did something with my face, trying to make it smile, and I had to reach down my throat and pull out my voice with my hand, but I got it and I said, 'I'll get mine by and by.'

The girl's mouth popped open. 'Well, I never—' she began.

But Kelly knew he had me. He waved me away. 'Go on, go on. Get out of here.'

I turned away and started walking, not fast but not poking. I went past workers, stepped over lines, ducked under staging, squeezed by shapes, through the access hole in the midship bulkhead, up the jack ladder to the third deck, up another ladder to the fourth deck, headed aft. I didn't see anybody, didn't see anything. I knew where I was going. I didn't want to go. My body just carried me and my mind just pushed me along. I didn't feel rash nor reckless, nothing like that, I felt low, dispirited, black as I've ever felt. Really a black boy now.

But I knew I was going to have to say something to Madge if I got shot on the spot. Not to rack her back or to cuss her out. That wasn't going to be enough. Not now. Not after having been tricked into listening to that bastard tell that joke. I was going to have to have her. I was going to have to make her as low as a white whore in a Negro slum – a scrummy two-dollar whore . . . I was going to have to so I could keep looking the white folks in the face.

And when Monday came I'd come on back and work as a mechanic. And if they put me in the Jim Crow Army I was going to take that too. Ben could talk all he wanted to. He was right. I knew he was right. But I was going to take it if they put it on me. If I had to fight and die for the country I'd fight and die for it. I'd even go so far as to believe it was my country too. But I'd be damned if I was going to be afraid to make this woman because she was white Texas.

So I started over where she was working. She was over to one side by herself, leaning against some staging. There were a lot of other workers around, but I didn't see them; all I could see was her standing there between me and my manhood.

She saw me coming and looked me square in the eyes, hers bright with a sudden excitement. One of the mechanics she was working with spotted me too and walked quickly to her side as if his presence would protect her. But his being there didn't mean a thing to me. I was going to say, 'Look, bitch, let's stop all this jive and get together like we want.'

My heart was in my throat and I felt like jelly. We kept looking at each other and I knew she expected me to say something. I knew she wanted me to. I knew she knew what I'd say. I didn't know what her reaction might be; I didn't even think about it. I won't say I didn't want her. It built up fast and shook me like a chip hammer digging in my navel. I wanted her then more than I wanted all the Alices in the world. I don't know how to case it. She looked like a big overpainted strumpet with eyes as wild as Oklahoma.

But when I got to her I lost my nerve. I couldn't say a word. I just couldn't do it, that was all. She was pure white Texas. And I was black. And a white man was standing there. I never knew before how good a job the white folks had done on me.

I turned and kept on by. I cursed myself for a coward. I called myself a fool. I told myself there was nothing to it. Hell, she was a cheap bitchy tacker. And I was still a leaderman. We were both workers. What could she say? How could she resent my speaking to her? The white guys treated some of those white women like they were bitches in heat. A lot of 'em were prostitutes anyway; they were always firing some of 'em for tricking on the job. And this woman looked like a slut on the make. Anybody in the world could understand how she'd get a proposition. A white guy might ask her outright how much was it worth – or sold for anyway. But I didn't even have the nerve to speak to her. That was what really got it, when I really knew. I had gotten up that morning and gotten myself ready to die. And I could have gone out and done it. I could have kept walking into .45 slugs until the weight of 'em pulled me down, so help me God. But I just couldn't walk into this woman with so much white inside her.

I knew she knew just what had happened. A white man wouldn't have known it. Some white women might not and she had seen my nerve desert me. I've never felt so cheap, so small and inconsequential, so absolutely subhuman. I couldn't stand myself; couldn't stand thinking about myself. It was physical torture.

I kept going toward the gangway port. Once I stopped I knew she was watching me. I knew her mouth was twisted in a sneer the size of a dill pickle. I wanted to turn around and go on back and talk to her. Even then I could have saved a little pride. I knew she would know I'd funked, then braced myself for another try. I knew she wanted me to make it. But I couldn't, just couldn't, that was all.

I wouldn't even try to make Sad Sammy believe it, and he'll believe anything. Because I didn't even believe it myself, even while it was happening. I didn't know whether it was all the things that had happened to me put together – that was what I wanted to believe – or whether it was just the pure and simple colours of America.

I had known white girls in both California and Ohio. I had gone with a little Italian girl in Cleveland for almost a year. Then there had been a tall brown-haired girl who worked as a stenographer in a downtown office who used to let me take her out now and then. She'd lived over on 100th Street near Euclid and used to walk up and meet me at the Chauffeurs Club. Both of them were good girls, as good morally as most.

And when Val had his joint in the alley off Cedar and Eighty-sixth Street a lot of gine white women in the money used to come out there to hear Art Tatum and Lonnie Johnson. Many of them would get drunk and cut out with any coloured guy available. And out at the Cedar Gardens the Avenue slicks laid about to catch them on the rebound. It wasn't any secret. The white men knew all about it. If the black boys played too rough the white men would put the cops on them and get them sapped up.

So it wasn't that Madge was white; it was the way she used it. She had a sign up in front of her as big as Civic Centre – KEEP AWAY, NIGGERS, I'M WHITE! And without having to say one word she could keep all the white men in the world feeling they had to protect her from black rapists. That made her doubly dangerous because she thought about Negro men. I could tell that the first time I saw her. She wanted them to run after her. She expected it, demanded it as her due. I could imagine her teasing them with her body, showing her bare thighs and breasts.

155

Then having them lynched for looking.

And that was what scared me. Luring me with her body and daring me with her colour. It ate into me, made me want her for her colour, not her body. In order to have her I'd have to challenge her colour; I couldn't take the dare. Just twenty steps and thirteen words – but I couldn't make it.

So I went outboard and down the wooden gangway, roughing people out of the way. I felt castrated, snake-bellied, and cur-doggish, I felt like a nigger being horse-whipped in Georgia. Cheap, dirty, low. I wanted to grab some bastard and roll down the stairs. My face felt tight. The taste of white folks was in my mouth and I couldn't get it out.

What I ought to do is rape her, I thought. That's what she wanted.

I went down to the dock, searched in the scrap-iron pile until I found a two-foot dog, heavy on one end with weld burrs. One blow with that would crush a chump's skull. Gripping it tightly in my right hand, I went along the dock. The sun was hot, unbearable. My skin felt scorched; my mouth was dry. My eyes felt half open, dead, ringed in steel. I walked with a steady hard motion, planting each step like driving piles. I shouldered into guys, split between couples, walked in a straight line. At the end of the dock I passed the guard in his little shanty, kept on toward the copper shop. It wasn't until then that I knew where I was going. I was looking for my white boy again. He'd been elected.

I was going to walk up and beat out his brains. Then I was going to find Madge, wherever she was, make my bid and make it stick. After that I could go up and sit in the gas chamber at San Quentin and laugh. Because it was the funniest goddamned thing that had ever happened. A black son of a bitch destroying himself because of a no-good white slut from Texas. It was so funny because it didn't make sense. It was just the notion. If you could just get over the notion you could laugh yourself silly.

I entered the copper shop from the front, kept on back toward the punch press the white boy operated. He wasn't there. I asked an old fellow working on the bench where the boy who ran the machine was.

'Johnny Stoddart?' he asked. Then he looked at me. He saw the dog in my hand. He saw my face. His eyes bucked. 'What do you want with him?' he asked.

'None of your goddamned business,' I answered evenly.

He opened his mouth as if to say something else, thought better of it. But he wouldn't turn his back to me; instead he backed away a distance, turned quickly, and started down toward the office. I stood there for a moment looking about. I felt weighted, baulked, baffled. It was as if this boy, Johnny Stoddart, had let me down by not being there so I could beat out his brains, had betrayed me.

I went out the back doorway, turned to the right. I whistled a sharp, high-breaking scale, levelled off on 'Don't Cry, Baby.' My lips felt stiff, inflexible. As I turned the corner of the corrugated building I threw the dog against the tin wall out of sheer frustration.

It sounded like a cannon shot and just missed hitting my boy in the face. He was coming down the other side and I hadn't even seen him. We both jumped back from pure reflex. Then recognition came into his eyes and his face turned greenish white. It froze him, nailed him to the spot. For a moment I was stunned. I'd never seen a white man scared before, not craven, not until you couldn't see the white for the scare.

Murder touched me then. Not the notion but the actual; the physical; the impelling vicarious urge to take

157

my iron dog and beat him to a pulp. Then all at once I felt sorry for him. Sorry for anybody who had to be that scared and keep on living.

Suddenly I was laughing, doubling over, laughing all down in my belly. I was thinking, without knowing why, about the other night when I took the garbage out for Ella Mae. Something had moved in the dark and made a funny noise that scared the hell out of me. I had dropped the garbage and damn near killed myself stumbling over the steps trying to get out of the way. Whatever it was lit out the other way. I ran into the house, got my pistol and flashlight, came back to investigate with the cocked pistol in my hand, and found the tiniest little kitten you ever want to see trying to hide in the irises. I was thinking about that and laughing like hell; and thinking about how all my life I'd been scared of white folks because they were white and it was funny as hell to find out white folks were scared of me, too, because I was black.

The white boy came out of it and colour came back into his face and it got beet-red. White came back into his soul; I could see it coming back, rage at seeing a nigger threatening him. Now he was ready to die for his race like a patriot, a true believer. I could see in his mind he wanted to kill me because I had seen him lose it. He hunched his shoulders, bowed his head, and started into me. And then he lost his nerve. He shook himself steady, straightened up, looked around for a weapon. He didn't see any, so he said, 'I'll fight you.'

I smiled at him. 'I don't want to fight you,' I told him. 'I want to kill you. But right now I'm saving you up.'

I could see the fear coming back and see him fighting against it.

'If I catch you around my house again I'm gonna shoot you like a dog,' he threatened, and wheeled away.

I turned and watched him for a moment, feeling good,

feeling fine, loose, free. I had gotten over the notion; I had spit the white folks out my mouth. There wasn't anything they could do to me now, I told myself; nothing they could say to me that would hurt. I was ready now, solid ready, to walk right up to Texas.

I kicked my tin hat back at a signifying angle, pushed back toward the dock. Before I got there the whistle blew for lunch.

CHAPTER
15

I went over to the canteen, got some hot stew, a piece of pie, and coffee. Looking around for a place to eat, I saw Madge sitting on the ground with her back propped against a stack of pipes in the shade of a shed beside the pipe shop. An older woman stopped and put her lunch down beside her, then got into the line at the canteen.

I hesitated a moment to see if anyone else would join her, then started toward her, my heart pumping like a rivet gun and my legs wobbly weak. Something drew her gaze and she looked up into my eyes. We held gazes until I stopped just in front of her. Her eyes were bright, liquid, and her face was slightly flushed. She had peeled off the leather jacket and was clad in a white waist, open at the throat. Her breasts were loose and ripe as cantaloupes.

I opened my mouth, couldn't make it, swallowed, and tried again. 'Just where do you get that stuff?' I said. 'Just who do you think you are?' My voice came out of the top of my mouth, light and weightless and stilted.

I had expected her to do anything but what she did. She fluttered her mascaraed lashes at me like an 1890 slick chick and gave me a look of pure blue innocence. 'I don't think you know me,' she said in her flat Southern drawl. Then she let recognition leak into her look. 'Oh, you're the boy I had the fight with the other day.' Now she gave me a ravishing smile – at least that's what it was supposed to be – and her manner became easy, friendly, without tension of any sort. 'Yo' name is Bob, isn't it? Rest the weight, Bob, you must get tired of toting it around all day.'

All I could do was stare at her. After all that tremendous anxiety I had gone through; after all that murderous build-up, that hard hollow scare; after all the crazy, wild-eyed, frightened acts she had put on, the white armour plate she'd wrapped herself up in, the insurmountable barriers she'd raised between us, here she was breaking it down, wiping it all out, with a smile; treating me as casually as an old acquaintance. It was too much, just simply too much, for one person to be able to do. I must have looked very funny at that moment, for she burst out laughing.

'Don't take it so hard,' she said. 'Lotta folks fight. I think it's 'cause they like making up so much.'

I sat down beside her, put my stew, pie, and coffee between my legs. But I couldn't eat it; if I had taken a bite I would have thrown up. I was sick as a dog. I didn't look at her. I took a long deep breath, looked at the ground. I didn't know whether to laugh or cry.

'I suppose you know you got me demoted,' I said finally, realizing instantly it was the worst possible thing I could have said. It acknowledged her power over me, and that was wrong.

Now she could play it any way she wanted, magnanimous or condescending. Instead she played it true to form. 'You oughtn'ta called me no slut,' she slurred. 'You don't know me that well.'

I jerked around and looked at her. She wore a maddening, teasing smile and her eyes were laughing at me. I went so blind mad I was petrified. Not mad at her; at myself for being pushed around by a notion. If you could just get over the notion, women were the same, black or white.

I knew that getting mad was bad, it gave her the lead. So I dug myself out, got a smile to match her own, and said, 'You'll make a man slap you one of these days, do you know that?'

'Now you know, I don't hardly understand you,' she said, taking a bite of pork-chop sandwich and fluttering her mascaraed lashes. 'You talk so funny.' She giggled, 'Is this the first time you ever talked to a white lady?'

'Look, baby, let Texas rest. You know the score, probably better than me. Let's stop clowning and get together—' I broke off. 'Look, what you doing tonight? How 'bout running with me? I know some fine spots where it'll be okay.' I could see her drawing in a little and I rushed on. 'You won't be the only white girl there.' Then I said, 'Look, baby, you really get me.'

At that she turned and said, 'You talks so fast, first you wanna jump on me and now you wanna date me.' Then she killed me with her smile.

'Look—' I began again, broke off as the other women came up with a piece of pie and two cups of coffee.

'I brung you some coffee, Madge. I declare, how you eat those dry poke-chop sandwiches is—' She was rattling off in a Southern dialect broader than Madge's when suddenly she caught sight of me. She had seen me without seeing me. She had thought I was just sitting there eating my lunch, as close to a white girl as I could get, and she'd been prepared to endure it since the joint wasn't Jim Crowed. But when she realized that I was among those present she stopped abruptly, her voice suspended in mid-air and her mouth hanging open. Her eyes went quickly to Madge's, seeking an explanation.

Madge took the coffee and placed it on the ground beside her. 'I'd rather choke than stand in that durn line,' she said casually, and then as if it was the most common-place thing in the world, she introduced me. 'Elsie, this is

Bob. He's a leaderman with the sheet-metal gang. Me and him had a fight but we done made up. Elsie is my sister-in-law,' she said to me.

'Hello, Elsie,' I said.

Elsie gave me a sharp quick glance, then looked away. She set her coffee carefully on the ground, then carefully sat herself down. Her actions were slightly dazed, as if she was trying to acquaint a slow mentality to the situation. Finally, when she got it all straightened out, she gave me a perfunctory smile.

'Howdedo,' she said, fanning herself with a piece of newspaper. 'Sho is hot.' She laid the paper down and opened her lunch. 'Lotta coloured boys working in 'dustry nowadays, right 'long with white people,' she observed, taking out a ham sandwich and nibbling at it daintily. 'You frum the South?'

I could feel Madge's gaze on me, and although I didn't look I knew she still wore that teasing smile. 'No, I'm from Ohio,' I said.

Elsie brushed it aside. 'I always says it ain't no more'n right. Coloured folks got much right to earn these good wages as white while we fighting this war. It's partly their country too, I always says. I was telling Lem – your uncle,' she said to Madge, 'just the other day that coloured folks got just as much right to earn these wages as we has. We believe in democracy over here and as I says to Lem, if we can just keep these Reds frum getting hold of the country we can keep our American way of living so everybody'll be happy.'

'Elsie is a democrat,' Madge put in. I couldn't tell whether to lessen the tension or prepare myself for the worst.

'So am I,' I said; I didn't want any argument either, but I couldn't help but add, 'Not a Southern one, however.'

'There's some mighty good coloured boys frum the

South,' Elsie went on through a mouthful of food. She washed it down with coffee. 'I declare, the coffee they make . . .' She grimaced. 'Now me and Madge are from Texas – Breckenridge, Texas. We went to Houston when the war broke out, then we got an itching to come to California.'

'I hear there're shipyards in Houston,' I began, but she didn't give anybody a chance to talk.

'Course it's different in Texas. The coloured folks there like to be by themselves, so we just let 'em go ahead and don't bother with 'em. Don't have no trouble and everybody is happy. I used to tell my husband – that's Madge's brother, he was killed in an automobile accident in Amarillo – I used to tell Henry that if everybody understood coloured folks like we do in the South there wouldn't be all this trouble.' She gave me a bright, toothy smile. 'Now tell the truth, you'd rather be with your own folks any day, wouldn't you?'

I got salty. 'If you're trying to tell me in a nice way you don't want my company—'

She threw up her hands and cut me off. 'I declare, you coloured folks frum California is so sensitive. Coloured boys in Texas know better'n to sit beside a white woman. Not that I mind if Madge don't. It's just that most coloured folks like to stay to themselves. That's why we ain't never had no trouble in Texas. All these riots in Detroit and New York and Chicago – it come from all this mixing up. I always say it ain't because white people is all that much better'n coloured folks – there's some mighty good coloured folks and some white people ain't worth their salt. And it ain't because white people hate coloured folks neither. We love coloured folks in Texas, and I bet you a silver dollar coloured folks love us too. I even know coloured folks what's educated. There's a coloured doctor in

Amarillo went to school and graduated. It's just that white people is white. We're different frum coloured people. The Lord God above made us white and made you folks coloured. If He'da wanted to, He coulda made you folks white and us people coloured. But he made us white 'cause he wanted us the same colour as Him. "I will make thee in My Image," He said, and that's what He done. And the sooner you coloured folks learn that, the sooner you understand that God made you coloured 'cause he wanted to, 'cause when He made us in His Image He had to make somebody else to fill up the world, so He made you. Not that I say coloured folks should have to serve white people, but you know yo'self God got dark angels in heaven what serve the white ones – that's in the Bible plain enough for anybody to see. And the sooner you coloured folks learn that, then the better off you'll be.'

'Don't pay no 'tension to Elsie,' Madge said to me as soon as she caught an opening. 'She just homesick, that's all.'

'Yes, I'm homesick, I'll tell anybody,' Elsie confessed. 'Too many Jews and Mexicans in this city for me, and if there's any folks I hate it's—'

'Your husband Elsie's brother?' I asked Madge, cutting Elsie off.

Madge gave me a startled, sidewise glance, then laughed. 'No, Elsie married my brother. My husband's in the service in—'

'Tell the truth!' Elsie broke in. 'You know well as you sitting there George is in Arkansas with another woman. He's too old for the service anyhow.'

Madge didn't like that. 'I heered he joined up. Lem told me—'

'Lem ain't told you no such thing,' Elsie snapped. 'I declare—'

I had to break it up again. 'You and Elsie live together?' I asked.

'No, Elsie lives with—' Madge began, but Elsie hunched her. 'Don't go telling your business to ev'ybody come along,' she said, then turned to me. 'I declare, boy, you ain't et a thing, and lunchtime is almost—' The whistled stopped her that time.

'Just like a clock,' I said.

'Now you got to slip off and eat on the job when you oughta be working,' she said.

'I'm not hungry anyway,' I said.

Elsie closed her lunch pail and got up, but Madge took a moment to gather up the scrap paper. When Elsie turned away I leaned over and whispered to Madge, 'I'm coming up to see you tonight.'

'You better not,' she threatened, looking panicky for an instant, then she giggled. 'You don't know where I live anyway.'

Elsie heard us whispering and turned back. 'Come on,' she said peevishly. 'I do declare, I don't know what's come over you since you come to California.'

Madge moved slightly, blocking Elsie from view, and I formed the words with my lips: 'Look for me around eight.'

'You go 'head!' Madge snapped at Elsie, wanting her to get away so we could have a last moment together. 'You know we can't leave no paper laying around.' Then she leaned over me to pick up a scrap of newspaper and I could see her breasts hanging loose inside her waist. She gave me plenty time to get my gaper's bit, then fluttered her eyelashes, straightened up, and went off with Elsie, pitching her hips. I sat there and watched them shake, too weak to move.

After a moment Ben, Peaches, and Conway came by on their way back to the dock. 'What you doing, taking your vacation?' Ben asked.

I picked up the stew, pie, and coffee, dumped them into a trash container, then joined the three of them.

'He's dreaming 'bout his white chicks,' Peaches said slyly.

I gave her a sharp look, wondering if she had seen me talking to Madge. Then I laughed and leaned over toward her. 'If you Negro women would give a man a break now and then we wouldn't have to—'

But she cut me off. 'That's what you all say. You niggers make me sick.' It must have been her pet peeve. 'If a coloured girl asks one of you niggers to take her to the show you start grumbling 'bout money – liable even ask her to pay the way. And then the raggedest-looking old beat-up white tramp can come by and get your whole pay check. You dump like a dumping truck.'

Ben saw that she was half-way serious and started teasing her. 'That's just what's wrong with you Negro women – always fighting and fussing. A man takes his life in his hands just to live with you. Always got your mouth stuck out and mad about something. Now take a white woman – all she wants you to do is love her.'

'I like big fat white women,' Conway started, ' 'cause there's so much of 'em that's white. An' I like old white women 'cause they been white so long. An' I like young white women 'cause they got so long to be white. An' I like skinny white women 'cause—'

A couple of white fellows passed and glanced at Conway, and Peaches snapped scornfully, 'Oh, shut up, Conway. You'll be up there begging me for some all afternoon.'

Ben gave a loud guffaw and Conway looked embarrassed. We started talking about the work and Ben got on Tebbel. Conway looked like he wanted to say something about me but thought better of it. When we came

167

to the landing stairs Madge was standing at the fountain. I half turned towards her and winked, but she must have thought I was going to say something to her, for she gave me one glance and went into her frightened act again. I gritted my teeth. That's okay, baby, I thought; you don't scare me now.

'What the hell's matter with that woman?' Ben asked. 'Is she—' He broke off and looked at me. 'That the cracker you had the trouble with?'

I nodded.

'What the hell is she trying to do, make as if she's scared of Negroes?'

'If she knew what I know 'bout you three she better be scared,' Peaches cracked.

'Bob don't want no stuff 'bout the woman,' Conway growled. Then he asked me, 'Hear any more 'bout it yet?'

'Not yet,' I said.

They didn't ask any more questions.

CHAPTER
16

On the way home I stopped at a café and had a couple of fried pork chops, some French fries, and baked beans. I was sitting at the counter with a bunch of other workers and all of a sudden I thought of Madge and had to laugh. The people turned and looked at me like I was nuts. But I couldn't stop laughing; every now and then I'd break out again. I really didn't know whether I was laughing at Madge or myself; we were both very funny people.

I got through, got up, paid the girl, and went out. The chops were heavy in my stomach but they gave me drive. I knew what I was going to do; I was going down to the hotel and see the dame. But I didn't want to think about it; I didn't want to get mixed up with a lot of crazy thoughts. So I kept looking at the people on the street as I drove home. I pulled up in front of the house and cut the motor before I realized I was there. I gave a little laugh and went inside.

I took so long bathing and getting dressed, Ella Mae said, 'So you got another heavy on tonight.'

'I'm just a playboy at heart,' I laughed, trying on another sport shirt.

I was wearing my beige gabardine pumps, grey flannel slacks, camel's-hair jacket, but I couldn't find a shirt that satisfied. I wanted to look sharp but I wanted to feel comfortable too. I could wear an outfit over on the Avenue and feel strictly fine, but if I went downtown in it I felt gaudy. Now I was trying to get a combination I'd feel all right in if I had to take the dame out somewhere. I finally decided on an aqua gabardine shirt. Then I stepped into the kitchen to let her gape me.

'See what I mean?' I said.

She tried to look scornful. 'You just think you look cute. You'll stumble in here 'bout four o'clock all messed up and wanna kill everybody.'

I grinned. 'I'm going out with my white chick tonight. She takes good care of me.'

'You're saying it for a joke,' she said derisively, 'but I believe you, you're just the type.'

'You know I like my white women, baby,' I teased. 'Couldn't get along without 'em.'

'You just like all the other niggers,' she came back. 'Get a white woman and go from Cadillacs to cotton sacks.' Then she added offhandedly, 'Alice called while you were in the tub,' and gave me a sharp look, catching me off guard. 'Oh, so, it's like that now. Just last week you were bragging 'bout how you were gonna marry her.'

I got my face under control again and said, 'Now you know I'm waiting for Henry to die so I can marry you, baby. What do you say we bump him off?'

She went on washing the baby's diapers, ignoring me. I stepped into the front room and called Alice. She answered the phone.

'Hello, baby. Bob,' I said.

'Bob, I've been trying to get you.' Her voice sounded as though it was under wraps; it was still low, controlled, but it wasn't mellow.

'I stopped and ate on the way home,' I said.

For a time she didn't say anything, then she asked,

'Bob, did you do what I asked you to?'

I knew what she meant but I said anyway, 'What did you ask me to do?'

'Let's don't play games with each other, Bob,' she said. 'You know what I asked you to do.' There was strain in her voice.

'I didn't do it,' I said.

She waited for me again and when she saw I wasn't coming, she asked, 'Are you going to?'

'No,' I said.

There was another blank and when her voice came now it was a little desperate. 'Do you love me, Bob?'

'Yes,' I said. I was fighting against her, trying to keep her from touching me. I didn't want to get all mixed up, mad or remorseful or even sensible; I wanted to go see Madge and to hell with everybody.

'You have a funny way of showing it,' she said.

'I told you, baby,' I said. My voice was getting heavy.

She was silent again for a time, then she asked, 'Am I going to see you tonight?'

'What for, so we can have another argument?'

'I want you to take me out to Hollywood. Lawson's going to lecture,' she said. 'Afterward we can have a snack and go to a night club if you like.'

Now it was my turn to hesitate. I tried to think of some way to let her down light but couldn't think of anything she wouldn't know was a lie. Finally I said, 'Not tonight, baby.'

'I want to talk to you, darling,' she said. I could tell she didn't want to let me go.

But I wanted her to hang up; it was getting inside of me, touching me. 'Not tonight, baby,' I said gruffly. 'I've got something to do tonight. I'll see you tomorrow night.'

I could hear her sighing over the phone. 'Tomorrow night might be too late, darling.'

I didn't say anything at all.

Finally she asked, 'Is this goodbye, Bob?'

'Look baby,' I said. 'I'm not in the mood to listen to your all this and heaven too.'

She hung up. 'Goddamnit!' I said. Now I was beat. I didn't even feel like going to see Madge any more, but I knew I had to.

I went out, drove down to Forty-ninth Street, and turned over to Broadway. I stopped at a Thrifty's drugstore and bought a bottle of brandy – '27 Years Old,' it said on the label. Then I got on Figueroa and kept straight down to the Hotel Mohave near Third Street.

It was a narrow four-storey building with a dry-cleaning joint on the first floor. The hotel entrance was to one side, a narrow stairway leading to the second floor with a round white dirty globe over the doorway. The neighbourhood was spotted with vacant lots and cheap hotels, a stagnant part of town between the downtown section to the east and the residential district to the west.

I drew up across the street and tried to spot Madge's room. Don had said it was a second-floor front but I didn't know which side. There were double windows on each side with drawn venetian blinds and a bare centre hallway window. Both front rooms were dark.

I knew these joints; if I walked in there dressed as I was, everybody who saw me would be hostile and curious; and the chances were somebody would call the police and have me arrested on general principles.

So I drove down the street until I came to a beer joint with a telephone sign outside. It was one of those dingy, dirty joints, but the moment I stepped inside everybody in the joint got on their muscle.

I stifled an impulse to say, 'Don't worry, folks, I don't want to be served,' said quickly in the direction of the bar, 'Just wanna use the phone,' kept on back to the booth. I found the Mohave's number and dialled.

A dried-up querulous voice said, 'Hotel Mohave.'

'I'd like to speak to Madge Perkins in room 202,' I said.

'She's out,' the voice said impatiently.

I hesitated. 'Do you know when she'll be back?'

'Don't know,' the voice said, and hung up.

I went out, turned around, and drove down on the same side as the hotel, parked several doors up the street, and waited. That way I'd see her when she came in. I got a swing programme on the radio and puffed a cigarette. People passed, glanced at me, then turned to stare with hard hostility when they saw I was a Negro. It was a rebbish neighbourhood, poor white; I'd have felt much better parked in Beverly Hills.

After a while I became conscious of somebody watching me. I looked around, didn't see anyone. Then I noticed that I was parked in front of a rooming house. Someone inside, maybe the landlady, had noticed the car, and several faces were peering furtively around the corners of the curtains in the front room. It made me nervous. I knew if I stayed there for any length of time they'd call the police. Any Negro in the neighbourhood after dark was a 'suspicious person.' So I pulled up beyond the hotel and watched the entrance through the rear-view mirror.

It seemed as if I'd been there for hours. I glanced at my watch. It was only eight-thirty. I got out, walked across the street, and took another gander at the second-storey front. Both rooms were still dark. For a moment I debated whether to call again, decided against it. I knew there wasn't any use trying to get by the desk. If I went up there and told the guy who owned the voice I'd talked to over the phone that I wanted to see Madge Perkins in

202, he was liable to shoot me on sight or drop dead of heart failure.

Suddenly I decided to give it up, go over, and take Alice out to Lawson's lecture, and afterwards take her to the Down Beat. Madge wasn't worth the effort, I thought. The whole idea of going to bed with her to get even with Kelly and Mac and the other peckerwoods out at the yard seemed silly now. She wasn't nothing but trouble any way you looked at it, I told myself; and I'd always figured myself too smart to let the white folks catch me out there on their own hunting-grounds.

I mashed the starter and drove out Figueroa, thinking about what a fool I'd been to go down there looking for Madge in the first place. Nobody but a pure and simple chump would skip a date with a chick like Alice for an off-chance shot at a tramp like Madge. I was feeling so good about it I'd forgotten all about the row I'd had with Alice the night before. My mind had jumped back to the good times we'd had together, and I felt relieved and kind of half-way clever, as if I'd gotten out of a trap the white folks had set for me.

Fifteen minutes later I pulled up behind a Pontiac coupé parked in front of the Harrisons' house and started to get out. Then I saw Alice coming down the walk from her house with Leighton. All thought and emotion just stopped, went blank. I got out slowly and waited for them.

'Why, it's Mr Jones.' Leighton recognized me, sticking out his hand. He gave me a cordial, friendly smile. 'How are you tonight?'

I shook his hand. 'Fine,' I said. 'How are you?'

'Well . . .' He hesitated, then said, 'I'm fine too,' giving a friendly laugh.

Finally Alice said, 'Hello, Bob,' without asking any questions or showing any surprise.

I looked at her then. She was sharp in a hunter's-green suit and white, lacy-looking blouse. But her skin looked too white, as if she had powdered it with chalk. I got the evil thought that she was trying to make herself look as white as possible so people would think she and Leighton were a white couple.

'Lo, baby,' I said. I waited for a moment, thinking she might give an explanation, and when I saw she wasn't going to, I said, 'I know this is impolite and all that, but may I talk to you a moment . . .' I hesitated, then added, 'In private.'

'I'm sorry, darling,' she said, giving me her social worker's smile. 'We're going to the lecture and we're late now. Tom gave me a ring after you said you couldn't go.'

'Well . . .' I began, then stepped aside to let them pass. 'That's fine.' After a moment I added, 'Enjoy yourselves.'

Her expression softened, went tentative. 'Would you like to go with us?' she asked.

'By all means, come along,' he corroborated quickly. 'We'd be delighted.'

It was an embarrassing moment. I wasn't going to have him share my girl with me; but I didn't want to say anything rude. 'Well, I really can't,' I fumbled. 'I have an appointment.'

Now he looked embarrassed. 'Well, I hope to see you again soon, Mr Jones,' he said, sticking out his hand. We shook hands again.

'Well, yes,' I said, turning to look at Alice.

For a moment I thought she might send Leighton on by himself; there was a slight concerned look in her eyes. Then she braced herself and said, 'Call me tomorrow, darling,' and walked on toward the coupé.

I turned back toward my car, stopped with my hand on the handle of the door, and looked back at the coupé. She was already seated and Leighton was going around the front toward the other door.

I climbed in, swung around in a sharp U, making my tyres cry, and headed back toward town. At Western I turned south to Jefferson, east toward the South Side. I felt for the brandy bottle, uncorked it, tipped it to my lips, and drank.

It really galled me to have a white guy take my girl out on a date. I wouldn't have minded so much if he had been the sharpest, richest, most important coloured guy in the world; I'd have still felt I could compete. But a white guy had his colour – I couldn't compete with that. It was all up to the chick – if she liked white, I didn't have a chance; if she didn't, I didn't have anything to worry about. But I'd have to know, and I didn't know about Alice.

At first the brandy made me hate her with a blue violence. I wanted to knock her down and kick her. I told myself if I ever saw her again she'd have to come crawling to me on her knees. When I came into Central I was so blind with anger and chagrin I almost ran into a bus broadside. Then suddenly I was ravenous.

I went out to the new barbecue place at Forty-second Street and ordered Virginia ham. But half-way through it I got the sudden picture of Alice sitting in Leighton's coupé, smiling with appreciation at something he'd said. She'd be interested and attentive, I thought, because Leighton was white and she couldn't help but want to impress him with her culture and intelligence.

I pushed the stuff away from me, got up and went over to the cashier's, paid for it, and went out. I turned my car around, started downtown. I could imagine Leighton taking her someplace after the lecture that the 'known' Negroes, like me, couldn't go. Perhaps to one of the swanky joints out on the strip – the Troc, maybe. She'd be gay and unrestrained with him, I thought; not tight and frustrated like she'd been with me the other night. She'd know that everybody would think she was white. Then she'd be able to tell me what a nice time she'd had with Tom.

At Fifth I turned west, found a parking space, went into the Blue Room. The joint was crowded. There were a couple of white sailors at one end of the bar and a white girl with her coloured girl friend down near the middle. The rest were coloured, mostly railroad men. I leaned over a guy's shoulder and ordered a double brandy, took it down to the juke box at the front, and put a nickel on King Cole's 'I'm Lost.'

All of a sudden I knew that I was getting ready to go back and see Madge. Getting charged. Getting my gauge up to be a damned fool about a white woman, to blow my simple top, maybe get into serious trouble – about a slut any white bum could have at will. Just to get even with Alice – with Kelly too, and Mac, and all the rest. It was crazy; I knew it was crazy, like a sign I once saw that said, '*Read and run, nigger; if you can't read, run anyhow.*'

'Simple son of a bitch!' I said aloud.

A little black gal at the end of the bar turned around and gave me a qualitative smile. 'Whatttt?' She had a soft, caressing voice.

'I was talking to myself,' I said self-consciously.

The girl next to her looked around then. The black gal said, 'Well, how 'bout you?'

I leaned over her shoulder, put my empty glass on the bar, patted her hair as I drew away. 'I'd like to see you sometime,' I said, and her eyes got to telling me about it. 'But not tonight,' I said, and it went out of her eyes.

CHAPTER
17

I went out, got in my car, and turned back toward Figueroa. When I pulled up in front of the hotel I glanced at my watch. It was nine after eleven; I had no idea it was that late. I cut the motor, took another long swig, then got out and started up the front stairs with the bottle in my hand. I didn't give a damn if the clerk was still on duty and had the whole police force with him. I was rocking and scared of nobody in the world, on a live-wire edge and ready to pop.

The hall light still burned but the desk was deserted. I'd primed myself to give the clerk an argument, to tell him this was America and he could go to hell; and when I found him gone I felt a slight letdown. I turned, went down to the front, knocked at 202. No one answered. I tried the knob; the door was locked. I knocked harder. Finally a sleepy Texas voice asked, 'Who's there?'

'Bob,' I said. 'Let me in.'

There was a silence for a moment then she asked, 'Who?' as if she couldn't believe her ears.

'Bob – from the shipyard,' I told her. 'I told you I was coming to see you.' My tongue was thick and I had trouble with my words.

'You better get away from here,' she threatened.

'Open up the door,' I said. 'Don't be so simple all the time.'

'If you don't get away from there I'll call the police and have you put underneath the jail,' she said in a fierce whisper as if standing close to the door.

'Call the police then,' I growled, rattling the knob.

'I'll scream,' she threatened.

'Scream then,' I said.

She didn't reply and I started hammering on the door. 'Well, wait a minute, can't you?' she whispered, unlocking the door. She opened it a crack. 'You wanna wake up everybody and let 'em see what's happening?'

I pushed inside, said, 'I don't give a damn.'

She quickly closed and locked the door, then wheeled toward me. 'You can't stay here, you'll get us both in trouble.'

'To hell with the trouble,' I muttered, turning to face her. 'Have a drink?'

She backed against the door. 'Well, wait till I get dressed, can't you? Are you in all that big a hurry?'

I put the bottle on the floor by the bed and stood looking at her a moment. She had on a nubby maroon robe and her blond hair, dark at the roots, was done up in metal curlers tight to her head. Without lipstick or make-up she looked older; there were deep blue circles underneath her eyes and blue hollows on each side of the bridge of her nose. Tiny crow's-feet spread out from the outer corners of her eyes and hard slanting lines calipered obliquely from her nostrils, dropping vertically from the edges of her mouth. Her mouth was big, hard, brutal, with lips almost colourless; and her eyes were wide, blue, staring, almost popping, but now there was a muddy look in them. Beneath her robe her breasts seemed lower, big and loose, and her hips lumped out from her waist like half-filled sacks. For bedroom slippers she wore a pair of worn-out play shoes that had once been red. She had big feet and her ankles were very white, laced with blue veins, and dirty on the bone.

Then I moved in, trapped her against the door.

She jerked to one side, turning, and went half across the room. I lunged, grabbed for her, caught her wrist, and pulled her back. She got rougher and began struggling in earnest. I got her by both arms, put my one-eighty pounds into it, and pushed her down across the bed. She twisted out from underneath me, turned on her stomach. I grabbed her by the shoulder and tried to turn her over toward me; but she rolled clear over me on the other side, and then started fighting with her fists. I grabbed her arms again and pinned them to her sides. She started kicking at me. We tussled silently back and forth across the bed until we were both panting for breath.

She was big, strong, and quick, and it was all I could do to hold my own. 'Gawddamn you!' she grated once, but that was the only time she spoke. I didn't say anything. We stopped for a moment by common accord, resting. Her face was a hard, glowing red and her blue eyes were dark and furious. Her mouth was a hard brutal line.

I relaxed my hold and she snatched a hand loose and hit me in the face. I made a sudden rough grab for her and we both rolled over on the floor. We kept rolling until we were in the middle of the floor and I got her flat on her back and pinned her down.

She stopped struggling and went limp, and the strangest look came into her eyes.

'I dare you to, nigger,' she said. 'Just go 'head. I'll get you lynched right here in California.'

'Aw, go to hell,' I growled.

'My Gawddd, now you wanna beat me,' she said, and all of a sudden started crying. 'I don't know what made me let you in, you cruel black bastard.'

She looked like hell. She was really a beat biddy, trampish-looking and pure rebbish; and since I'd already lost my live-wire edge, I wondered what the hell I'd seen in her in the first place. I just stood there and looked at her and wondered.

And on top of all of that she began acting coy. 'Take off my shoes,' she said, holding out her feet.

'Take off your own goddamned shoes.'

'You think 'cause I let you in you can do anything you want,' she flared. 'Well, let me tell you—'

'Aw, go wash your face,' I said. 'You look beat.'

That startled her. She must have thought her being white made her look good to me under any circumstances.

'Wanna drink?' I offered, waving toward the bottle on the floor by the bed.

'That's all you niggers do,' she said, getting up. 'Lie up and get drunk and dream of having white women.'

'Now listen, don't start that—'

'I don't drink noway,' she cut in. 'I'm a Christian woman.'

I started laughing.

She opened her robe. She was naked except for her shoes.

'Ain't I beautiful?' she said. 'Pure white.'

She had a big mature body with large sagging breasts and brownish-pink nipples the size of silver dollars. Her stomach was soft and puffy and there were bulges at the top of her big wide thighs. Once upon a time she had had a good figure, but age was in it now.

'This'll get you lynched in Texas,' she said.

Just the notion; just because she was white. But it got me, set me on edge again. I sat down on the bed and reached for the bottle.

She kicked off her shoes and ran across the room, big,

gawky, awkward, and grotesque, but with a certain wild grace in her every awkward motion.

'You can't have none unless you catch me,' she teased.

I watched her through lowered lids. My tongue was thick and swelling and my stomach was hollow and weak.

'Sit down,' I choked in a thick voice. 'This ain't Texas.'

She came over and stood beside the bed. 'You know what I'll do?' she began. I didn't answer and she started laughing. 'You dare me.' I still didn't say anything.

'The preacher said niggers were full of sin,' she said. 'That's what makes you black. Take off your clothes.'

I laid there and called her everything but a child of God, talking in a slow, slightly slurred voice.

When I reached for her, she jumped back and wriggled free. 'You know what you got to do first,' she teased.

Then I grabbed her and we locked together in a test of strength in the middle of the floor; I had her by the wrists, trying to break her down.

'Take it, you can have it,' she hissed, hunching her shoulders and trying to break my hold by bulling.

Someone knocked at the door and said in a low, hard voice, 'Cut out that racket or I'll throw you out.'

We didn't pay any attention. I took a deep breath and bore down. She began getting blood-red all down from the face in her neck and shoulders. She was almost as strong as I, but not quite. I slowly broke her down to the floor, and she looked me in the eyes, hers buck-wild.

'All right, rape me then, nigger!' Her voice was excited, thick, with threads in her throat.

I let her loose and bounced to my feet. *Rape* – just the sound of the word scared me, took everything out of me, my desire, my determination, my whole build-up. I was taut, poised, ready to light out and run a crooked mile.

The only thing she had to do to make me stop was just say the word.

I gave her one last look, saw her mouth come open as though she were going to scream. Then I got the door unlocked, hit the stairs fast, and was just getting in my car when I heard her call my name.

I looked up. She had the blinds drawn back from the window.

'Wait,' she whispered.

I climbed in the car without replying, snapped on the juice and mashed the starter, then snapped it off just as the motor caught. My passion was gone; I was tired, sore, and deflated; a hangover was taking ahold fast. I hated her guts. But I waited anyway.

In a few minutes she came down, made up like a hustler, and putting her foot on the running board fluttered her mascaraed lashes at me. 'Gawd,' she said peevishly, 'you're sure a scary nigger. Let me in.'

That one really burned me. I was through and I knew it; the white folks had won again and I wanted out. But I couldn't let her get away with it. I didn't want her to have that satisfaction. So I said coldly and deliberately in a hard, even voice: 'You look like mud to me, sister, like so much dirt. Just a big beat bitch with big dirty feet. And if it didn't take so much trouble I'd make a whore out of you.'

She turned a dull dirty red and I could see her eyes getting ugly even in that light. I saw her look up and down the street, then she said, 'Just let me see a policeman, you nigger . . .'

I dug off and didn't even look back.

CHAPTER
18

That night I dreamed that a white boy and a coloured boy got to fighting on the sidewalk and the coloured boy pulled out a long-bladed knife and ran at the white boy and began slashing at him and the white boy broke and ran across the street digging into his pocket and at a grocery store on the other side the coloured boy caught up with him and it looked as if he was going to cut him all to pieces but the white boy brought his hand out of his pocket and every time the coloured boy slashed at him he hit at the back of the coloured boy's hand. The white boy was crying and hitting at the back of the coloured boy's hand with his fist and the coloured boy was screaming and cursing and jumping in at the white boy to slash at him with the knife; but he couldn't cut the white boy because the white boy kept ducking and dodging and hitting at the back of his hand. Finally the white boy hit the back of the coloured boy's hand that held the knife and made a slight cutting movement and the knife fell from the coloured boy's hand. When I saw the blood start flowing from the back of the coloured boy's hand I knew the white boy had a small-bladed knife gripped in his fist. The coloured boy picked up the knife with his left hand and began slashing again and the white boy kept on ducking and dodging until he hit the back of the coloured boy's left hand and cut the tendons in that one also. Then the white boy began chasing the coloured boy down the street stabbing him all about the head and neck with the tip of the small-bladed knife. Everybody standing around looking at the white boy chasing the coloured boy down the street thought he was beating him with his fist, but I knew he was digging a thousand tiny holes in the coloured boy's head and neck and that it was only a matter of time before the coloured boy fell to the street and bled to death; but the white boy wasn't crying any more and he wasn't in a hurry any more; he was just chasing the coloured boy and stabbing him to death with a quarter-inch blade and laughing like it was funny as hell.

I woke up and I couldn't move, could hardly breathe. The alarm was ringing but I didn't have enough strength to reach out and turn it off. My hangover was already with me and my body trembled all over as if I had the ague.

Somewhere in the back of my mind a tiny insistent voice kept whispering, *Bob, there never was a nigger who could beat it.* I blinked open my eyes, closed them tight again. But it kept on saying it. And I knew it was a fact. If I hadn't had the hangover I might have gotten it out my mind. But the hangover gave me a strange indifference, a weird sort of honesty, like a man about to die. I could see the whole thing standing there, like a great conglomeration of all the peckerwoods in the world, taunting me, *Nigger, you haven't got a chance.*

I agreed with it. That was the hell of it. With a strange lucid clarity I knew it was no lie. I knew with the white folks sitting on my brain, controlling my every thought, action, and emotion, making life one crisis after another, day and night, asleep and awake, conscious and unconscious, I couldn't make it. I knew that unless I found my niche and crawled into it, unless I stopped hating white folks and learned to take them as they came, I couldn't live in America, much less expect to accomplish anything in it.

It wasn't anything to know. It was obvious. Negro people had always lived on sufferance, ever since Lincoln gave them their freedom without any bread. I thought of a line I'd read in one of Tolstoy's stories once – 'There never had been enough bread and freedom to go around.' When it came to us, we didn't get either one of them. Although Negro people such as Alice and her class had got enough bread – they'd prospered from it. No matter what had happened to them inside, they hadn't allowed it to destroy them outwardly; they had overcome their colour the only way possible in America – as Alice had put it, by adjusting themselves to the limitations of their race. They hadn't stopped trying, I gave them that much; they'd kept on trying, always would; but they had recognized their limit – a nigger limit.

From the viewpoint of my hangover it didn't seem a hard thing to do. You simply had to accept being black as a condition over which you had no control, then go on from there. Glorify your black heritage, revere your black heroes, laud your black leaders, cheat your black brothers, worship your white fathers (be sure and do that), segregate yourself; then make yourself believe that you had made great progress, that you would continue to make great progress, that in time the white folks would appreciate all of this and pat you on the head and say, 'You been a good nigger for a long time. Now we're going to let you in.' Of course you'd have to believe that the white folks were generous, unselfish, and loved you so much they wanted to share their world with you, but if you could believe all the rest, you could believe that too. And it didn't seem like a hard thing for a nigger to believe, because he didn't have any other choice.

But my mind kept rebelling against it. Being black, it was a thing I ought to know, but I'd learned it differently. I'd learned the same jive that the white folks had learned. All that stuff about liberty and justice and equality... All men are created equal... Any person born in the United States is a citizen... Learned it out the same books, in the same schools. Learned the song too: '... o'er the land of the free and the home of the brave...' I thought Patrick Henry was a hero when he jumped up and said, 'Give me liberty or give me death,' just like the white kids who read about it. I was a Charles Lindbergh fan when I was a little boy, and thought George Washington was the father of my country – as long as I thought I had a country.

I agreed with the Hearst papers when they lauded the peoples of the conquered European countries for continuing their underground fight against 'Nazi oppression'; I always bought the Los Angeles Sunday *Times* too, and the *Daily News*; read the *Saturday Evening Post* and *Reader's Digest* sometimes out at Alice's house while I was waiting for her to dress; I even got taken in by Pegler plenty times. Like the guys said out at the yard, 'Ah believe it.'

That was the hell of it: the white folks had drummed more into me than they'd been able to scare out.

I knew the average overpatriotic American would have said a leaderman was justified in cursing out a white woman worker for refusing to do a job of work in a war industry in time of war – so long as the leaderman was white. Might have even called her a traitor and wanted her tried for sabotage.

It was just that they didn't think I ought to have these feelings. They kept thinking about me in connection with Africa. But I wasn't born in Africa. I didn't know anyone who was. I learned in history that my ancestors were slaves brought over from Africa. But I'd forgotten that, just like the aristocratic blue bloods of America have forgotten what they learned in history – that most of their ancestors were the riffraff of Europe – thieves, jailbirds, beggars, and outcasts.

So even though the solid logic of my hangover told me that Alice's way was my only out, I didn't have anything for it but the same contempt a white person has for a collaborator's out in France. I just couldn't help it. That much of the white folks' teaching was still inside of me.

I knew I could marry Alice – the chick loved me. Could marry her, go back to college and get a degree in law, go on to become a big and important Negro. I knew that most people would consider me a lucky black boy.

I knew I would be lucky too. Lying there with the hangover beating in my head like John Henry driving steel, I could see it from every angle – I couldn't keep from seeing it. I didn't have the strength to keep it from my mind.

In the first place my old man had been a steel-mill worker at National Malleable in Cleveland, Ohio, when I was born, and my mother had died when I was three. I had two brothers older than I, and we'd been poor boys. My old man had married again and had three other children by our stepmother and I lived in a cold attic room for twelve long years. Shep, my oldest brother, went East when he finished Central High and the last I heard of him he was in the rackets in Washington, D.C. Dick wanted to be an artist and fooled around with the group at Karamu; he's still in Cleveland, some sort of politician. I was the ambitious one, I'd wanted to be a doctor. I'd gotten my two years at Ohio State by washing dishes in the white fraternity houses about the campus. But when my old man took sick in '38 I had to stay home and dig in with the rest; and I never got back. I puttered about with pottery at Karamu and worked with the theatre group for a time – met some fine chicks, too, but none like Alice.

All I had when I came to the Coast was my height and weight and the fact I believed that being born in America gave everybody a certain importance. I'd never had two suits of clothes at one time in my life until I got in this war boom.

In the three years in L.A. I'd worked up to a good job in a shipyard, bought a new Buick car, and cornered off the finest coloured chick west of Chicago – to my way of thinking. All I had to do was marry her and my future was in the bag. If a black boy couldn't be satisfied with that he couldn't be satisfied with anything.

But what I knew about myself was that my desire for such a life was conditional. It only caught up with me on the crest of being black – when I could accept being black, when I could see no other out, such a life looked great.

But I knew I'd wake up someday and say to hell with it, I didn't want to be the biggest Negro who ever lived, neither Toussaint L'Ouverture nor Walter White. Because deep inside of me, where the white folks couldn't see, it didn't mean a thing. If you couldn't swing down Holywood Boulevard and know that you belonged; if you couldn't make a polite pass at Lana Turner at Ciro's without having the gendarmes beat the black off you for getting out of your place; if you couldn't eat a thirty-dollar dinner at an hotel without choking on the insults, being a great big 'Mister' nigger didn't mean a thing.

Anyone who wanted to could be nigger-rich, nigger-important, have their Jim Crow religion, and go to nigger heaven.

I'd settle for a leaderman job at Atlas Shipyard – if I

could be a man, defined by Webster as a male human being. That's all I'd ever wanted – just to be accepted as a man – without ambition, without distinction, either of race, creed, or colour; just a simple Joe walking down an American street, going my simple way, without any other identifying characteristics but weight, height, and gender.

I liked my job as leaderman more than I had ever admitted to myself before. More than any other job I could think of; more than being the first Negro congress-man from California. But it was just the same as all the rest: if I couldn't have everything that went along with it, if I couldn't be in authority over white men and women just the same as any other leaderman, to hell with it too.

I knew that that was at the bottom of it all. If I couldn't live in America as an equal in the minds, hearts, and souls of all white people, if I couldn't know that I had a chance to do anything any other American could, to go as high as an American citizenship would carry anybody, there'd never be anything in this country for me anyway.

And I knew I was a fool. That was the hell of it. All it did was give me a grinding headache to go along with the rest of my hangover, and a blinding sense of confusion. I didn't know whether I was going or coming. If it hadn't been for my riders I wouldn't even have made the effort to get out of bed. I took a couple of anacins and some coffee and that helped some.

When I went outside some of the confusion left me. It was a clear morning; the sun was coming up and the air smelled good. It was one of those mornings that ought to have made me feel good to be alive. But as soon as I got behind the wheel I began remembering all the crazy things I had done the night before. Fighting with Madge until I'd already gotten her down, then jumping up running at the sound of the word 'rape,' letting her go untouched. I'd set out to grind her down but in the end I was the one who was defeated. Maybe I would have been anyway. Maybe there just wasn't any way of winning. Like the man said, 'I can't win for losing.'

No wonder I dreamed such crazy dreams and woke up full of philosophy. I felt chagrined, as foolish as a chump in a prostitute's room without the price of a lay.

But I made up my mind not to let it ride me. I had done it and that was that. All I could do now was try not to think about it, try to get through the day. I never wanted to see her again as long as I lived.

And then as soon as I got inside the yard I found myself looking at the white women, long-faced and urgent, thinking of Madge again. I wanted to see her, to meet her eyes – even if it wasn't any more than just walking past her. It was so strong I had to stop dead still and fight it out in my mind before I took another step.

I turned around and went back to Mac's office to quit. I wanted to clear my tools and get out of the yard as fast as possible. But Mac kept me waiting while he talked to six white guys who came in after me. He just didn't want to talk to me. I didn't get sore. I felt too low. I just left because I got sick standing there in the stuffy, smoky office and my stomach started peeling in my mouth.

When I got on the job I found Tebbel cursing out the Jews. I didn't want to listen, didn't want to argue. But I knew if I left I'd start looking for Madge. That woman spelled trouble, and trouble was on my mind.

Tebbel said the Jews controlled all the money in the world; that the Jews had started the war to make money; and that all Jews were Communists.

'That I gotta see,' I said.

But no one paid any attention to me. I supposed they were so happy to find somebody cursing out somebody else besides the 'niggers' they didn't want it interrupted.

He said that F.D.R. was a Jew, that his real name was

Rosenveld; that almost all movie actors were Jews; that Eddie Cantor's real name was Izzy Iskowitz; Jack Benny's was Jack Kubelsky; Charles Chaplin's was Tonstein; Douglas Fairbanks' was Ullman; that Nelson Eddy's old man was a rabbi.

'You left out Jesus Christ,' I said. 'What was his real name?' But nobody paid any attention to that either.

He looked about him furtively to see if any Jews were within earshot, then produced several faded coloured circulars from an old envelope he had in his pocket. 'Here's where you get the facts,' he said.

We gathered about to look. They were circulars distributed by Pelley Publishers, Box 2630, Asheville, North Carolina, advertising anti-Semitic booklets. '*Hidden Empire – The Complete Story Of Jewish World Control,*' one read, '*6 for* $1.00 . . . 100 *copies*, $12.50.' Then another: ' "*Dupes of Judah*" – *How Jews Launched the World War.*' A third read: '*Stop Being Fooled by Jewish Wailings! Open Door to Knowing. The Christian-Gentile people of the United States have the right to know what the nation's Jews are doing and planning, to destroy Constitutionalism and substitute an Asiatic Sovietism* . . .'

I stopped looking after that. I wanted to laugh but my head was splitting with a hundred-degree headache and I was scared of jarring loose my brains.

Ben gave him a contemptuous look. 'Now show us what you got hidden in that other pocket about Negroes,' he said.

Tebbel reddened slightly. 'You just want to argue,' he grated. 'I like coloured people. I was raised with them.'

I heard Peaches whisper, 'Now if he says he had an old black mammy, I'll – I'll—' She choked.

'Who the hell gives a damn whether you like coloured people or not?' I said.

Conway gave me a half smile and Bessie said, 'You tell
'im!'

'These damn fascists come over here and the first thing
they start campaigning against is the Jews,' Ben began,
but Tebbel cut him off.

'I'm Irish,' he stated hotly. 'Nobody in the world is
any more anti-fascist than the Irish.'

'All you foreigners—' Ben started again, but Tebbel
cut him off again:

'Who's a foreigner? I'm a hundred per cent American.
My grandfather fought in the Civil War.'

'On which side?' Zula Mae asked.

I cut out. I'd listened all I could.

It was pulling at me, eating into me, to go find Madge.
The weight of chagrin was still in my mind; the thought
of having been a fool gnawed at me. *Read and run,
nigger* ... I knew it was time to run. I glanced at my
watch, saw that it was a little after nine, went down on
the yard, and found a phone booth and called Alice. I
didn't know what I was going to say to her – I couldn't
think about her straight – but I had to hear her voice.
Had to know that she was there; had to lean on her for a
moment until I got myself steadied.

Some smooth-voiced chick answered the phone and
said that Miss Harrison had a conference the first thing
that morning; would I leave my number and have her
call me back when she was free.

I said, 'I'll call again.'

I felt let down and a little scared. A truck rumbled by,
almost hit me. I jumped back out of the way, stumbled
over a six-inch pipe bend, sat down on a greasy spot of
concrete. Killing myself already, I thought wryly; got up
and started over to Mac's office. I'd quit, get cleared,
and get the hell away. But I stopped with my hand on
the door, turned around, and went back. I just couldn't

leave it like that; I just couldn't do it.

I looked around for Don and saw him ducking through the access hole so I started after him. I knew I didn't want to see him but in the back of my mind I figured if I walked along with him he might accidentally lead me to Madge, and I wouldn't be seeking her deliberately.

He'd stopped outside in the companionway to bull with a guy and when I came up he looked around at me and they both stopped talking. The other guy went back to work and Don and I walked off a piece.

'You look as if you made a night of it,' he said.

'Killed myself,' I managed to say. 'I started off tryna kill my grief but I went along too.' I knew it sounded corny but it was the best I could do.

'Your girl friend looks as if she had a night of it too,' he said casually.

'You seen her?' I asked quickly. The words popped out of my mouth so fast I couldn't stop them.

Don blinked. 'Haven't you?' he countered.

I realized that he'd tricked me, but I tried to laugh it off anyway. 'We musta been drinking the same stuff – billa.'

He gave that slight smile. 'How'd you make out?'

I tried to look innocent. 'Are you kidding?'

Then she walked straight into us. Her hood was kicked back on her head, making her taller than either of us, and her shoulders were held high and square. Her face seemed slightly swollen on the left side and there were deep dark circles underneath her eyes which the heavy coating of powder couldn't hide. There was a hard savage glint in her eyes and her mouth was spread, squarish at the corners in a hard brutal set. She didn't look whorish now; she looked plain mean.

She stared at me, stared right through me as if I wasn't there, didn't give a flicker of recognition. Then she turned toward Don and came into him like a prize fighter.

'Damn you, Don, can't you get me some good sticks?' she said in a flat grating voice. 'They got a new nigger in the tool crib now and she don't know her ass from a hole in the ground.'

Don blinked. Neither of them looked at me. All three of us knew she didn't care about the rods; she just wanted to call me a nigger and took that way to do it.

'What are you doing down here?' Don asked her.

'I'm looking for you,' she grated.

'Are you sure?' he asked in a soft baiting voice.

Red came up in her face like a sunrise. 'What in the hell do you mean, am I sure?'

'I mean I'm not your leaderman,' he said evenly. 'I don't have anything to do with the kind of rods they give out. Why don't you see your own leaderman?'

'Well, it's your job that's gotta be done,' she snarled. 'And if these tacks don't hold, just blame that nigger in the tool crib.'

I started to call her on it then. But I knew she was raking me through Don and if I said anything to her she'd have jumped red raving.

But Don did it his way. 'How'd you make out last night?' he asked.

She had started away, now she wheeled back, but her gaze sought me first, slashed at me, then pinned on him. 'Now what the hell do you mean?'

'You told me you were going out with a new boy friend,' he said. 'Remember? I was just wondering what kind of a guy he turned out to be.'

'I didn't tell you any such a goddamned thing,' she stormed.

He blinked again, his eyes giving off sparks behind his rimless spectacles, then spread his hands. 'All right, it wasn't you. It must have been somebody else. I just drove by your place early this morning and thought I saw you getting out of a car.'

I jerked around to look at him. She gave me another quick killing look, then levelled a furious challenging stare on his benign face. 'You better mind your own goddamn business, thass what! You just better!' she whispered savagely, turned, and stalked off.

My eyes grew narrow and feverish. It crowded back into me – to go get her, to have it out.

Don said, 'She's touchy today, isn't she?' looking at me. I was embarrassed under his scrutiny, didn't understand his game. Right then I didn't care. I just wanted to get away from him.

'See you, Papa,' I said as lightly as I could and walked off before he could stop me.

I went back to the booth and called Alice again. This time I got her. 'It's Bob, baby,' I said, swallowing. 'Look, if I pick you up in about an hour, can I take you to lunch?'

'Where are you now?' she asked.

'Oh, I'm on the job,' I said. 'But I'm going to check out in a few minutes. I want to talk to you.'

There was a long pause and when she spoke again her voice sounded distant. 'What can we possibly talk about, Bob, that we haven't talked about before? You reject everything I say to you. All we do is quarrel.'

The receiver got so heavy I could hardly hold it. 'Okay, baby,' I said. 'I'll see you.'

I hung up, went back out on the yard, stood for a long time in the hot sunshine. Beyond was the road leading down to the outfitting dock, flanked by the various shops, dropping off in the blue-grey stretch of the harbour. Off to the left was a row of hulls in various stages of erection, spaced apart by the crane-ways. Cranes were silhouetted against the sky like long-legged, one-armed spiders, swinging shapes and plates aboard. Over there the workers walked with care. Everywhere was the hustle and bustle of moving busy workers, trucks, plate lifts, yard cranes, electric mules, the blue flashes of arc welders, brighter than the noonday sun. And the noise, always loud, unabating, ear-splitting. I loved it like my first love.

But now I was cutting out, I told myself. Atlas wasn't for me any more. I was getting the hell out of L.A. Away from Alice too. Going to 'Frisco, maybe. Las Vegas. Somewhere. I shook my head. Goddamnit, maybe she just don't know how much I need her, I thought. Maybe she thought it was easy for me to do the things she wanted. Maybe it was easy to some folks, I thought. But not to me. I'd already read and I was running. *Read and run, nigger* . . .

But when I started moving again I knew I was looking for Madge. I went up to the fourth deck first, found the team she'd been working with, but she was nowhere in sight. I searched the ship from fore to aft, from the superstructure down to the flat keel, but I didn't find her. I went out on the dock, walked down to the water, looked out across the harbour. But I couldn't stand still; I felt as if a thousand things were tearing at me, pulling at me. My feet felt weighted, my mouth sour. My coveralls chafed. My jacket was hot. I peeled it off, unbuttoned the top buttons of my coveralls, kicked my hat back from my eyes, dug a cigarette from a squashed pack and lit it.

Then I started looking for her again, with seven devils beating in my head. I just couldn't help it. I had to talk to her. Had to get it out my system and all of Texas wasn't going to stop me.

I had to do something to bring her down, to hurt her in some kind of way, humiliate her, make a fool out of her like I'd made out of myself, or I just wouldn't be able to keep out of trouble, I knew. I wouldn't be able to think straight about Alice either, after she'd gone out with Leighton last night.

So I climbed back to the weather deck and started off again. My head felt swollen; heat was growing in my brain. Somebody slapped me on the back. I jumped a good six feet, whirled with my dukes up.

Herbie Frieberger said in his loud jubilant voice, 'Jesus Christ, you're jumpy. What the hell's the matter with you?'

'Man, goddamnit, are you fighting or playing?' I said. 'How many bowls of Wheaties did *you* eat this morning?'

He looked aggrieved. 'I've been looking for you all morning to get that grievance, fellow. Jesus Christ, is this all the thanks I get?'

'I haven't got any grievance,' I grated.

He looked blank. 'What about what we were talking about?' He frowned. 'Don't you remember? I told you to write out the grievance and give it to me and I'd present it before the executive board.'

I tried to quiet my nerves and be pleasant. But it was no go. 'Look, Herbie,' I said. 'I'm not gonna make any grievance. I'm gonna let it go.' My voice was raw and shaky; all of a sudden I felt sick.

'But I thought you wanted—' he began.

I cut him off. 'All I want is peace,' I said. I was tired, tired, tired. 'Just peace, Herbie. Is that too hard for you to understand?'

Herbie looked at me for a long moment. 'You're lucky you're not a Jew,' he said.

CHAPTER
19

When one of Kelly's flunkeys came up at about a quarter of twelve and said there was a call for me, all I thought was, Please just let it be Alice. I held my breath all the way down to the tool crib, and when the girl gave me a different number to call I went dead inside. For an instant I started not to call it, then I went ahead on the off-chance.

'Alice?'

When I heard her voice, light and gay, 'Darling, I've changed my mind again. Isn't that just like a woman?' I let my breath out in a long soft sigh and felt the life come back into me.

'My luck is really getting good,' I said. 'This is the very first time a woman's prerogative has ever worked in my favour.'

'There's no such thing as luck,' she teased. 'It's only the correct application of effort, energy, evaluation—'

'And eccentricity,' I supplied, laughing. 'Do you know you've just won the Robert Jones medal for distinguished service?'

'And by what action, General Jones? Certainly not merely because I am exceedingly glamorous, talented, intelligent, wealthy, famous, and unattached?'

I laughed again. She was determined to keep the mood light, and that was fine by me. 'I'll just keep my medal, baby, and give myself instead,' I said, then asked, 'Do you have your car?'

'I'm at the parking lot now. I decided at the last moment that I couldn't live without you.'

'You sound groovy,' I said, then, 'Listen, you know the drive-in out on Avalon just beyond the riding academy? I'll meet you there in half an hour.'

'I'll be there, darling.'

I never knew until that moment just how much she meant to me. It really built me up, made me feel wanted again, important too. A guy just had to feel important to somebody, even if only to himself. A woman's a wonderful thing, I thought – when you love her.

On the way out I passed Kelly and gave him a broad wink, laughed out loud at the startled look that popped on his face.

The noon whistle blew as I was weaving my way through the machine shop and I joined the densely packed, gouging, pushing, fighting crush leaving the ship, stepping on one another's feet, ramming the edges of our hard hats into one another's eyes. But it didn't bother me; I felt at peace with everybody. Anyway, I never minded the scramble nor the hard, hurried push, liked it, in fact.

I went over to Mac's office, told Marguerite I had an appointment with the dentist, and had her write me out a two-hour pass. The gatekeeper asked sourly when did I work; and I told him executives never worked, he should know that. When I opened the door of my car heat rolled out as from a furnace. I had to open all the doors and stand there for a moment until it aired. Then I got in, squirmed down in the soft springy seat, and felt good all over.

Traffic was loose on the harbour road, making driving friendly, but the big Diesel trailers, long as freight cars, hogged the road in passing. The hot dry air was filled with motor smell, pungent, tantalizing; it poured in through the open windows over me, making me want to just squat on the highway and drive a thousand miles.

The vertical sun had a hard California brilliance, powder-white and eye-searing. When I reached into the glove compartment for my sunglasses I felt the gun I'd put there Monday to kill Johnny Stoddart. I jerked my hand back as if I'd touched death, felt the shock run clear down into my soul. To realize that I'd been so close to murder, now that things had begun to look up, disturbed me more than anything that had ever happened to me in all my life and choked me up again with the old scared feeling. I knew I'd been pushed, but it really jarred me to know that I'd been pushed that far. It gave me a funny feeling of having been drawn outside of myself, of having been goaded beyond my own control. Now I could understand something of Alice's reactions – she must have seen the trouble in me.

But the day wouldn't hold it, cleared it from my mind. It was California on parade, one of those days that relax you like a light massage. If your thoughts will free you, a day like that will make you new. I began feeling excited about seeing Alice – more excited than I'd ever been before. I knew she'd never have called me back if she hadn't really cared. I got something of the same thrill I got the first time I ever dated a girl – a live, tingling expectancy.

What I needed was to marry her, I thought. To settle down before they settled me – in San Quentin or some place. Then I got a strange yearning to have some children – two boys and two girls. I'd never thought seriously about children before, not about having any of my own; and now suddenly I wanted some, wanted the responsibility of raising them, supporting them, educating them;

wanted to watch them grow. The girls would certainly have to look like Alice; if they didn't I'd never forgive myself.

Then I had to laugh. It must be the heat, I thought deprecatingly. Or maybe the gas fumes were making me high. Me, a papa. I'd make one hell of a papa, I thought; every time I came home late my children would wonder whether the white folks had killed their papa at last.

But it wasn't such a crazy dream. It was just that I'd never felt any stability, had never really felt confident that the white folks would let me have the next day coming up. And since I'd begun earning enough money to live my own life I hadn't felt that my life belonged to me. Any moment the white folks might ask me to check it in.

A guy couldn't live like that, I knew. I couldn't, anyway. There wasn't enough of me; there wasn't enough of any man, just by himself. And as long as I was black I'd never be anything but half a man at best. I knew I had to get an anchor and hang on or I'd really be gone with the wind, as the good Southern lady said. I knew I'd have to give in, to both Alice and the white folks; but I didn't mind that now. Because now I knew I had to duck or get my goddamn brains knocked out. That much I'd learned since Monday morning. Death had been right on top of me and I hadn't even realized it.

I spotted Alice's maroon Olds two-door sedan as I drove up, spic and span and freshly Simonized, in the circle of cars about the place, so I parked in the lot to one side and walked over. It was a typical southern California drive-in, a circular glass-enclosed building shining with chrome trimmings with a counter inside and cars parked spokewise outside. Pretty girls in very brief red and gold costumes like those of ballet dancers, showing a lot of leg and thigh in the hopes they might be 'discovered' by some Hollywood talent scout, scampered in and out, waiting on the customers.

Alice had been watching through the rear-view mirror, and when she saw me coming around the back of the car she turned and smiled. She had on a beige gabardine dress, open at the throat, and tortoiseshell sunglasses; and her hair was loose and windblown, falling all over her shoulders. She looked fresh and feminine, a chick you'd be proud of anywhere, and her smile was wide and warm.

'Hi, darling,' she greeted, leaning over to open the door. 'You look like a worker in a CIO win-the-war poster.' Her voice was low and mellow, but there was an intimacy in it that made me the one and only.

I climbed in beside her, laughing; pulled shut the door. 'I'm the twelve million black faces,' I said.

She took off her sunglasses and set up her mouth. 'Let me kiss one of your faces.'

'I didn't bring but this one.' I tossed my hard hat on the back seat, leaned over, and kissed her lightly. 'You taste good.'

She gave a girlish giggle. 'I bet I'd be delicious with cold beer.'

'Unh-unh, you're more the sparkling burgundy type,' I contradicted.

She curled up in her corner of the seat and drew her legs beneath her. 'I have such a rotten disposition I doubt if I'd be palatable,' she said with mock ruefulness.

I had to laugh out loud. I'd never seen her in just that mood before, gay and whimsical, so completely cut loose from her social worker's attitude. But I liked it.

'We ought to do this more often,' I said.

'What, speculate on our savouriness?' she asked, raising her brows. 'Do you by any chance think that you are more palatable than I?'

The little blond waitress came up just in time to hear the last of it and she gave a spontaneous giggle. Alice blushed and looked disconcerted, but the waitress gave her a friendly smile and attached the tray to the car door. I ordered a couple of chicken sandwiches and milk, and Alice ordered a sandwich of tuna-fish salad and iced tea.

When the waitress left I said to Alice, 'See, you got caught.'

She laughed. 'Wouldn't it be funny if she thought we were cannibals?' Then after a moment she said wistfully, 'I'd love to go to the beach today and just laze in the sun.'

'Let's do.'

'Oh, I can't. I have another conference at three.' She sighed. 'Life is just one damned thing after another.'

'You're not just saying it,' I echoed.

We were silent for a moment and I looked around at the people in adjoining cars. With the exception of us, they were all white. I noticed several of them glancing furtively at us and I figured they were trying to make out what nationality Alice was. Now I felt self-conscious, slightly ill at ease. I wondered if I'd ever feel perfectly at ease around white people.

Alice hadn't noticed; she was looking over toward the riding academy where three white girls were cantering their mounts around the oval.

'Take me riding Sunday morning, darling,' she said impulsively.

I felt myself frowning. 'I don't know of any place in the city we can go now. The place in Watts is closed for the duration and you know how most of these other places are – they don't even want us to park and watch.'

She didn't answer right away and I wondered for a moment if she'd been riding at the white places. Then I thought about her going out with Leighton the night before, and while it didn't exactly bother me, I had to say something about it.

'Did you have a nice time last night?' I asked politely, and the next instant I could have bitten off my tongue.

She gave me a curious sidewise look and her face went sober. 'Yes,' she said. 'Did you?'

I winced and all of a sudden the pressure was back on me. 'Baby, let's don't do this to each other,' I said, but I knew that wasn't enough. I had to tell her why we shouldn't. After a moment I said simply, 'I love you.'

She turned slowly to face me and her eyes were like misty stars. 'That's the first time you've ever said that without any qualifying remarks,' she said with a look on her face that made her really beautiful.

'I've never meant to qualify it,' I said. 'You know us cullud folks just talk that way.'

After a moment she murmured, 'But yours comes from a lack of self-restraint, really.'

I watched the fluid motion of her long slender fingers as she absently fiddled with the steering wheel and thought wonderingly that I'd never noticed before how beautiful they were. Then I thought of what they said about being able to tell a Negro by the half-moons in their finger-nails, and reflected half laughingly on what they'd have to do if the nails were painted.

Finally I said seriously, 'I know. I wonder what's the matter with me, myself. Everything I do or say seems wrong. But I don't do it deliberately, it just turns out that way.'

'Your only trouble is maladjustment, darling,' she said. 'Please don't think I'm trying to rub it in, but there're simply no other words to express it. You don't try to adjust your way of thinking to the actual conditions of life.'

The waitress brought our orders and we were silent

while she served them. But now both of us had lost our appetites.

'When I do try to get pushed around,' I said, beginning to tighten up inside again. 'Sometimes I get to feeling that I don't have anything at all to say about what's happening to me. I'm just like some sort of machine being run by white people pushing buttons. Every white person who comes along pushes some button or other on me and I react accordingly.' I turned to look at her. 'Do you ever get that feeling?'

She was looking at me too, not critically as I'd expected, but with a strange deep sympathy. She didn't answer, but there was something in her look that just drew me right on out.

'Take for instance doing something as simple as going downtown to a moving picture show. Every white person I come into contact with, every one I have to speak to, even those I pass on the street – every goddamn one of them has got the power of some kind of control over my own behaviour. Not only that but they use it – use it in every way. Say if I ride the streetcar, the conductor can make me stand there waiting for my change or he can make me ask two or three times for a transfer. Then when I get off and walk down the street the pedestrians can make me step aside to let them pass. The cashier at the theatre can sell me loge seats when she knows there aren't any, and the doorman can send me on up to the balcony, knowing that there aren't any loge seats, then the usher will find the worst possible seat for me. And there's the picture – it's almost certain to offend me in some kind of way. If there're Negro actors in it the roles they play will be offensive; and if it's a play with no part at all for Negroes, if you get to thinking about it, you resent the fact of seeing the kind of life shown you'll never be able to live. The hell of it is, it's not just one little thing – say if I bought the wrong ticket I could take it back and have it exchanged, but it's selling me the ticket and making me go through all the rigmarole. But it's not only that, it's the pressure they put on you of being able to do these things to you . . .'

My throat began feeling dry and I paused to take a swallow of milk. 'I don't mind some of it,' I went on. 'I know that most people don't have too much to say about the way they live. But I don't have anything at all to say about the way I live – nothing. Take my job – I've never been anything but a flunkey for Kelly, a go-between for him and the coloured workers. Many a time I've been standing down in the tool crib with the other leadermen discussing a new job with Kelly, but whenever I made any kind of suggestion or said anything at all, no matter how sound it was, Kelly just brushed it aside as if I hadn't spoken. I never did have any real authority. Sometimes Kelly'd even have other leadermen give me my assignments. And then the very first time I tried to use a little authority I got slapped down.'

'I understand, darling,' she said. 'But you shouldn't feel too badly about it. That is typical of most Negroes working in a supervisory capacity where white and coloured are employed. Many Negroes whom we think are in top positions are actually no more than figureheads and are much more frustrated than you. I can't give direct orders on my job either, although I am classified as a supervisor. Only suggestions. It almost drives me mad to see cases handled incorrectly and have no power to correct them. Oft-times I have the feeling that I haven't earned two cents since I've been on my job – that I'm just there, keeping someone else out of a job.' She sighed. 'But that is simply one of the conditions of life.'

'I know,' I said. 'But it rankles just the same. I don't like to be pushed around all the time. A guy wants to feel he can control at least some of his life. All this morning—' I caught myself about to tell her how my resentment toward Madge had built up to the place where all that morning it had been controlling me like a puppet on a string. Instead I said, 'I don't want to always be thinking about my race either. I get awful goddamn tired of it. But the white people make me think about it in every way. I never get a chance to think like an ordinary guy.'

'I must tell you again, Bob darling,' she said. 'You need some definite aim, a goal that you can attain within the segregated pattern in which we live.' When I started to interrupt she stopped me. 'I know that sounds like compromise. But it isn't, darling. We *are* Negroes and we can't change that. But *as* Negroes, we can accomplish many things, achieve success, live our own lives, own our own homes, and have happiness. There is no reason a Negro cannot control his destiny within this pattern. Really, darling, it is not cowardly. It is simply a form of self-preservation.'

'Listen, baby, it's not that I want to argue. I don't want to ever argue with you any more. And I've already made up my mind to conform – so it isn't that. But please don't tell me I can control my destiny, because I know I can't. In any incident that might come up a white person can use his colour on me and turn it into a catastrophe and I won't have any protection, any out, nothing I can do about it but die. And if that's controlling my destiny—'

'That isn't true, Bob,' she said patiently. 'I will admit that we are restricted and controlled in our economic security, that we have to conform to the pattern of segregation in order to achieve any manner of financial success. And I will grant you that we are subject to racial control in securing education, in almost all public facilities, welfare, health, hospitalization, transportation, in the location of our dwellings, in all the component parts of our existence that stem directly or indirectly from economy.

'But, darling, all of life is not commercial. The best parts of it are not commercial. Love and marriage, children and homes. Those we control. Our physical beings, our personal integrity, our private property – we have as much protection for these as anyone. As long as we conform to the pattern of segregation we do not have to fear the seizure of our property or attack upon our persons.

'And there are many other values that you are not taking into consideration – spiritual values, intrinsic values, which are also fundamental components of our lives. Honesty, decency, respectability. Courage – it takes courage to live as a Negro must. Virtue is our own, to nurture or destroy.

'After all, darling, these are the important things in life. These things that are within us that make us what we are. And we can control them. Every person, no matter of what race, creed, or colour, is the captain of his soul. This is much more important, really, than being permitted to eat in exclusive restaurants, dwell in exclusive neighbourhoods, or even to compete economically with people of other races. It depends, darling, on our own sense of values.'

For a long time after she'd stopped talking I didn't say anything at all because I was just getting it. If somebody had told me this a long time ago, made me see it in just this way, it would have saved me a lot of trouble. Because I was seeing it then for the first time. No matter what the white folks did to me, or made me do just in order to live, Alice and I could have a life of our own, inside of all the pressure, away from it, separate from it, that no white person could ever touch. I saw that then, and I turned to her, tense and serious.

'Will you marry me, Alice?'

I never saw her mouth go so tender as when she said, 'Yes, Bob. Didn't you know that I would?'

I went all buttery inside. 'When?'

'Whenever you want.'

'Next month?'

She nodded. I leaned forward and kissed her again with long and steady pressure. Her eyes closed, her lashes lowering like two tiny fans on her cheeks, and her body flowed forward as her lips came out to meet mine, soft and resilient and budding and full of hope, like the beginning of a new life. That was when I knew it, when I lost all doubt. I could take anything the white folks wanted to put on me, as long as I had this. Because this was it; I knew this was it; this was the number that John saw.

When we broke apart she sat there for a time, relaxed, with her eyes closed; and when she opened them they held a little laugh. 'Will you apologize to the girl you had the fight with?' she asked.

I began laughing too, deep inside. 'You never give up, do you, baby?' I said, adding, 'You know I will.'

Suddenly she said, 'I don't want you to.'

We both laughed together, so wonderfully happy. 'You only win,' I said.

After a moment she started to tell me how she came to know Stella. I tried to stop her, but she had to tell me, she said, she had to get it out from between us. A girl friend of hers had suggested they go there one night after they'd attended a concert at the Hollywood Bowl. She'd gone back once with the same girl. While she'd been hep to the play, it had only been curiosity on her part; she'd never been up with it, never even gone as far as she had the night I was with her. But what was great about it was that I believed her.

After that we had a togetherness we felt nothing could destroy. We felt we'd gotten over the river Jordan into the promised land. Did you ever just know you were right? No matter whether you were gambling or working or operating on a guy, you just had that feeling and you knew it. That was the way it was with us.

'I'm part you now and you're part me,' she said.

'I'm all you.'

'No, I'm all you, if anything.'

'Unh-unh, we're both it.'

Then we were laughing again.

We'd be married sometime the middle of July, we planned.

'People will think funny things because no one ever marries in July,' she said.

'What do we care what people think?' Then I said, 'I'll sell my car and buy us a house. A fellow offered me two grand for it just a couple of weeks ago.'

'I saw the cutest little place for sale. On a little hill beside Monterey Road.'

'Way out there? It'll take me a year to get to work.'

'I'll drive you to work every morning, but you'll have to arrange to ride back with someone else. Although I could meet you downtown every evening – perhaps at the P.E. station.'

'Unh-unh, a bar's the place,' I said.

Then we became serious and talked about means.

'You can keep your job until the first baby comes,' I consented, feeling very male and important. 'But after that it'll be home, sweet home for you, baby.'

'It might be some time before we're able to afford a baby,' she pointed out. 'You're going to be a schoolboy for about three years – don't forget that, *Papa*.'

'Oh, we'll have the baby whether we can afford it or not,' I said.

She gave me a sly, sidewise glance and began giggling. 'How do you know?'

I was startled for a moment, then I began laughing.

She wouldn't help me to decide about my job. Whether to quit and go to another yard or stay on at Atlas as a mechanic. That was entirely up to me, she said. But she did point out that I might be better off if I stayed on at Atlas and tried to get my job back so I could keep my deferment.

'One thing,' I said. 'Wherever I go, I'll keep out of trouble. I'll get along and make good on the job. You won't have to worry about that.'

She leaned over and kissed me. 'Don't behave too well, darling. I might not love you so much.'

'Anyway, when I enter U.C.L.A. this fall I'll have to go on the graveyard shift, and there might be a better bunch of workers.'

It was exciting, planning for the future. It gave everything a new meaning, an importance it had never had before.

Suddenly I noticed something strange and looked around. All of the cars that had been there when we came were gone. I glanced at my watch. It was a quarter to two.

'I'll have to run,' I said.

'You'll have dinner with us. We'll tell Dad and Mother.'

'I know they'll jump for joy.'

She laughed. 'Oh, they like you, really, darling. And they've already guessed how I feel.'

I paid the check and turned to kiss her. I didn't want to ever let her out of my arms, but finally I had to. Then I jumped out, hurried over to my car. I turned one way, she turned the other; we waved to each other. I'll never forget her smile just before she pulled away.

Driving back, I noticed the fields of young corn beside

the road and resolved right then to get some place where we could have a victory garden. It'd be fun growing things.

For the first time in my life I felt satisfied. I didn't think of marrying Alice as a way out. I felt that it was what I wanted, what I'd always wanted. I could see myself at forty, dignified, grey at the temples, pleading the defence of a Negro youth. 'Gentlemen of the jury, let me tell you about frustration, a social disease, a disease imposed on peoples of minority groups over and above their control. It is this frustration that drives these youngsters to crime; it is as if society picks them up bodily and hurls them into it. Gentlemen of the jury, I say to you, it is as unjust to condemn this youth for a disease that society has imposed on him . . .'

Goddamn, I sounded like Clarence Darrow himself, I thought, laughing out loud. Then I sobered. Maybe by that time people would have gotten over the notion, I thought. Maybe they wouldn't be so prone to believe that every Negro man was the same, maybe they would have realized how crazy the whole business was. I sure hoped they'd have some goddamn sense by the time my son was grown.

But my mind wouldn't hold it. My thoughts were full of Alice. I just shook my head. It was one of those miracles. I was a different guy; didn't think the same; didn't feel the same. That was what it did for me. Set me up. Big tough world, but I got you beat now, I thought exultantly. *Peace, Father, it is truly wonderful.*

CHAPTER
20

When I checked back in I decided suddenly to have a talk with Mac. I was worrying about my job deferment. At the last minute I didn't want to have to go into the Army and lose everything – Alice and my dream and even my good intentions. So I swallowed my pride and turned toward the tin-shop office.

Mac kept me waiting again; but I waited. Finally when he saw I wasn't going to leave he beckoned me over.

'What's on your mind, Bob?' he asked, his big sloppy body overflowing his huge desk chair, and his eyes twinkling in his jolly red face as if I was the one guy he wanted to see the most.

'I'd like to talk to you about staying on in my job,' I said, swallowing. 'I promise you, you won't have any more trouble out of me.' It was hard getting it out but I made it.

'Think you've learned your lesson, eh?' He beamed. 'Got that chip off your shoulder, eh?'

I swallowed again, felt my Adam's apple bobbing in my throat. 'Yes sir,' I said in a high, weightless voice.

'That's fine,' he purred, looking about. I was suddenly conscious that everybody in the office was listening. 'Think you can co-operate with the other workers now without losing your temper?'

'Yes sir.'

He wagged his finger at me and said laughingly, 'Now you're just trying to keep out the Army – that's it, isn't it?'

'I'll admit I don't want to go into the Army,' I said. 'But that's not the reason I want to keep my job.' I paused, then told him, 'I want to get married.'

'Well! Married, eh?' His big jolly face took on a congratulatory expression. 'Marriage'll do you a lot of good, boy. Settle you; make you more reliable.' He paused, then showed a friendly interest. 'One of the girls in the yard?'

'No, sir, she's a social worker,' I said. 'A supervisor in the city welfare department.' It did me a lot of good to tell him that.

'Oh!' His face went suddenly sober and a peculiar distrustful look came into his eyes. 'Did you ever hear of Executive Order No. 8802?' he asked abruptly.

I didn't get the connection right away but I said, 'Yes sir, it's the President's directive on fair employment.'

He gave a deep belly grunt and some of the twinkle came back into his eyes. '*Directive!* That's right! The President's directive. It's a good thing,' he said, and his gaze came up in a swift, sharp, searching look.

I knew I should have let it go right then and there, but the half-sneering way he said it got under my skin. 'I think it's a good thing too,' I said. 'I think it oughta be enforced.'

Now his face got sober again. 'We enforce it here at Atlas. To the letter! You know that!' When I didn't reply right away he pressed me, 'You know that, don't you?'

Now I was sorry I'd said anything at all because I had to say, 'Yes sir,' to keep out of an argument.

He nodded, then went reflective. 'But your case doesn't come under that. There's no discrimination involved in your demotion whatsoever. People who want to agitate might tell you that, but it isn't so . . .'

All of a sudden I caught the connection between Alice being a social worker and the Executive Order – Mac figured she'd been talking to me, probably trying to get me to use the no-discrimination angle.

'I'd have done the same to any other leaderman who'd cursed a woman,' he went on. 'Been forced to. A matter of discipline.' He paused, waiting for me to say something.

There wasn't anything for me to say.

Then he beamed at me. 'I tell you what I'll do with you, Bob. You go back up there and work under Tebbel for a while. Prove that you're dependable, trustworthy, that you can keep out of trouble. Take your punishment like a man, then make a comeback. That's the American way, my boy. Prove yourself. Then come back here and see me. I'll see if I can get Kelly to put you back as a leaderman.'

I swallowed, took a breath. 'When must I come back?'

He looked impatient. 'You'll know that better than me. Whenever you feel I can put dependence in you; when you think you can handle a little authority without losing your head again.'

I had to get some help from Alice before I could say it that time. 'Yes sir. I'll do my best.'

I noticed Marguerite looking at me curiously when I went out. I wondered what she was thinking.

On the way across the yard one part of my mind kept telling me that I'd made a mistake speaking to Mac – that he'd figure I was trying to jive him and never reinstate me. But the other part of my mind argued that it had done some good. I had let him know I wanted my job bad enough to get along with the white workers in order to keep it. And I'd humbled myself, if that was what he wanted. Then there was always a chance that he might really mean it. Perhaps if I worked hard and kept out of arguments he really would reinstate me. I'd have to take people at face value, I told myself; have to believe they meant what they said instead of always picking it to pieces.

Then too it was a cinch Tebbel wouldn't be able to keep it. He didn't know enough about the work for one thing. And another thing, his race baiting was going to get him into trouble with those guys in my gang sooner or later. He'd say the wrong thing once too often and one of them would hang him. I didn't want anybody to get into any more trouble; there'd already been too much excitement about the whole thing. If I'd just let it die down, maybe the whole thing would come out right – I'd come to work one Monday morning and Kelly would tell me to take over my gang again.

I was thinking so hard about it, I was up on the third deck before I realized it. Everybody in my gang was working like mad. Two fire pots were going and all three girls were soldering. Red was helping Homer hang his duct; they were crouching on the staging beneath the upper deck bolting the stays, puffing and blowing. Conway was riveting a joint; Arkansas was bucking for him. Pigmeat was drilling rivet holes. The place was smoky, smelly, sweltering; and the din was terrific. They were knocking themselves out.

'What're you folk doing?' I shouted. 'Working for E buttons?'

Several of them heard me; they slowed up, looking as guilty as if I'd caught them in something wrong. I wondered what the hell it was all about. Then Conway stopped for a moment to explain. 'Tebbel got Kelly to give us a good job for a change. Soon as we's finished here we's going up and work on deck, in the superstructure.'

Ben was working near enough to hear over the din.

'Ole Marsa's gonna free us at last,' he cracked; but even he seemed happy over the prospect.

Smitty stopped his work and came over beside me. 'It show you how them dirty sonabitches do,' he said. 'Just soon's they get you out and a white boy in your place they start giving us better jobs.' Maybe he thought he sounded sympathetic, but he looked gleeful.

Tebbel just stood to one side and looked like the cat who ate the canary. I knew what Kelly was doing. The superstructure was a plum job – cool, airy, with a good view of the harbour; and the guys could stroll out on deck and enjoy the sunshine. He was selling my gang on Tebbel, fixing it so they wouldn't want me back. They'd all think just like Smitty – what Mac had done to me might be a dirty trick, true enough, but a white leaderman could get them better jobs, after all.

Red and Homer got their duct tied and swung down from the staging. 'Damn, I'll sure be glad to get out of this hole,' Red said, flexing his muscles back into place. Then he turned to me. 'What you gonna do, Bob, you gonna stay on with us?'

'I don't know yet,' I said.

'Hell, if it was me I'd quit,' Homer said.

'Ef'n it were me I'd get some bumbs and set 'em all over everywhere and blow up the ship,' Pigmeat said.

'Boy, hush!' Conway said. 'The FBI'll have you for sabotage.'

I noticed that none of them said anything about wanting me to stay on as their leaderman. It looked like I was out to stay.

Then George came up. 'Say, Bob, why don't you go up and look over the job?' he said as if to sort of apologize for the way they felt. 'Tell us what we got to do.' He looked around at Tebbel, lowered his voice. 'You know more 'bout this work than Danny do anyway.'

'Okay,' I said, giving a half-smile. 'I will.' I wanted to get away from them for a moment; I felt pretty low.

I climbed to the superstructure, bumping into other workers absent-mindedly, trying to make up my mind whether to quit at the end of the day or stay on. It was five after three then . . . It'd be easier to quit, I thought. But the proof would be to stay on there and make a comeback. I kept on up to the bridge, glanced idly at the gun installations down on the deck, debating whether to talk it over with Alice. I decided not to do it; I'd make the choice myself, stop leaning on her for every little thing. I looked into the chartroom, wandered out again, went down to the weather deck, and wandered over toward the railing.

But I couldn't make up my mind. Then I remembered I'd promised George to look over the job, went back to the deck-house, and strolled through the companionways, peeping into various rooms. I didn't know what they were all for; various lockers and the officers' quarters, I imagined. I'd have to get a print to tell anything about it. Of course the ventilation didn't look as though it ought to be very complicated, I thought. The place could ventilate itself.

Pipe fitters and electricians were at work in some of the rooms. Outside a woman painter was spraying the bulkheads with red lead. There wasn't a great deal of activity; the superstructure would be the last place to be outfitted – start at the bottom and work up.

I was going aft to take a gander down into the engine-room when I noticed a closed door, put my hand on the knob, and pushed inside to see what it might hold. It was dark inside after the glaring sun on the deck, but I saw an extension cord running underneath the door, traced it to the lamp hooked over a clip tacked to the bulkhead, snapped on the light.

I just had time to notice that it was a cabin with facing bunks and two portholes to starboard tightly covered with old newspaper when someone grunted sleepily, 'Unh!' I jerked around. There was a saggy mattress on one of the bunks and a bigbodied woman with dyed blond hair was lying on it, sleeping, with her face to the wall.

All of a sudden she came awake, said, 'Damn!' then wheeled over quickly and sat up, blinking at the light. Her big blue mascaraed eyes were full of sleep and there were deep lines in the heavy coat of powder on her face where the witches had been riding her.

'I was feelin' bad and just thought I'd lie down for a—' she started alibi-ing rapidly in her flat Texas voice; then broke off. 'Oh, it's you!' she said.

I'd gotten Madge completely out of my thoughts and running into her like that startled me. I stood for a moment, looking at her stupidly as if she was some strange sight. Then I caught myself and said, 'Oh, I didn't know you were here.'

'I bet you did,' she said, trying to look coy.

I snapped off the light, started to beat it. I didn't want to see her now; I'd gotten over it. All I wanted to do was get away from her.

'Wait a minute,' she said. 'What's your hurry? You come in here and wake me up and then wanna rush off.' I could hear her sighing like an animal, see the vague outline of her body as she flexed the sleep out of it.

Voices sounded in the companionway outside, footsteps came our way. I groped quickly for the light, snapped it on again. I didn't want to be caught in the dark with her. And just in case somebody walked in I tried to make it look legitimate. 'I'd like to apologize,' I began in a fairly loud voice. 'I was upset that morning and—'

'Shut the door, fool!' she said as the voices drew nearer; jumped up and shut it herself, slid the latch on. She stood with her back toward it, looking at me.

The footsteps stopped outside and somebody tried the latch. Then a voice, a sly feminine lilt, a laugh, and the footsteps went on.

My lungs hurt from holding my breath. I let it out, got another lungful. 'Let me get the hell out of here,' I said, trying to push her aside. 'You're simple.'

By then I realized that some of the workers must have been using the cabin for loafing, sleeping, gambling, and assignation, and I didn't want to be found there with her under any circumstances.

But she wouldn't let me by. She put the palms of her hands over my ears, pressed the tips of her fingers against the back of my head, and pulled my face toward hers. She had a sharp mixed odour of sweat and powder, pungent and perfumed.

I broke away, gave her a push. She went back three steps, caught herself. 'Goddamnit, don't le's fight,' she said.

'Why don't you get some sense?' I said. I began inching back toward the door, scared any moment she might start to perform. It was funny the way I was trying to slip away from her without starting any ruckus; but it wasn't funny then. I was tense, nervous; really scared of that dame. 'Look,' I said, 'I'll call you up tonight.'

'You look, yo'self,' she said. Footsteps sounded in the companionway again. I had the door unlocked, but I locked it again, snatched my hand away as if it were hot.

I knew I should have run, got the hell away from that crazy bitch no matter who was out in the companionway. But I couldn't; all I could do was just stare at her. All she had was her colour, so help me, but it put me right back on that weak-kneed edge.

But I came out of it. I said in a low, level voice, 'Look, baby, I don't want you. I don't want no part of you, that's final.' And I meant it.

'You're a liar,' she hissed.

Someone tried the handle of the door, rattled it. 'Why is this door locked?' a voice with authority asked. 'Is it supposed to be locked?'

'Nooo, not as I know of,' another voice replied. The lock was tried again.

'Is there anyone in there?' the first voice asked.

My eyes sought Madge's, warning. Hers were panicky, trapped. Neither of us breathed.

'I say, is anyone in there?' the voice asked again. 'Do you suppose there's anyone in there, Mr Nelson?'

'Well . . .' The second voice hesitated, then said, 'There must be. It's locked from within.'

The first voice was crisp this time. 'Open up, this is the Navy inspector.' I waited. A fist banged on the door. Then it said, 'Get a burner, Mr Nelson, we'll take off the lock.'

I let out my breath, gave Madge a last warning look, then said aloud, 'Okay, I'll open up, just a minute.'

Madge came into me from the angle, caught me off guard, flung me toward the bunk. The side of my right leg, just below the knee, clipped against the side of the bunk, broke me into a spinning fall. My head hit against the bulkhead and I sprawled face down on the mattress. I wheeled over, got one foot on the deck, and was coming up when she began to scream.

'*Help! Help! My God, help me! Some white man, help me! I'm being raped.*'

I saw the stretch and pop of her lips, the tautening of her throat muscles, the distortion and constriction of her face, the flare of her nostrils and the bucking of her eyes with a weird stark clarity as if her face were ten feet high.

I was in the middle of a breath and the air got rock-hard in my lungs, like frozen steam, and wouldn't budge. My whole body got rigid and my head swelled as if it would explode. My eyes felt as if they were five times their natural size; as if they were bursting in their sockets, popping out of my head. Then cold numbing terror swept over me in a paralysing wave.

'*Stop, nigger! Don't, nigger! Nigger, don't! Oh, please don't kill me, nigger . . .*'

I heard the sudden shouts from outside; the banging on the door, the startled curses, the savage commands. 'Open up this goddamn door, you black bastard! Open up, I say, or by God—' The confused orders, 'Get a torch! Get a sledge hammer! Call that chipper over here.' Heard the scuffling sounds of abrupt activity. Footsteps running, going and coming. New voices. More shouts.

But my mind could not rationalize it, could get no sense out of it. I could see and hear but could not move.

I watched Madge fumble at the latch, rattle it. She slammed against the door once but didn't open it. From without it sounded as if we were struggling, brought on a new chorus of pleading. Then she turned and sprang toward me, rolled me over on the bunk, beat at me with her fists, clawed at my face, scratched me with her nails, bit me on the arm.

Abruptly a raw wild panic exploded within me. The overwhelming fear of being caught with a white woman came out in me in a great white flame. I gave one great push, threw her off of me and half-way across the room, jumped to my feet, grabbed at the first thing I touched, and leaped at her to beat out her brains. She had landed off balance and when I hit at her she ducked, went sprawling on her back on the deck. I went to swing again, slipped, and my foot sailed in the air and I sat down on the end of my spine on the iron deck. Pain shot up my spine like a needle, shocked the fury out of me. I braced my hands on the deck, pushed to my feet. She lay there without moving and looked up at me. But there was no fear in her face.

I stood trembling in a strange bewilderment. The din of activity from without vaguely penetrating my consciousness – the shouts, the threats, the pleas – had no meaning in my mind. My reason was shattered; my senses outraged.

There were only the two of us in pressing chaos. Looking at each other; our eyes locked together as in a death embrace; black and white in both our minds; not hating each other; just feeling extreme outrage. I felt buck-naked and powerless, stripped of my manhood and black against the whole white world.

Then I came out of it. Sanity returned. I started toward the door to open it. 'Wait, I'll let you in,' I shouted above the din. 'Wait, this woman is crazy!'

I touched the latch; snatched my hand away. It was burning hot. 'Wait, goddamnit!' I shouted, looking around at Madge. She hadn't moved; she lay on the deck in a daze. Her mouth was half open and her eyes looked glazed. I thought for a moment she was dead.

Sparks showered into the room where the burner had cut through. I stepped over and shook her to see if she was alive, fighting against panic. Without moving she said in a low flat voice, 'I'm gonna get you lynched, you nigger bastard.'

Out of the corner of my eye I could see the door swinging inward; people were surging into the room from the companionway. I saw a hundred million white faces, distorted with rage.

For one fleeting moment I tried to talk. 'Goddamnit, listen,' I shouted.

A fist in my mouth cut it off. The sight of one hard

hating face across my vision shook loose my reason again. Now I was moved by a rage, impelled by it, set into motion by it, lacerated by it. I started hitting, kicking, butting, biting, pushing. I carried the mob outside into the companionway, striking at faces, kicking at bodies. Somebody fell and I stepped on him. The soft roll of muscle over bone sent goose flesh through me. I looked up, saw a white guy wielding a sledge hammer, his face sculptured in unleashed fury. A flat cold wave of terror spread out underneath my skull, freezing the roots of my hair.

I wheeled into the tight mob of bodies, half squatted, put my arms about three pairs of legs, straightened up with the strength of insanity. I threw them back over my shoulder in the direction of the guy with the sledge, started a mad surging rush forward that got me through to the midship companionway; went into a flailing spin that freed me for an instant, started down the jack ladder toward the engine room.

A guy leaned over the hole and swung at my head with a ball-peen hammer. I was going down forward with my hands on the railings and saw the hammer coming. It didn't look like a hard blow; it looked as though it floated into me. I saw the guy's face, not particularly malevolent, just disfigured, a white man hitting at a nigger running by. But I couldn't do a thing; I couldn't let go the railing to get my hands up; couldn't even duck. I didn't feel the blow; just the explosion starting at a point underneath my skull and filling my head with a great flaming roar. And then what seemed like falling a million miles through space and hitting something hard to splatter into pieces.

CHAPTER
21

I came to once as I lay crumpled on the deck at the bottom of the ladder. A lot of guys were kicking me. Then again when I was being lifted from the ambulance on a stretcher. I was in a sort of half and half state when the doctors began working on me. I remember swallowing some pills and getting a shot in the arm; and I felt it when they shaved my head and clamped the metal stitches in my skull. They were doing something to my mouth when I just drifted on away.

When I came to again I was in the room back of minor surgery, lying on a cot. My mouth felt dry, cottony; and my head throbbed with a steady ache.

Then I saw the guard sitting in a chair by the door, puffing slowly on a pipe. He was huge, tremendous, the biggest man I'd ever seen, with a squarish, knotty, weather-reddened face, and small colourless eyes, cold and inscrutable. When he saw I was looking at him he got on a look of joviality that didn't change the expression of his eyes at all.

'You're a lucky boy,' he said in a big intimidating voice, and got that phoney lipless smile that the coppers down at the old Thirty-seventh Street station in Cleveland were famous for when they beat a Negro half to death with a loaded hose. 'No bones broke. All in one piece. Just skinned up a little.'

I looked away from him without replying, threw back the covers, propped myself up on my elbows. The slight movement sent the pain through my body. I was nude. My knees, elbows, and one wrist were bandaged and taped and I was splotched all over with mercurochrome. I reached for my head, felt the thick turban of bandages. My face felt raw and my lips were swollen several times their natural size. I explored with my tongue and felt teeth out in front but I couldn't tell how many. I hurt in the groin as if I was ruptured.

I lay back and closed my eyes and tried to remember just what had happened. But my brain was fuzzy. It wouldn't come back clear. I remembered Madge screaming. Then I'd gone panicky. Then I remembered her lying there on the deck, saying, '*I'm gonna get you lynched* . . .' Well, she got me lynched all right.

But something was missing. Something important. Then suddenly I knew what it was. I hadn't even tried to rape her; I'd been trying to get away from her. I'd gone up there to case the new job for the gang and had run into her accidentally. She'd kept me there, cornered me, hadn't let me go. I'd wanted to go, but she hadn't let me. She couldn't get away with that. This wasn't Georgia.

I opened my eyes, propped myself up on my elbows again, and said, 'I didn't bother that woman. She's crazy!' My voice was a lisp. My lips felt like two big balloon tyres beating together. I had to push the words half formed through the gap in my teeth.

'I don't have nothing to do with that, sonny,' the guard said jovially. 'You'll have to tell it to somebody who knows more about it than me.'

'I'll tell anybody,' I lisped belligerently.

'There ain't anybody to tell,' he said. 'Now ain't that hell?'

I'd see somebody first thing in the morning, I thought,

swinging my feet over the edge of the bed and sitting up.
I was dizzy and had to brace myself with my hands. Hell,
I'd see the president of the company. I'd get it straightened
out. I wouldn't make any charges against the fellows for
beating me up; I'd let that go. But I'd make the company
pay my hospital bill, pay for fixing my teeth. And I'd get
that bitch fired if it was the last thing I did. She couldn't
get away with that, even if she was a white woman. But
I wasn't worried, wasn't in any particular hurry.

'You wanna get dressed now?' the guard asked, nod-
ding toward a cabinet. 'Your clothes are in there.'

When I stood up to go after them my knees wobbled;
I had to catch hold of the foot of the bed to keep from
falling. I felt out of balance, uncoupled, like a little tin
soldier out of whack.

When I took down my things I noticed dried blood
about the collar of my coveralls and the upper part of my
underwear shirt. I must have bled like a hog, I thought.
Leaning against the cabinet to steady myself, I got into
my underwear and coveralls without tearing off the
bandages. But when I bent over to draw on my socks I
almost fell forward on my face. And my ankles were
swollen so I couldn't lace up my boots.

The guard sat there watching me curiously. 'Just as
good as new,' he remarked jovially. 'By God, I never saw
a man what could take so much punishment.'

I didn't see my watch, billfold, key ring, leather jacket,
tin hat, or identifications. 'Where are my other things?' I
asked, lisping the words carefully.

He chuckled. 'That tap on the noggin ain't bothered
your memory any,' he said, pulling my watch, keys, and
billfold from his pocket. 'Here you are, sonny. You're
lucky somebody was good enough to turn 'em in.'

I didn't ask about my badges and identifications; I was
through, I wouldn't need them any more anyway. The

228

crystal of my watch was broken and it had stopped. I checked my keys; they were all there. I thought of my brass tool checks but didn't ask about them. I'd get all that straightened out in the morning. Then I looked to see if anything had been taken from my billfold. My driver's licence, draft classification, a small snapshot of Alice, and the other papers were there, but my money, two tens and four ones, was gone. I didn't ask about it either. I'd make the whole goddamned bunch sorry for everything that had happened, I resolved, stuffing all of it into my pocket.

'That's a pretty gal's picture you got there,' the guard observed. 'Is she white?'

I didn't reply.

'Better get your medicine too,' he said.

I looked on the bedside stand, saw a bottle of brown pills and a paper cup of water that had been sitting there until bubbles had formed in it. I picked up the bottle, dropped it into my other pocket.

The guard stood up. In his uniform, the regular olive drab with the Sam Browne belt and the auxiliary police insignia on his sleeve, he looked impressive, six feet four or more, and a good two-fifty pounds. 'Wanna go 'long with me now?' he said, opening the door into minor surgery.

I took a deep breath and went out ahead of him, weak and wobbly. There were two white-clad doctors, a nurse, and several patients in minor surgery. They stopped in the middle of what they were doing to stare at me. I looked straight ahead, stepped out into the yard.

It was dark; I had an idea it was pretty late. On the ground hundreds of lights made a sort of sketchy daylight, but overhead it was night. Here and there the arcs of welders were blue-white flashes. The shipways were to my back, big dark eerie shapes with a million lights;

but I didn't look about. Workers scurried about, trucks moved by, the noise was still there; the work went on. I had an idea it was the graveyard shift.

'We'll go over to the truck gate,' the guard said.

I headed in that direction; he fell in beside me. When we came to the glass-enclosed guards' room he held open the door. I went inside. There was a slanting draftsman's desk against the window toward the entrance, littered with pads, papers, temporary badges, and the usual forms gatekeepers have to make out before permitting vehicles to enter.

Two heavy-set gatekeepers in blue uniforms with holstered pistols sat on high stools, their feet hooked in the rungs and their elbows propped on the desk, listening to a short, pudgy, grey-haired man in the uniform of a guard captain who stood before them. He had a round rosy face and twinkling grey eyes, but at sight of me his eyes got hard.

'That the boy?' he asked the guard.

'This is him,' the guard said.

For a moment all of them looked at me curiously. Then one of the gatekeepers chuckled. 'Damn if they didn't beat hell out of you,' he said.

The guard captain said, 'You're lucky you're in California. In my home state we'd have hung you.'

I didn't say anything; I expected that out of the guards. Most of them were Southerners anyway. I was just waiting for him to get my time card so I could sign out and go home.

Instead he picked up the phone from the end of the desk and dialled. When he got an answer he said, 'Send somebody out here to Atlas to pick up that coloured boy on that rape charge.' He listened a moment, then said, 'Yeah, you got a warrant for him. . . . Okay, I'll expect you.' He hung up and turned to look at me again. 'You'll

230

get thirty years in this state, boy.'

I was slow getting it. My first reaction was surprise. 'What the hell?' I lisped. 'You having me arrested?' I kind of half thought maybe they were joking.

Everyone in the room gave me a quick, startled look. Then the big guard said, 'That's right, boy. The lady swore out a warrant.'

No one else said anything; they just looked at me.

I didn't get scared right away; I'd been thinking so hard about what was going to happen to her when the people knew the truth. I was even kind of amused to think she was simple enough to think she could get away with that in California. But my mind began going over the evidence. I still wasn't alarmed.

Then it smacked me, shook me to the core. I don't know what set it off; it must have been deep inside of me – always inside of me. I knew in one great flash she really could send me to the pen for thirty years. My word against hers, and all the evidence on her side. I knew there was no way in the world I could prove I hadn't tried to rape her.

Before, up in the room with her, with the mob beating at the door, I'd been instinctively scared of being caught with a white woman screaming, 'Rape.' Scared of the mob; scared of the violence; just scared because I was black and she was white; a trapped, cornered, physical fear.

But now I was scared in a different way. Not of the violence. Not of the mob. Not of physical hurt. But of America, of American justice. The jury and the judge. The people themselves. Of the inexorability of one conclusion – that I was guilty. In that one brief flash I could see myself trying to prove my innocence and nobody believing it. A white woman yelling, 'Rape,' and a Negro caught locked in the room. The whole structure of American thought was against me; American tradition had convicted me a hundred years before. And standing there in an American courtroom, through all the phoney formality of an American trial, having to take it, knowing that I was innocent and that I didn't have a chance.

I was scared more than I've ever been scared in all my life: a rational, reasonable, irrefutable, cold-headed scare. But I wasn't panicky. My mind got sharp, cunning; I thought of only one thing – *escape*.

A truck drove up, stopped to be inspected. One of the gate-keepers started out the front door; the other one reached for a form to copy the licence number. I swung a long left hook into the big guard's belly with everything I had, went out on the shoulders of the gatekeepers, roughing him to the ground. I stumbled over him, beyond, caught on my hands and one knee, felt the gravel bite into my palms, the pain rack me from the knee; heard the guard captain shout, 'Don't shoot! Catch him!' The instinct of self-preservation got me up and moving; I'd lost a boot and shook the other one off; heard the sudden clatter of action behind me, dug steps with a high-kneed, churning motion, trying to get some speed. It took a flat twelve hundred years to get to the back of the truck, around it, on the other side; and another dozen centuries to get across the lighted stretch of driveway before I reached the darkness of the parking lot.

I didn't think; my mind was following the blind line of action, concentrating on the problem of getting greater motion out of my body, nothing else.

I figured my car was way down to the left, ducked sharp between two cars, skinned my shin against a bumper, stumbled over something in the dark, fell flat, and got up again. I ran past my car and didn't see it, wheeled and sent a stabbing gaze along the row, rigid, tense, desperate, but not terrified. I spotted it three cars back, heard the guards looking for me two rows over, squatted on my hands and knees and walked back to it bear-fashion, hid below the fenders of the cars.

I thought I never would get the door unlocked; to get the key in the ignition took even longer. Out of the corner of my eyes I saw the guards coming toward me. I was parked in a double row with the cars heading in, V-shaped and tight together. A double line of six-by-sixes separated the two rows, served as barriers. There was a vacant space in front of me, at a sixty-degree angle. I cut sharp and headed into it without a thought of whether I could make it; took the double line of six-by-sixes on the starter before the motor caught; heard the back bumper hook into an adjoining fender and the motor roar at the same instant. Noise shattered the night as I yanked the fender off, sideswiped the car in the other line, straightened down the driveway.

Down in the lighted section by the central drive somebody ran out in front of me. I headed into him, missed him by a breath as he leaped away, made a screaming left turn toward the harbour road, but not quite tight enough, and dented my fenders fore and aft against the protective posts.

A P.E. train was coming toward the crossing and I didn't have time to shift. I got across ahead of it so close I heard it ping against my rear bumper as it swivelled the rear end out of line. I had to fight it out of a ditch, felt it lurch crazily beneath me, pulled it right into the harbour road on one thin prayer.

I hadn't turned on my lights and at the first turn a big, fast-moving Diesel cutting a long bend on the wrong side almost ran me down. I reached down and switched on the bright lights, noticed that fog was settling on the night, turned on my fog lights, and stood my stocking foot on the gas as if I was weighing myself. The snaky

233

road came up over the hood, bent, straightened, and came up again. Behind, motor roar spilled like a P-38. The hood squatted so low it looked as though the crankcase would rub.

I started to brake for a left turn into Figueroa, saw a truck coming, and knew I couldn't make it, kept on over to Alameda. Outside of Wilmington a siren blew for me, but I didn't even slow. All I could think of was flight, desperate, cold-headed flight.

I came into the jog beyond the refineries where the P.E. tracks crossed again so fast I couldn't make the bend, went down the tracks, jumped into the gulley, heard water splash, came out on the road down on the floor, hanging to the wheel for dear life. I thought for a moment I'd wrecked it that time, but when I stepped on the gas it took life again.

Then I caught a stretch of open road, watched the needle climb. The speed cooled me slightly and the Buick drove itself. Thought came back into my mind, made me calculate. I looked at the gas. The needle was on '1'; I knew that'd give me three with the two reserve – three gallons. I could get some gas. Then I remembered suddenly that I didn't have any money. Finally I realized I couldn't use my car anyway; the cops would be on the lookout for it; they'd get the description and the licence number from the yard.

Scare hung over me like a cold grey shroud, but I knew I was thinking straight. I knew I had to get out of California before daylight, go somewhere and hide until I got healed up. Las Vegas, maybe. All kinds of strange Negroes had gone to Las Vegas; I could hide there in one of those whorehouses for a time without attracting any attention. After that I'd go east, to Harlem, maybe, take another name, and start life over. Because I knew I couldn't beat that rap that Madge had hung on me.

But first I'd have to get some money. I had about a hundred and ninety-odd dollars in my room. That was as far as I'd let myself think. I'd keep on the dark side streets, do about thirty-five. I kept down to Fiftieth, turned left back to Untility Fan, came into Long Beach by the cannery, turned left again to Fifty-fourth, right to Central, right on Central to Fifty-first, left over to San Pedro. I was about to turn down Wall when I suddenly realized I'd better call first.

I turned around, drove back Fifty-first to the barbecue joint just before Central, parked half a block up the street, got out, and walked the rest of the way in my stocking feet. Before I went in I took a gander up the street, then peeped inside through the window. The place was filled with a lot of noisy, laughing, half-drunk people, men and women, all coloured. I braced myself and went in, kept on through to the phone booth at the rear. People turned and looked at me. One woman giggled, and another cracked, 'What run over him?' but the guy with her said, 'Tend to yo' own damn business.'

Ella Mae answered my ring. 'Look, I'm in trouble—' I began, but she cut me off.

'Is that you, Bob?'

'Yeah, listen—'

'Don't come home,' she said in a whisper. 'The police are here—' Her voice broke off. I heard a scuffle. In the background I could still hear her telling me not to come home, but yelling now. Then a man's voice said, 'Listen, Jones, the best thing you can do—'

I hung up, hurried out of the joint without looking to right or left. So the L.A. cops were already looking for me; that meant I'd have to keep out of public places. I began feeling pressed, trapped, conspicuous. I turned around, started to go back to the filling station at Fifty-fourth and try to get some gas on credit, then remembered

that my ration book was at home. Every time I passed a
car I drew up into a knot inside. I felt as though I were
driving around a hook-and-ladder truck.

Finally I remembered a woman I knew who lived on
Crocker. She worked in private family but was off on
Thursday nights and she might be home. She had a couple
of roomers, but they'd either be asleep or out and I had
to take that chance.

I drove over to Crocker, pulled up far enough in the
driveway beside the house so the car couldn't be spotted
from down the street, got out, and knocked at her
window. There was no answer at first and I knocked
again. A female voice said, 'Who is it?'

'It's me, Bob, Hazel,' I lisped. 'I'm in a little trouble
and I want to use your phone.'

'You don't sound like Bob,' she said sceptically. 'What's
the matter with your voice?'

'I got some teeth knocked out,' I lisped.

'Oh!' Then she said, 'What kinda trouble? You ain't
stole nothing, have you?'

'No, I hit a peck with my tyre iron,' I lied. 'The police
are looking for me.'

She was silent for a moment. 'All right, come around
to the back door.'

I went around the yard, felt the cool damp grass on my
stocking feet. She opened the door into the kitchen
without turning on the lights. In the darkness she was
just a big vague shape.

'I oughtn'ta be doing this,' she grumbled. 'No telling
what kinda trouble you might be getting me into.'

'I won't be long,' I promised.

'You know where the phone is.' Then after a moment
she asked, 'You ain't killed nobody?'

'No, he's not bad hurt.'

She paused for a moment to look at me in the darkness,

then asked, 'What you doing with all them bandages on your head? Somebody beat you up?'

'The police,' I lied.

'Oh!' She started away, stopped. 'Don't bother 'bout the door when you go out.'

The phone was in the kitchen, I dialled Alice in the dark. She answered the phone herself; she had an extension in her room and always answered calls after midnight.

'It's Bob,' I lisped. 'I'm—'

She cut me off immediately. 'If you're drunk, Bob, I don't want to talk to you. We waited dinner for an hour—'

'I'm not drunk,' I cut her off. 'I got some teeth knocked out. I'm in trouble. And I'm in a hurry—'

'What sort of trouble?' Her voice was sharp, anxious.

'I got in a jam at the yard,' I lisped, talking low so Hazel wouldn't hear.

'Talk louder,' she said. 'I can't hear you.'

'I got in some trouble at the yard,' I said, talking louder. 'I got messed up with that white woman I had the argument with and she's charging me with rape—'

'Rape!' Her voice was shocked, incredulous.

'Look, I can't explain now. I'm in an awful hurry,' I said. 'The police are looking for me. I didn't do it – you know that – but I'll have to explain when I see you.'

'Oh, Bob, you would have to get into something like that,' she said. Her voice sounded tearful.

'I tell you I haven't done anything,' I said impatiently. 'But nobody will believe it. Right now I've got to get away. What I want is to get whatever money you have on hand – and your car. I can't use mine and I can't go home to get any money – the police are there. I'll drive over to Western and—'

'But if you haven't done anything, why do you have to run away—'

'I told you, they're charging me—'

'But this sounds foolish. No one can just be charged – What can they do?'

'They can put me in the pen for thirty years,' I said. 'Look, let me explain when I see you—'

'But if you're innocent the worst thing you can do is run away.'

'Listen,' I began. 'You don't understand. I didn't do anything, but I can't prove it. I was in the room with the woman when she started screaming—'

'Screaming!' She got shocked all over again. 'Did you assault her – physically, I mean?'

'I can't explain now,' I said again. 'It just happened I got caught with her and she started hollering, "Rape." I'll tell you about it—'

'But I won't help you run away,' she cut in, getting her Americanism to working. 'That doesn't make any sense. I'll engage Blakely Moore to defend you. If you're innocent, Bob, you'll be acquitted. You forget there are laws. A person just can't charge you with a crime you haven't committed.'

'Look, Alice, this is serious,' I said. 'This isn't just talk any more. I don't expect you to keep our engagement. That's off, of course. But I need some help. I know what I'm doing. You're still talking in the air. But I know if I go before trial I'll be convicted. I know I haven't got a chance. I'm telling you—'

'But you can't know that if you are innocent,' she argued.

'Okay, I don't know it, but that isn't the point right now.' My mouth felt sore and ragged and I was at the end of my patience. 'The point is will you let me have some money and your car? I've got to get away. After I'm gone you can have Moore investigate—'

'If I thought it was for your own good I wouldn't

hesitate,' she said. 'But I know it isn't. You're excited and frightened and aren't thinking straight. This is the state of California – I was born here. Why can't you be sensible for once – give yourself up and I will bring Blake down with me the first thing—'

'Will you do it or won't you?' I cut in.

'No, I won't,' she said. 'I'll do anything else – within reason. But I won't help you escape. If you're innocent you have nothing to fear. I'll fight it through the courts with you until—'

I hung up, sat there for a moment, debating whether to talk to Hazel again and get what money she had. Finally I decided against it. It might get her into trouble.

All of a sudden my body began shaking; I began going hot and cold all over as if I had chilblains. I peered around in the darkness to see if she had anything to drink out there, found a pint bottle half full of some kind of whisky. I tilted it to my mouth, drank, swallowed, choked, then drank again. Then I remembered my pills. I shook some of them loose in my palm, I don't know how many, got a half glass of water at the sink, washed them down.

I heard motor sounds outside, thought it might be the police, ran out the back door across the yard to the fence separating the properties, ready to jump over and run through to the other street. The car passed. I went around, got into my car, backed into the street.

Instinct carried me over toward Central, into the heart of the ghetto. I parked in a dark spot in the middle of the block back of the Dunbar Hotel. I hadn't felt any pain before I'd telephoned Alice, but now I ached in every joint.

The bandages had fallen from my knees, had worked off my elbows. I pulled up my coverall legs, fingered the lacerated kneecaps. I must have landed on my knees when

I fell off the jack ladder. Then I groped around underneath the seat on the floor until I found my first-aid kit, felt for the bottle of mercurochrome, slowly and painstakingly painted the lacerated spots. When my eyes became more accustomed to the darkness I wrapped fresh bandages about my knees, taped them, tried to bandage my elbows again but couldn't make it.

As long as I'd kept moving my mind had remained concentrated on the action. But now a dull hopelessness settled over it, an untempered futility. I felt pressed, cornered, black, as small and weak and helpless as any Negro share-cropper facing a white mob in Georgia. I felt without soul, without mind, at the very end. Everything was useless, fight was useless, nothing I could do would make any difference now. I switched on the ignition, looked at the gas. It was on 'Empty' – I didn't know how long it had been there. I didn't want to get into some white neighbourhood and run out of gas. If I had to be caught I'd rather be caught right there in the heart of the Negro district. Chances were they'd catch me before daybreak anyway.

I went back over everything that had happened, detail by detail. I could think about it now: it didn't make any difference at all. I felt very calm and reasonable. They were going to catch me and give me thirty years in prison. For raping a white woman I hadn't even tried to rape.

Then it burst wide open in my mind. I wasn't excited. I looked at it objectively, as if it concerned somebody else. I'd kill Johnny Stoddart and let them hang me for it. All they could ever do to me then would be to get even. I was going but I'd take him with me.

I opened the glove compartment, got out my pistol I'd put there Monday afternoon, snapped on the overhead light, looked to see if it was loaded. Satisfied, I put it back, snapped off the light, mashed the starter, turned on the headlights, I felt for a cigarette, didn't have any. I noticed that my hands were trembling, but I didn't feel nervous.

I went ahead to Central, turned south to Slauson, doing a slow twenty-five, observing all the traffic rules, stopping at the boulevard stops, putting out my hand when I turned. At Slauson I turned toward Soto, stopped at Soto for the red light.

A police cruiser pulled up beside me. The cop on the outside gave me a casual glance, saw that I was a Negro, and came to attention. He leaned out the window and said, 'Pull over to the curb, boy.'

For just an instant I debated whether to try to make a break, but I knew I didn't have enough gas to get away and there was no need of getting another whipping for nothing. I pulled over to the curb, cut the motor. The cops pulled up ahead of me, got out, and came back.

'Let's see your operator's licence,' one said.

I fished out my billfold, handed it to him.

He looked at it, turned the leaf and looked at my draft classification, then caught sight of Alice's picture. He showed it to the other cop. They grinned.

One turned his flashlight on me. 'Whew!' he whistled, then said, 'Get out!'

It wasn't until then I remembered about my pistol but it was too late to worry about that now. For an instant I hesitated, debated whether to try; then I thought. What the hell's the use? got out, and stood beside the running board.

'Who you been fighting, boy?' one asked.

It startled me. I knew then that they didn't know I was wanted; they'd just stopped me because I was a black boy in a big car in a white neighbourhood.

'I was in an accident at the plant where I work,' I lisped.

'Where's your shop identification?'

'I left it at home.'

'What you doing out in this neighbourhood?'

'I was on my way home.'

He turned to the other cop. 'Let him go?' he asked.

The other cop shrugged.

The first cop flashed the light into the car, looked about the seats, pulled open the glove compartment, and brought out the pistol.

'Aha!' he said.

The other cop took me by the arm while the one with the flashlight locked the car ignition, rolled up the windows, and locked the doors. Then they got on each side of me, walked me back to the cruiser. One sat in the back with me; the other one drove.

They held me at the desk. Finally a lieutenant came out and looked at me. 'Aren't you the boy they want in Pedro for that rape at Atlas?' he asked.

I didn't reply. He slapped me.

'Answer when I speak to you,' he said.

I still didn't answer. He looked as if he was trying to decide whether to get rough with me or not, then turned impatiently to the cops who picked me up. 'What we got on him here?' he asked.

'Gun in his car,' the copper said.

The lieutenant turned to the desk sergeant, 'Lock him up and call Pedro. We'll let them have him first.' Then he stood there, looking important for a moment, and went out through a door.

The desk sergeant motioned the jailer to take me away. He took me back and locked me in a cell with a guy with a cut head. He lay on his bunk, moaning slightly. I imagined he was more scared than hurt. I stood there, leaning against the bars, not thinking about anything at all. Some time later, I don't know how long, the jailer came and took me out again, and two other policemen took me out past the sergeant's desk again and put me in a car and drove me down to San Pedro.

They put me in a cell by myself this time. It was a dirty grimy cell, stinking of urine, sweat, and fifth. The cotton mattress was bare, stained in several spots, looked as though it might be crawling with lice. I didn't give a goddamn; I stretched out on it. I didn't think I'd ever sleep again.

CHAPTER
22

I dreamed that when I came to Johnny Stoddart's house it was dark and I walked up to the door and pushed the bell, then I rapped on the door panel and shouted, 'Western Union,' and a light came on inside and the door was unlocked and I put my left hand on the knob, pulled my gun with my right, and rode it in.

Johnny Stoddart's eyes popped and his face drained colour and he stood in rigid amazement all dressed up to go to work and over his shoulder I saw his wife coming from the lighted kitchen to see what it was all about. I put the gun to his heart and pulled the trigger three times, the sounds exploding in the house and echoing in the street, and the slugs knocking him back a little. He kept clinging to the knob of the door as he started going down, crumbling slowly to the floor as if he was squatting down and it was painful and finally his hand let loose the door-knob and his chest hit his knees and he pitched doubled-up at my feet.

I looked down at him and knew he was dead and felt a crazy exultation, as if I had conquered the world and gotten past, gotten through, wrapped up in the glory of immortality, as free, goddamnit, as Thomas Jefferson, aw, goddamnit, you had me, but I'm out now – *out* – I'm broken out, and now all you white sons of bitches can go to hell. It was all I could do to keep from emptying the gun into his body.

Then I saw the woman's face and it was stretched in vertical lines with the mouth opening and closing soundlessly as she stood in the kitchen doorway with her hands held rigidly in an odd pose in front of her and I turned and walked slowly back to the street and all inside of me felt swollen and bursting with joy as if I'd just hit a hundred-thousand-dollar jackpot. I wanted to run and leap and shout and roll in the goddamned street.

I walked past houses and felt good, fine, wonderful, and felt something heavy in my hand and looked down and saw the gun and without being aware of what I was doing sat down on the curb and took out my handkerchief and began wiping it carefully for fingerprints then thought of the white boy falling dead at my feet and all of a sudden just burst out laughing like hell.

The woman ran out into the street and began yelling, 'Murder! Murder! Murder!' in a high hysterical shriek and I jumped up and dropped the gun and started to run and the woman kept screaming, 'Police! Catch him! There he goes! Murderer!' and the voice pushed me on.

After a moment I heard footsteps behind me and looked over my shoulder and saw the biggest man I ever saw in the uniform of a Marine sergeant with rows of stripes and decorations on his chest and I turned and dove for his legs but he leaped over me and turned on the balls of his feet and I staggered to my feet and dodged him and ran around the corner and a dog came out of the shadows and started barking and in the distance I could still hear the woman screaming.

The Marine was trotting along behind me chuckling to himself and after we'd run about a block I stopped and wheeled around and swung at him and he caught my arm, twisted it behind my back and put a half-nelson about my throat and marched me down the street. I didn't struggle. I knew it wasn't any use. We came to an alley and he pushed me down it and stopped and turned me around to face him, releasing his hold, and I couldn't see his face but his breath smelled like a gin barrel.

'Whatcha do, boy, kill somebody?' he asked in a husky chesty whisper and I knew he was reeling drunk. 'Yeah, I killed the son of a bitch, what you gonna do about it?' He asked, 'Was he a Jew?' and I said, 'Naw, he was a goddamned peckerwood like you,' and for an instant he didn't move, didn't make a sound. I couldn't hear him breathing and I looked for him to hit me, probably beat me to death, and I didn't give a goddamn. Then he began chuckling and I could smell his breath on me again and he asked, 'Whatja kill him for?' and I said, 'He called me a nigger.' He laughed louder and louder until his big booming laugh woke up the neighbourhood and he said, 'That's right, you kill 'em every time.' He laughed some more then he said, 'I always wondered 'bout you folks whether you ever wanted to kill us like we wanna kill you.' He stopped and panted and wiped the tears out of his eyes and said, 'I'm from Florida and ev'ybody I knew said they'd killed a nigger or two – at least one nigger – and I used to b'lieve 'em and I got to packing 'round my rifle looking for a nigger to kill till my old man found out what I was doing and said I couldn't kill no niggers until I got to be twenty-one and by that time I'd joined the Marines so I ain't never got to kill a nigger.' He sounded regretful looking at me and I got to wondering if he was thinking about killing me so I told him, 'I raped a white woman too,' and that tickled him all over again and he laughed loud and long and said, 'Hell, I've raped all kinda women, white women, black women, yellow women, red women, and the only reason I ain't raped no green women is 'cause I couldn't find none.' Then he stopped and laughed again and said, 'I done killed all kinda sonabitches, raped all kinda women' – pointing to the decorations on his chest – 'see these, the Purple Heart, the Bronze Star, the Presidential Memorial Citation, even a Good Conduct Medal. I got these for killing a lot of sonabitches I ain't even seen until after they was dead.

'Hell, boy, so you killed a man because he called you a nigger,' he said and laughed, 'and raped a white woman all in one night. Was she the man's woman you killed?' 'Naw,' I said, 'she don't even live nowhere near here,' and that started him off again. 'Goddamn you're some boy,' he said, 'rape a white woman in one part of town then run clear across town and kill a white man 'cause he called you a nigger.' He stopped and wiped the tears out of his eyes, and said regretfully looking at me, 'I ain't killed a nigger yet.' Then he drew slowly back and let it go and I saw it coming big as a house but there wasn't anything I could do but wait for it . . .

I woke up on the floor. Somebody was banging on the bars, saying, 'Damn if you didn't fall right off your bunk. They musta been after you.'

I must have thought he was the Marine because the first thing I felt was I didn't give a damn whether he killed me or not; I had made it. Then I saw he was the jailer and the day came back. When I tried to stand up nothing worked; I tried three times, finally made it by pieces. I was sore, stiff, ached in every joint. My head throbbed and the wound beat with my heart. My mouth felt useless, swollen shut; my tongue felt too big; I was thirsty, lousy, and really beat – low in the mind as a man can get. I rubbed the sleep out of my eyes with my knuckles, stood blinking at him.

He unlocked the door. 'Come on,' he said. 'You're lucky. Judge Morgan wants to see you in his chambers.'

I stepped into the bull pen, followed him dumbly. We went through some gates, down some corridors, came into an office with a big ornate desk and some big maroon leather chairs. There was a deep green carpet on the floor and two windows with clean white venetian blinds. In the distance was the harbour in the high bright sun.

'We'll just wait here,' he said, standing.

I stood a little away from him without replying. The dream was so real I kept thinking they had me in for murder. Then I began remembering the incidents of the day before, the stretch of Madge's big brutal mouth yelling, 'Rape,' the hammer floating at my head and not being able to dodge it, coming to on the hospital cot. Then the break, the drive back to town. When my mind came to the talk with Alice I tried not to think about it, but it came back anyway. Now she'd know once and for all. They had me and they were going to throw the book at me. I didn't have any hope at all of beating it; I didn't even feel like making the effort any more; I'd just as soon take a plea and get it to hell over with. I felt like a different person, I didn't have any fight left, didn't even hate the peckerwoods any more, didn't have anything left in me at all any more. What I hated most about the whole thing was I had to keep on living in the goddamned world.

Two men entered the room through the other door and broke my train of thought. One was a short, squat, quick-motioned man with a heavy-featured, pallid face and a half-bald head. He had on tortoiseshell glasses, a wrinkled brown suit, and talked in a brisk, rapid voice, slurring his words. He took the seat behind the desk, motioned the other man to be seated, looked over at me, and asked the jailer, 'Is this the boy?' all at the same time.

The other man was big, grey-haired, athletic-looking, more deliberate in his motions. He was poised, immaculate in an expensive-looking grey flannel suit, with a thoughtful, serious expression on his face. He lowered himself carefully in the chair beside the desk, crossed his legs, and studied me.

'Yes, Your Honour, Robert Jones,' the jailer replied to the squat man behind the desk, taking hold of my arm at the same time.

'You needn't hold him,' the judge snapped. 'He's not going to bite us.'

The jailer let go my arm, stood away from me again.

The judge said, 'The president of Atlas Corporation, Mr Houghton here, has interceded in your behalf, Jones. He has come down here expressly to talk to you.' His rapid, casual voice got sharp. 'I want you to listen to him.'

The first time I tried my voice wouldn't come at all, then I tried again and lisped, 'Yes sir,' in no more than a whisper.

Mr Houghton cleared his throat and got on a look of deep concern. 'I talked with Mrs Perkins last evening and again this morning,' he began. 'She is a tolerant and intelligent woman, I am happy to say, capable of weighing personal vengeance against national good. She realizes that, should she press charges against you, it might in all likelihood create racial tension among the employees and seriously handicap our production schedule, so she has consented to withdraw her charge against you, and Judge Morgan has informed me that this is permissible.' He had a cultured, scholarly voice, authoritative but un-emotional. 'It is a patriotic gesture comparable only to the heroism of men in battle, and I have the highest admiration for her.'

I knew right off what had happened; they'd grilled Madge and learned the truth, or learned enough to guess at the rest. His conscience bothered him too much for him to let me take a strictly bum rap, but he'd never come right out and say it; he'd cover for her till hell froze over and make himself believe that he was doing it for the best. But I didn't care how he played it – I was beat.

'I genuinely regret that circumstances permit you to escape punishment,' he went on, 'for you, more than any criminal, should be punished. You had no motive, not even an understandable excuse. Yours was a crime of uncontrolled lust – the act of an animal. And for it to be you, out of all other Negro employees at Atlas, to commit this crime is doubly disheartening, not only to the people of your race but to those of us who have always had the welfare of your people at heart.' He paused and got out his I-trusted-you look. 'You were given every opportunity to advance. You were the first Negro to be employed in a position of responsibility by our corporation and you were in a position to represent your race, to win for them advantages heretofore denied. You were selected because you were considered the highest type of Negro. We made you a leader of your people, such as Joe Louis, the prize fighter, Marian Anderson, the singer, and others. We had confidence in you. To do a thing like this, at a time when Negroes are making such rapid progress, when Negro soldiers are earning the respect of the nation, and when Negro workers are being employed in all branches of industry is more than a disgrace to yourself, it is a betrayal of your people . . .'

He was very, very smooth, but I wanted him to hurry and get it over with.

'Mr MacDougal and Mr Kelly both tried very hard to make you a success on that job,' he went on. 'They wanted you to set an example for other Negro employees, to open the way for those with more than average skill. I, personally, am anxious that Negroes make a good record in industry, and it is indeed regrettable, I assure you, to learn that you are not to be trusted to work alongside white women employees.

'That is all I have to say to you,' he concluded, rising. 'But I hope, seriously, that you will think about it.'

He had to say all that, I thought, just to cover up for a no-good cracker slut who just happened to be born white instead of black.

He turned to Judge Morgan. 'Good morning, Your Honour, and thank you.'

'Delighted,' the judge mumbled, half rising.

Mr Houghton went out.

'And let that be a lesson,' the judge said briskly, and began shuffling some papers on his desk he had brought in with him.

'I see they want you in Los Angeles for carrying a concealed weapon,' he remarked, then looked up at me. 'Suppose I give you a break, boy. If I let you join the armed forces – any branch you want – will you give me your word you'll stay away from white women and keep out of trouble?'

I wanted to just break out and laugh like the Marine in my dream, laugh and keep on laughing. 'Cause all I ever wanted was just a little thing – just to be a man. But I kept a straight face, got the words through my oversized lips. 'Yes sir, I promise.'

'Good,' he mumbled, standing up. 'Don't worry about that charge in Los Angeles.' He shook his finger at me, said, 'Make a good record, get an honourable discharge. It will do you a lot of good after this war.' Then he spoke to the jailer. 'Have somebody go along with this boy to the recruiting station.'

'Yes, Your Honour,' the jailer said, taking me by the arm again.

We went out, back through the corridors, kept through to the desk this time. 'Judge Morgan wants to send somebody with this boy to the recruiting station,' the jailer said to the sergeant on duty.

The sergeant didn't even look at me; he called over to a cop by the door in a bored, indifferent voice, 'Here's another soldier.'

'Come on, boy,' the cop said.

The two Mexican youths he had with him grinned a welcome.

'Let's go, man, the war's waiting,' one of them cracked.

'Don't rush the man,' the other one said. 'The man's not doing so well,' and when I came closer he said, 'Not doing well at all. Looks like this man has had a war. How you doing, man?'

They were both brown-skinned, about my colour, slender and slightly stooped, with Indian features and thick curly hair. Both wore bagged drapes that looked about to fall down from their waists, and greyish dirty T-shirts. They talked in the melodious Mexican lilt.

'I'm still here,' I lisped painfully.

They fell in beside me and we went out and started up the hill toward the induction centre, the three of us abreast and the cop in the rear.

Two hours later I was in the Army.